The Travel Nurse Series

COVID'S SILVER LINING

By

Ken Schroeder

Table of Contents

Chapter 1:
The Calm Before the Storm

Nancy adjusted her surgical mask and stepped into the trauma bay.

The light overhead was harsh and sterile, casting a sharp glow across the empty gurney in front of her. The smell of antiseptic hit her nose; a sharp, familiar scent that clung to the walls, the scrubs, the air itself. She didn't flinch. The sound of distant monitors beeped in steady rhythm, a reminder that somewhere in this building, someone was hanging on. A stretcher wheel squeaked in the corridor. Someone called out for a saline push. Fluorescents buzzed. Vitals blinked. The day had started, but it had not yet unraveled.

Her shift had begun like most others: a sprained wrist from a bike accident. A toddler who had swallowed a bottle cap. A man with a fever. The usual current of small emergencies.

Today still moved with a rhythm she had known for decades.

Mercy West in St. Louis wasn't just a hospital. It was her second home. She had walked these halls since her hair was dark and her back didn't ache at the end of a 12-hour shift. She'd seen the place during snowstorms and summers, budget cuts and remodels, quiet mornings and frenzied midnights. New policies came and went. So did interns. But Nancy remained.

Her coworkers called her steady. Reliable. Unshakable. The kind of nurse you wanted nearby when the pulse dropped and the panic rose. Newer nurses watched her like apprentices with a master craftsman, trying to absorb how she made chaos look choreographed. Nancy didn't just do her job she conducted it. Trauma became a symphony in her hands IVs here, compressions there, a sharp word to an intern, a reassuring squeeze to a patient's shoulder.

What most didn't know was that her calm under pressure wasn't learned in nursing school.

It was forged beside a man whose life depended on it.

Her husband, Jim, had spent three decades with St. Louis PD. She learned early what it meant to be alert ready. They had lived a life built on late-night calls, silent glances, and prayers that the phone wouldn't ring. That steady vigilance followed her into the ER, and it had never left.

In fact, it had only deepened.

Especially after the transplant.

***

It had been six months since Nancy had walked into Barnes-Jewish as a donor and walked out minus a kidney. Her left one, to be exact. She gave it freely without hesitation to the man she had shared her life with for 37 years.

Jim's kidneys had been declining steadily, worn down by years of untreated hypertension and a lingering autoimmune condition. For months, she had watched the labs creep toward irreversible numbers. Creatinine climbing. GFR falling. He had stubbornly resisted dialysis. And when the nephrologist finally said, "We should start talking about transplant," Nancy had already made up her mind.

There was no one else. Their children were tested, but none matched. Friends offered, but none cleared. And then Nancy still healthy, still working full-time, still stronger than women half her age got her bloodwork back and saw the note from the transplant coordinator: **MATCH**.

Jim had cried. She didn't.

She simply packed a bag, signed the forms, and showed up.

The procedure had gone smoothly. Her recovery, fast. She was back on her feet in three weeks, working part-time again in six. Jim had taken longer. He'd needed physical therapy, lab draws, home IVs. But each week, his color returned. His appetite grew. The shadows under his eyes faded.

Now, each morning, Nancy checked on him before she left for work. Made sure his meds were lined up in the tray. That the bandages over the port site were clean. That the fridge had juice and protein shakes and, of course, the mushroom ravioli he liked too much.

She sat up slowly, muscles stiff from the late shift. Her body hadn't fully recovered from donating a kidney six months ago, no matter how much she pretended otherwise. The scar on her left side still tugged faintly every time she twisted out of bed.

Nancy reached across the table and squeezed his hand. His fingers were still cool from the fridge shake.

"I gave you one of my kidneys. I think I've earned the right to be overbearing."

Jim smiled. "It's yours. I'm just borrowing it."

He always tried to walk her to the door.

Today was no different.

The parking lot at Mercy West was more crowded than usual for a Tuesday. She had to circle three times before finding a spot near the loading dock. Inside, the mood had shifted. The lobby was quieter. Staff moved briskly, no small talk.

The receptionist wore gloves now. So did the security guard.

Nancy scrubbed in twice at the sink before stepping into the ER. The soap stung the healing cracks on her knuckles.

Carla met her at the nurse's station, sipping from a dented thermos.

"You're early," Carla said. "Or just paranoid?"

"Little of both."

"You miss us that much, even after major surgery?"

"Turns out retirement is boring," Nancy said, pulling on gloves. "Besides, Jim's doing better."

"Yeah? The kidney holding up?"

Nancy smiled. "Better than I am some days."

Carla handed her the updated board.

"You might want to sit down."

"I never do."

"Six new respiratory cases since this morning. Two are on BiPAP. One coded in triage. We got him back, but barely."

Nancy scanned the chart. Orange tabs suspected viral. Red confirmed.

"Still no word from CDC?"

"They're sending updates by fax," Carla said dryly. "Faxes, Nancy. Like it's 1998."

Nancy rolled her eyes. "What are they saying?"

"Zoonotic virus. Jumped from animal to human, probably from a wet market.

Maybe a bat. Maybe a pangolin. Take your pick."

"And their guidance?"

"Assume every patient is contagious. Full PPE. Hourly sanitation. No unnecessary contact."

Nancy raised an eyebrow. "So basically, don't breathe."

Carla gave a tired smirk. "Pretty much."

****

The day rolled forward in a series of fast, blurry waves. A middle-aged woman gasping with every breath. A young man in a hoodie whose lips turned blue mid intake. A nurse from another hospital who showed up short of breath and refused to sit down.

"I can't be sick," she kept repeating. "I have a 2-year-old."

Nancy calmed her, gently eased her into a bed, called for labs. Her own hands shook only after she stepped out of the room.

In the hallway, the air felt denser. The noise sharper.

A code rang out from Radiology.

Nancy ran without thinking.

****

She checked her phone during a break.

Jim: *Had soup. Took a nap. Watched the dog sleep. Exciting stuff.*

She smiled and typed: *You're not missing much. It's chaos here.*

She hesitated, then added: *Love you.*

Then hit send.

***

Behind the nurses' station at Mercy West, someone had taped up a cartoon of a skeleton holding a coffee mug that read, *"I survived night shift."* The paper edges curled from too many 3 a.m. shifts. Nancy smirked every time she passed it.

Carla strolled by with two trays of syringes like she was delivering room service. Sharp, fast-talking, with a ponytail that never drooped, Carla had become the unofficial morale officer of the ER. Just as she rounded the corner, a new intern flew out of the charting room, eyes glued to his clipboard.

He clipped her elbow.

The tray launched.

Syringes scattered across the floor like spilled pencils.

"Oh God, I'm so sorry!" the intern yelped.

Carla barely glanced down. "There goes my chance at Nurse of the Month."

Nancy, watching nearby, let out a quiet laugh. She crouched beside the red-faced intern, helping him collect the mess. "Don't jab yourself. HR has enough to deal with."

He nodded, eyes wide.

Carla tossed over her shoulder, "Interns. Walking disasters with ID badges."

Nancy joined her at the med cart. "He'll figure it out."

"Maybe. Or he'll go to law school."

Nancy smiled again tired but genuine.

The day rolled forward.

A teenager with a gym injury. A woman with back pain. A man convinced he had a heart attack he didn't.

Nancy worked the floor with quiet efficiency, checking vitals, updating charts, and soothing patients with that trademark calm. Her left side ached now and then not painful, just a reminder. The transplant scar was healing well. The surgeon had said it might pull a little for months. She didn't mind. Every twinge meant Jim was breathing easier.

At noon, she grabbed a sandwich from the break room and joined Mike by the TV.

"Another virus?" Mike said around a mouthful of soup. "They always say that."

The screen showed grainy footage of hazmat-suited medics in China. A voiceover mentioned a new coronavirus. Nancy paused mid-bite.

"It's spreading?" she asked.

Mike shrugged. "They love a good panic."

Nancy didn't respond. She just stared at the TV a moment longer than usual.

Then her phone buzzed.

Jim: *Took the dog for a short walk. No nausea. Appetite decent. Love you.*

She smiled faintly, texted back *Drink your water*, and closed the screen.

***

By mid-afternoon, something felt... off.

Three patients had come in within an hour all with fatigue, shortness of breath, and low-grade fevers. All otherwise healthy. No flu. No strep. No travel history.

Nancy noted the symptoms. Made her rounds.

Then the code came.

5:43 p.m.

"Code Yellow. Three incoming. Respiratory distress. ETA four minutes."

She looked up sharply. Three?

Carla was already suiting up.

"Same exposure?" Nancy asked.

Carla shook her head. "Different parts of town."

Nancy's jaw tightened. "Prep the isolation bays. Chest films. Full panels. Masks on. Double-glove."

She didn't wait for a reply.

The ambulances arrived within minutes.

The first: a man in his sixties, gasping despite oxygen.

The second: a woman, unconscious. Vitals tanking.

The third: a college athlete no prior conditions barely responsive, bluish fingertips.

Nancy moved fast. She didn't panic. She couldn't.

She stabilized the man. Ordered blood gases. Checked vent settings. Wrote down chest x-ray orders on instinct. Issued instructions without raising her voice.

Her mind ran two tracks one in the room, and one at home.

Was Jim okay?

Had he taken his meds?

Was he safe?

She couldn't protect them both.

Not at the same time.

That night, she drove home with the radio off.

The air in the car felt tight.

She walked into the house and found Jim sitting at the kitchen table, a bowl of soup in front of him, the dog curled at his feet.

"You're late," he said.

"You're upright," she replied.

They both smiled.

"Everything okay at the hospital?" he asked.

She hesitated. "It's getting busy."

Jim leaned back slightly. "Bad-busy or flu-season busy?" Nancy looked at him.

"Let's just say I'm glad we didn't wait on your transplant."

He was quiet for a long time.

Then he said softly, "You saved me twice, you know. Once by marrying me. Once by giving me a part of yourself."

Nancy stepped forward and kissed the top of his head.

"We're not done yet," she whispered.

Outside, sirens echoed in the distance.

The rhythm had changed.

Chapter 2:
The Pandemic Hits Home

Nancy woke with a start, her breath catching as her eyes adjusted to the dim light filtering through the bedroom curtains. For a moment, she didn't move. She lay there, still and blinking, as if her brain was slowly catching up to her body. The sheets were tangled around her legs, warm from where she had slept.

It took her a few seconds to remember where she was. Not in the break room at Mercy General. Not slouched on a hospital cot during a two-hour reprieve between shifts. She strained to hear the familiar sounds of the ward—monitors, announcements, the squeal of gurney wheels—but there was nothing. Only the soft hum of the ceiling fan and faint city sounds beyond the window.

Home.

She was home. And somehow, that felt like something new.

Bits and pieces of the night drifted back. The hiss of running water, Jim's sleepy chuckle as she told him to move over in the shower, his hand brushing her wet hair from her face. She remembered leaning into him, the steam between them, his heartbeat steady against her back. Later, the two of them curled up under the blanket, limbs tangled, whispering a few quiet words that melted into sleep.

She reached toward his side of the bed, but it was empty. The pillow was cool. On the nightstand lay a folded note, his handwriting instantly familiar.

Good morning, babes. Felt better, so I'm heading to the gym. Call me when you wake up. Left your favorite soup on the stove. Love you.

Her lips curved softly. She could almost hear his voice saying it, half teasing, half tender.

She picked up her phone. 11:47 a.m. Nearly noon.

She had come home a little after three. That meant she had slept almost six hours, maybe five if she counted the time she sat on the shower floor letting the water run over her. She had no memory of crawling into bed after that. Time had simply blurred.

Her body didn't hurt in the way it used to after twelve-hour shifts. There were no sharp muscle cramps or throbbing blisters, just a deep ache in her chest, the kind that came from being stretched too thin.

She rubbed her eyes, reached for her phone again, and called him.

"Hey," she said, her voice still hoarse.

"Morning, sleepyhead," Jim replied, light and familiar. She could hear the faint echo of weights clanking behind him. "You left early," she murmured. "Didn't even kiss me goodbye." "I did," he said with a smile she could hear. "You just didn't wake up. You were out cold."

She laughed quietly, the sound rough but real. "You sound better."
"Yeah. Guess I just needed rest. How are you holding up?"
"I'm tired, Jim."

He paused, his tone softening. "Heading back in today?"
"In an hour," she said automatically, glancing at the notepad on her dresser filled with scribbled patient notes. "Maybe less."

She hadn't reviewed the notes since writing them. She didn't need to. The faces of the patients were still fresh in her mind. Their vitals. Their lab results. The endless list of what could go wrong and what already had.

Jim didn't say anything at first. That silence between them had its own language now. It wasn't awkward. It was loaded. Familiar. He knew her rhythms, and he could hear the weariness in her tone. But as always, he didn't linger in the dark corners. He found a way to pull her gently toward something lighter.

"I'll make dinner," he said. "That mushroom pasta you like. With the good parmesan. Not the bagged stuff."

Nancy's lips pulled into something close to a smile. Not a full one, not quite. But it was there, a flicker of warmth in the fog. "You're really betting on me making it home tonight?"

"I'm betting you'll need something besides hospital vending machine soup."

"You're not wrong," she murmured.

"I rarely am," he said with a lightness that managed to cut through her exhaustion.

"I'll keep a plate warm. Even if you're late. Again."

She was quiet for a beat. Then said, "It would've been our date night."

"I know," he said, quieter now. "We'll have it next week. The world won't stay like this forever."

Nancy swallowed the lump in her throat. She didn't say the thing that hovered at the edge of her thoughts, that maybe this *was* forever. That maybe they were already living inside the new normal. That the curve would never really flatten, not the one on the whiteboard and not the one pressing down on their lives.

But she couldn't say that out loud. Not to him. Not right now.

"I'll try to be home," she said instead. "By ten. Eleven at the latest."

"We'll see," he replied. Then added, "Don't forget your charger again. And eat something."

"I'll grab a protein bar."

"Eat something that has actual food in it."

"Fine," she said with mock surrender. "I'll eat the protein bar *and* a banana."

"That's my girl."

"Love you, my boy..." She said.

"Love you too my sexy head..." He whispered.

Nancy giggled and he matched her rhythm.

She hung up and stared at the screen for a moment longer than she meant to. Then dropped the phone onto the bed and let her body lean back against the pillows again.

Her eyes drifted toward the ceiling. She counted the slow turns of the fan. Each rotation felt like a second she didn't have.

Outside, the world was moving. People were waking up, brewing coffee, heading to work, walking their dogs. There was a normal tempo to things beyond these four walls.

But for Nancy, the tempo had become something else entirely.

A loop.

A relentless, repetitive loop of suffering. Of giving everything she had, only to feel like nothing changed. The patients came in. Some lived. Some didn't. The board never cleared. The oxygen alarms never stopped. There were moments when she looked around the ICU and wondered if any of it was helping. If they were buying minutes instead of years. If all their knowledge and effort and skill just delayed the inevitable.

She had been trained to stay calm under pressure. To act, not to dwell. But lately, the pressure never stopped. There was no come-down. No release. Only more need, more urgency, more chances to fail.

She couldn't remember the last time she had felt proud of her work.

And that thought terrified her.

***

The shower was lukewarm, but it didn't wake her up the way she hoped it would. Nancy stood under the stream until her skin prickled, watching the water trail down her collarbones, her spine, her thighs. A dull pull in her heart that made her feel like she had aged twenty years overnight was still there. She leaned her forehead against the tile and stayed there, letting the mist gently fog the mirror she couldn't bear to look into.

When she finally stepped out, she moved slowly, like someone recovering from something invisible. She pulled on a fresh set of scrubs, soft from too many washes. She held her ID badge and looked at her photo, a version of herself that had once smiled.

Her hair, still damp, was pulled back into a low ponytail without care. No time for neatness. No reason for it either.

She bypassed the stove and didn't even glance at the fridge. There were eggs inside, and a half loaf of rye bread sitting on the counter, still in its paper wrapper. But nothing pulled at her appetite. Not even in the way that hunger sometimes creeps up when you're tired enough to forget what the body needs.

On the far end of the kitchen, near the storage cupboard, a half-open basket still held the bananas Jim had picked up for her yesterday. Bright yellow, not a blemish in sight. He had said she needed to stop skipping breakfast, tossed a fresh bunch into the cart without asking, then kissed her temple in the checkout line like it was a routine they never had to name.

Nancy stared at them now. Reached for one. Then pulled her hand back.

Beside the coffee maker was the protein bar she kept meaning to eat. It had migrated from her work bag to the drawer, then onto the counter, and now sat waiting like a promise she wasn't sure she'd keep. She picked it up and slipped it into her bag without unwrapping it.

"I'll eat it later," she mumbled to no one.

She poured herself a cup of coffee and held the mug between both hands, letting the warmth ease into her palms.

Nancy walked into the living room and turned on the television, more out of habit than curiosity. The screen flickered to life, casting a soft glow across the room. The anchor's voice carried a practiced calm, steady and composed, but the headlines scrolling beneath told a different story; one filled with urgency, uncertainty, and the quiet kind of fear that didn't need to shout to be heard.

"Multiple states report new spikes in hospitalizations, many reaching surge capacity. Federal supplies are delayed.

Local systems are implementing emergency protocols." "Assume everyone is positive," the anchor said. "That is the latest guidance from the National Infectious Disease Center. All staff, all patients, no exceptions. New regulations recommend universal masking across healthcare settings, regardless of symptoms."

Once the coffee was finished, Nancy turned off the television and reached for her cloth mask, the one with tiny indigo patterns. Jim had teased her once, said it looked like something out of a vintage nurse's catalog. He had said it with affection, not mockery. She folded it in half and tucked it into her bag.

***

Outside, the sky was bright. The kind of cloudless day that should've signaled warmth, renewal, something fresh. But the air felt still. *Strange.* The neighborhood was awake, but subdued. A jogger passed by with a cloth mask pulled down to his chin, panting heavily. A young couple walked with their toddler, pausing at each house as if weighing whether it was safe to continue.

Nancy started the car and drove past rows of familiar houses. On her left, a man was spraying down his mailbox with disinfectant. A few kids sat on the curb, tossing a ball, but their laughter was low and distracted. Even joy had grown careful.

The drive to Mercy West was short, but traffic made it longer. Everyone seemed in a hurry to go nowhere. Horns honked more often, not out of frustration, but fear people flinching at proximity.

She reached the hospital and circled the lot twice before squeezing into a spot between a plumbing van and a compact car with a printed sign in the window:

"Thank You, Frontliners." A child had drawn hearts in red crayon around the edges.

Nancy sat in the car for a moment before getting out. Her hands were already reaching for sanitizer before her feet hit the pavement.

Inside the hospital, the difference was *immediate.*

There was movement, but it lacked flow. The receptionist wore gloves and didn't lift her eyes from her screen. A woman in a wheelchair was coughing into a surgical mask while her daughter filled out forms with shaking hands. The volunteer desk was empty. A sign had been posted in its place: "Temporarily Suspended."

Nancy moved briskly through the corridor. No greetings today. Just nods. Just eyes above masks that said everything without saying anything.

At the nurses' station, she headed straight to the scrub sink. The faucet creaked. She washed her hands for a full thirty seconds, twice. The soap stung her raw knuckles. Her skin had started cracking days ago, and now every touch felt like a warning.

She was drying her hands when Carla appeared beside her, cradling a dented silver thermos like it held something more precious than coffee.

"You look semi-human today," Carla said.

"I got six hours," Nancy replied.

Carla raised an eyebrow. "You should be in a museum."

Nancy pulled on her gloves and clipped her badge in place. "What's waiting?"

Carla handed her a clipboard. It was already smudged with ink and fingerprints. "Seven new admits. All respiratory distress. Two are on BiPAP. One coded around three. We brought him back, but he's not stable."

Nancy's eyes scanned the notes. "Any test results?"

"Only two. Both flu-negative. The rest? Labs are jammed. Everything's being routed through the main processing center downtown. They're behind by at least twenty-four hours."

Nancy's throat tightened. "And PPE?"

Carla gave a half shrug. "We've got about twenty gowns left. N95s are being signed out by supervisors only. The rest of us get whatever's in the bin." Nancy swallowed hard. "So we're rationing safety now."

Carla didn't reply. She didn't have to.

A few feet away, a flatline beep echoed from a nearby monitor. A voice on the intercom called a code in Room 6. The sound snapped through the air like a match being struck.

No one flinched. Not really.

Nancy turned her eyes toward the hallway but stayed rooted. She wasn't on that case. Not yet.

The helplessness in her stomach didn't come from panic anymore. It came from familiarity.

This was the new rhythm a shift where every effort felt like repetition. Every life saved is a pause before the next loss.

She had poured herself into this work for years and believed in it. But lately, belief wasn't enough. Passion didn't protect you. Not from fatigue. Not from failure.

And especially not from loss.

She reached for the pen clipped to her lanyard, and the motion felt heavier than it should have.

"Let's go," she murmured to Carla.

Carla took a long sip from her thermos and nodded. "Another day in the grind."

Nancy looked down the hallway at the closed doors, the flickering monitors, the shadows that moved behind privacy curtains.

Another day, yes. But something inside her had started to shift.

The work still mattered.

But maybe, just maybe, it was no longer *enough*.

***

The triage board had changed. Color-coded now, as if danger could be organized into neat categories. Red tabs marked the confirmed positives. Orange meant suspected. Blue stood for undetermined exposure risk. The orange ones were spreading across the shift schedule like ivy creeping up a wall, taking over quietly, relentlessly.

In Bay 2, a man in his forties sat propped up with oxygen tubes threaded beneath his nose. His breaths came in short, gasping pulls, like his lungs had forgotten how to stretch. Just across the corridor in Bay 6, a college student lay motionless, his eyes fixed on the ceiling. His sweatshirt clung to his body, drenched in sweat. He didn't speak. He barely blinked.

Nancy moved from one patient to the next with practiced focus, checking vitals, pulling labs, adjusting oxygen flow, and offering comfort to family members who could not come any closer than the other side of a glass panel or a choppy phone call.

Her hands never stopped moving. Her mask left a faint mark on her skin. Her gloves squeaked softly each time she touched plastic or metal.

Every patient wore a mask. Every nurse wore two.

By 9 PM, her body felt like it was moving through mud. Hours had blurred into one another, a stretch of nonstop movement without rhythm. Her legs ached from standing, her fingertips were wrinkled from constant glove use, and the back of her neck throbbed from the weight of the mask's elastic pulling at her skin.

She stepped away from the nurses' station for just a breath of space, leaned back against the wall near the supply closet, and reached into the inner pocket of her scrub jacket. Her phone screen lit up her face in the low hallway light.

A message from Jim.

Even before she read the words, just seeing his name steadied something in her.

Still thinking about that pasta. Come home if you can.

She closed her eyes briefly, exhaling through her nose. Then typed back slowly.

Things are bad here. Another wave just came in. We're short on gowns again. I may not be home for a while.

She paused. Then added: *Trying. Promise.* Her thumb hovered. She re-read it. Then retyped it with a little heart at the end.

Moments later, his reply lit up the screen.

I understand, my iron lady. I will wait for you. My lips want to kiss you so badly...

<3

Her breath caught for just a second. That was Jim. Always knowing how to cut through the static and remind her she was more than the role she filled at work. He never needed paragraphs. Just a few words that felt like arms around her shoulders.

The word *pasta* in his earlier message pulled her back to the morning.

She bent down and pulled her bag onto her lap. Somewhere in the side pouch, beneath folded papers and a half-used lotion bottle, was the banana she had grabbed on her way out the door...

She had promised to eat one...

The banana was warm now, and a little soft, its yellow skin dulled from the long day. She held it in both hands, letting her thumbs brush the spot where the color had darkened. Not spoiled. Just tired. Like her.

She peeled it carefully and ate it slowly, bite by bite, her mind circling around the fact that she was keeping the promise. Small as it was. It meant something.

She imagined Jim sitting on the couch, probably watching some crime show with one foot propped up and the pasta long gone cold in the kitchen. But waiting. *Always waiting for her at every meal.*

The last bite was bitter near the stem, but she didn't waste it. She slid the peel into the trash under the nurse's station, rubbed sanitizer into her hands, and stretched her shoulders.

She looked up at the triage board.

The orange tabs had multiplied.

One of them was blinking.

Nancy pulled her mask back up, tightened the loops around her ears, and glanced down the hallway as the sliding doors at the ambulance bay opened.

Another patient was coming in.

Another reason to stay strong.

***

By the time the wall clock in the hallway blinked 11:02 PM, Nancy was ready to call it. She had managed to get through most of her patients, logged the last round of vitals, and submitted her shift notes to the unit clerk. Her feet were sore in that familiar way, not screaming in pain but just humming with the weight of another day survived.

She leaned against the nurses' station, thumb hovering over her phone screen as she typed.

I am comingggggggg, she wrote to Jim, dragging out the letters like she used to back when they were younger and still found ways to flirt through exhaustion.

A small smile pulled at the corner of her lips. She could almost see him stretching out on the sofa, rubbing his eyes, reaching instinctively for the door when he heard her key.

She was just about to slide her phone back into her pocket when a voice down the corridor called out.

"Nance... we need you up front."

The shift wasn't over.

Not yet.

She made her way down the hallway, and what met her there was no longer manageable.

Stretchers lined the walls, pushed up like chess pieces without a board. One patient sat upright in what used to be a storage closet, propped with pillows and hooked to a portable oxygen tank. The air in the hall felt heavier, like even the building itself was exhausted from stretching to hold so much pain.

Near radiology, a young woman lay on a gurney, her head tilted against the painted cinderblock wall. Her eyes were open but unfocused. Her breaths came fast and shallow, like she was trying not to draw too much attention to the effort it took to stay conscious.

Nancy crouched beside her, her voice soft but steady.

"Sorry for the wait. We're short on space tonight."

The woman nodded faintly. "I get it. I flew in from Chicago two days ago. Felt fine. Thought it was just jet lag."

Nancy slipped the pulse oximeter onto her finger. Her pulse was rapid. Temp read 102.3. Her oxygen hovered in the low nineties.

"We'll start you on fluids. Get a full panel going. Chest X-ray too, just to be safe."

The woman blinked slowly. "Thanks for not yelling at me. I know people are scared."

Nancy paused for a beat, then met her eyes.

"We're not afraid of you. We're afraid of failing you."

The woman went still, her breath hitching for just a moment. Then, beneath her mask, Nancy saw the corners of her eyes crinkle with something like gratitude.

A tiny smile. The first sign of calm.

"Keep your mask tight," Nancy said gently. "I'll check back in a bit."

She stood up, stepping out of the way so the tech could wheel the woman toward imaging.

Her phone buzzed in her pocket. She didn't check it right away.

This, right here' this was the part of the job that held her in place when everything else inside her was shifting. She couldn't walk away. Not yet. Not when the need still outnumbered the hands available.

But part of her ached at the thought of Jim waiting in a quiet house, lights low, door unlocked.

Another hour, she told herself.

Maybe two.

Then she'd go home.

***

By 12 AM, Nancy stood outside the break room, her back pressed against the cold tile wall. The hallway was dim now, lit only by motion-sensitive overheads that flickered every time someone passed. Her hands were shaking, though she wasn't cold. Her body was simply running on fumes.

She pulled out her phone and dialed Jim. She didn't text. Texts felt too distant for what she needed to say.

He picked up on the first ring.

"Nance?"

Her breath caught in her throat. For a second, she didn't speak. Then, in a voice soft and breaking at the edges, she whispered, "I don't know when I'll make it home."

24

There was a pause. He let that sentence sit in the air, not filling the silence right away like he normally would. She could hear the faint sound of the ceiling fan in their bedroom. The creak of his weight shifting on the bed.

"Is it still bad?" he asked quietly.

"It's getting worse," she said. "I don't want to leave until I'm sure everything's stable. But things aren't... they're not stabilizing."

Another pause. Then his voice came back, lower, steadier.

"Okay. I'm upset. Not at you. Just at everything. At how this feels so out of your hands."

Nancy leaned her head against the wall, eyes closed. "I'm sorry, Jim."

"Don't be sorry," he said. "You're doing more than anyone else could. I wish I could bring you home myself. But if you can't make it... I want you to know I'm proud of you. Every single second."

She pressed her lips together.

"Try to sleep a little," she said.

"I won't, but I'll lie here anyway," he replied gently. "I love you, Iron Lady."

A weak laugh caught in her throat. "Love you, too."

She hung up and slipped the phone back into her pocket, already hearing her name being called again.

By 1 AM, the situation had shifted again.

Word had made its way through the staff lounge, passed between exhausted nurses and breathless techs with disbelief tightening their voices: Mercy West was now an active surveillance site.

The CDC had flagged them. Internal dispatch confirmed it. Screens lit up in succession as the email blast hit every hospital inbox. Alerts. Emergency response protocol updates. A blur of PDFs and rapid policy shifts. One nurse began printing out the documents to post at the main stations.

Carla dropped a thick stack of pages onto the metal table between them. Her hands were visibly shaking, though her voice stayed even.

"They've named it," she said.

Nancy's eyes moved to the header.

SARS-CoV-2. Coronavirus Disease 2019. COVID-19.

It looked sterile on paper. Cold. But the weight of the words pressed into her chest.

"They're calling it airborne now," Carla added, her voice quieter. "Not officially yet, but the memos are saying both droplet and aerosol precautions. That means full PPE. All the time."

Nancy's throat tightened. "We don't even have enough N95s to get through a regular shift, let alone what they're asking now."

"National Guard is distributing what they can from state stockpiles," Carla said.

"FEMA is being looped in. No timelines yet. Everything's reactive."

"And what does that mean for us?"

Carla looked at her squarely. "Mandatory overtime. Starting tonight. No opt-outs. No rotation."

Nancy turned her gaze toward the whiteboard, where patient initials and notes were now being tagged with bright orange and red tabs.

"And no backup?"

Carla shook her head. "Float pool is either sick or already reassigned. This is us.

We're the line."

They both went quiet. The kind of quiet that feels louder than words. Nancy glanced down at her gloves, then up again at the stack of protocols.

***

By 5 AM, Mercy West had settled into that exhausted rhythm only hospitals know. The kind where time stopped meaning anything, and actions repeated like muscle memory. The same steps, the same instructions, the same battles fought again and again with little to show for it.

Repetition without reward was dragging on everyone.

They gave everything they had every ounce of knowledge, every minute of rest, every calm tone offered to panicked patients, but the virus was faster. Meaner. Smarter. And the worst part was the helplessness that settled like dust in their bones. It was not just the fatigue from double shifts or aching backs. It was the crushing reality that sometimes, no matter how hard they tried, it would not be enough.

Nancy felt it too. She had felt it for days now, maybe weeks. A silent weight that followed her from room to room, whispering that all her training, all her drive, was barely keeping up with a problem that had no end.

Still, she kept moving.

She found Carla hunched over a chair in the break room, one shoe off and her thermos empty.

"Come on," Nancy said, tossing her keys up and catching them. "I'm driving you home."

"You sure?" Carla murmured. "I can call a ride."

"You're nodding off while sitting. I don't trust you behind the wheel. Let's go." They stepped outside into the half-light of early dawn.

The sky was the color of ash, not quite morning, not quite night. The air was cool but sticky, and the sound of distant sirens still carried, like background music to a nightmare no one could wake from.

Nancy unlocked the car with a tired flick of her wrist. Carla dropped into the passenger seat, her head already leaning against the window before Nancy even started the engine.

"I hate always leaving Jim waiting like this," Nancy said quietly as she pulled out of the lot. "He made pasta. He texted. He waited. I promised I'd eat a banana. First I forgot...I didn't even make it home for that, Carla."

Carla's eyes stayed closed. "You did eat the banana."

"It was brown and warm and half-mushed."

"But you ate it."

"Yes I did... But I felt guilty for always..."

Carla turned her head and cracked one eye open. "Nancy, you remember your vows?"

Nancy glanced at her. "Of course I do."

"I was there. I remember one part clearly. Jim said, 'I'll wait for you. In quiet rooms, on lonely nights, in silence, and in hope. I'll wait.' So if waiting is part of the job description, he knew exactly what he signed up for.

Nancy felt something stir in her chest. A laugh, fragile but real. "You memorized my vows?"

"I have a soft spot for romantics who pretend they're not," Carla said. "And besides, it was the prettiest wedding I ever went to where the groom quoted poetry."

They both smiled as the car rolled into Carla's neighborhood. Nancy pulled to the curb and parked.

"Get some sleep," she said.

"Only if you do."

"No promises."

Carla gave her a weak salute and climbed out. Nancy waited until she saw her reach the front door before pulling away.

The streets were quieter now, the early risers not yet out, the night shift just settling. She drove through the silence until she reached her own street.

She parked in the driveway and reached beneath the small ceramic planter by the steps. The spare key was still there, tucked into the dirt like a secret.

She let herself in.

The living room lights were off, but the television cast soft shadows on the wall. Jim was on the couch, wrapped in a throw blanket.

He was *shivering*.

And *coughing*.

Nancy froze in the doorway, her hand still on the knob.

"Jim?" she whispered.

He turned his head slowly. His face was pale, eyes glassy.

"Hey," he rasped, trying to smile.

She dropped her bag and rushed to his side. Her hands hovered over him, not quite sure where to begin. Forehead? Pulse? Should she grab the thermometer first or the pulse oximeter?

"I didn't want to call you," he said, voice hoarse. "You were already saving the world."

"You should've called me the second you felt anything," she said, kneeling beside him.

"I didn't want you to worry."

"Too late."

His breath hitched as he tried to sit up straighter. Nancy adjusted the pillows behind him.

"When did this start?"

"After you called. Just felt cold. Then the cough kicked in." She pressed her hand to his forehead. Warm. Too warm. "Any shortness of breath?"

"A little. Nothing serious. Yet."

Nancy stood, moving toward the kitchen, switching into nurse mode with a speed that startled even her. She needed water. She needed to check his temperature. She needed to know if they had a pulse ox that still worked.

But in the back of her mind, something else thudded louder than her footsteps.

This virus had found its way home.

No...no...no...

Nancy's panic mode was activated.

And suddenly, it wasn't just about survival anymore. It was about saving the one person she couldn't afford to lose.

Chapter 3:
When the Caregiver Becomes the Patient

Imagine a world where the streets have lost their rhythm.

Where laughter echoes from windows instead of parks.

Where playgrounds sag with disuse, swings creaking in the breeze.

Schools are silent. Pews are empty. Supermarket shelves carry only ghosts of what used to be.

The words *community* and *gathering* feel like historical terms, whispered from a safer past.

And masks? Masks are the new handshake. The new wedding veil. The new prayer.

It wasn't a war in the traditional sense.

But something had invaded just the same.

Invisible. Ruthless. Merciless.

***

Nancy sat at the kitchen table that morning, hunched over her old leather journal. The sun sliced across the wood in thin ribbons, lighting up a half-filled coffee mug and a single pencil worn to the nub. Her fingers hovered over the page. She had started writing again recently, mostly fragments, mostly quiet. It was the only outlet that didn't make her feel like she was screaming into a hurricane.

Her latest entry read:

A world paused, but not in peace.

We breathe behind fabric and fear.

The silence isn't rest; it's weight.

And even hope must wash its hands...

She tapped her pen. The fifth line never came.

From the hallway came a cough. A rough one. Wet. From the chest.

Nancy froze. Her breath caught halfway up her throat.

"Nance?" Jim's voice thinner than usual, hoarse.

The pen rolled off the table and clattered to the floor.

She moved.

***

In the hallway, she reached instinctively for the PPE kit she'd left by the door: gloves, N95, face shield. Her fingers moved through the motions like muscle memory precise, mechanical, deliberate. She could have done it blindfolded.

They had set up the guest room as a quarantine space four days ago. At first, it was precautionary Jim had insisted he was fine. Just tired. Maybe sinus pressure. Maybe the change in weather. But Nancy had seen too much, and the look in his eyes two nights ago had said everything his words didn't.

She knocked gently, then entered.

The air inside the room was thick. Warm. Unmoving. Jim was propped up against the pillows, pale and glassy-eyed, sweat glistening on his brow. The bottle of water beside the bed was still full. His glasses were fogged over.

"You didn't answer," she said gently.

He tried to smile. "You always were impatient."

"Not today." She stepped closer. "Let me take your temp."

He grumbled but didn't resist. She pressed the thermometer to his forehead and watched it climb.

101.8.

Higher than yesterday.

She checked his pulse. Elevated. His oxygen? 92%. Not critical. But heading in the wrong direction.

"Did you try to eat this morning?" she asked.

He shrugged. "Didn't feel like it."

"You need calories, Jim. Fluids too."

"I'm trying," he said, softer now. "It's just... tight. Breathing. Feels like I'm sucking air through a coffee straw."

Nancy didn't speak for a moment. She looked at him really looked at him. He was trying to be strong for her. And she was trying not to cry for him.

She knelt beside the bed. "We're going to stay ahead of this, okay? Fluids. Rest. Breathing exercises. You're not going to the hospital unless you absolutely have to."

"I don't want to die there."

"You're not going to die." Her voice cracked, just a little. "Not on my watch."

He smiled faintly, then coughed again.

***

At Mercy West, the air had changed.

Not just metaphorically. It *smelled* different. Like bleach and sweat and something else something you couldn't scrub out. Fear.

The staff didn't joke as much. No more teasing at the nurse's station. No half-burnt popcorn in the break room. No secret stashes of chocolate in the drawer beneath the printer. Everyone kept their masks on even when they weren't technically required to. Voices were clipped. Eyes rimmed red.

Nancy didn't stop to process it anymore. She just moved.

Her first patient coded before she finished morning rounds. A woman in her forties, previously healthy, who'd come in for shortness of breath and was now unresponsive. Nancy worked chest compressions like her own life depended on it.

She thought of Jim the entire time.

***

Later, she found Carla outside Bay 9, staring at the intake board with a sheet of CDC updates in her hand.

"They've changed the guidelines again," she muttered.

Nancy didn't even blink. "Let me guess. More PPE?"

"Double masking is now mandatory. Face shields in all zones. No shared electronics. No breakroom congregating. No touching anyone. Ever." "Why don't they just ask us to levitate while we're at it?" Carla gave her a tired look. "That would be less exhausting."

They stood in silence for a beat.

"Any word on staffing?" Nancy finally asked.

Carla's lips thinned. "Three more nurses out sick. One ICU doc is on oxygen himself now. We're absorbing their caseloads."

"So we're down to skeleton crews."

"Skeletons with cracked bones," Carla muttered. "They're drafting surgical techs to run meds and physical therapists to answer call lights."

"Are they trained for that?"

"Are we trained for this?" Carla shot back. "No one is."

Nancy stared at the wall. "Any fatalities overnight?"

"Two. One was an ER nurse from Jefferson Memorial. Thirty-three years old. Had asthma. Didn't make it past triage."

Nancy's heart thudded. Thirty-three. That was Carla's age.

Carla swallowed hard, as if she knew what Nancy was thinking. "I can't tell if I'm numb or just past the point of processing."

"Maybe both."

The intercom crackled.

"Code Blue. Radiology hallway. Immediate response."

Nancy ran. Again.

***

By mid-afternoon, the break room was silent. Nancy sat alone for five minutes just five to check her phone. A text from Jim lit up the screen.

Still breathing. Still tired. Don't forget to eat.

She typed: *Try to nap. I'll bring soup.* Then paused.

She added: *Love you.*

Then deleted it. Rewrote it. Hit send.

She sat there, unmoving, until her pager went off again.

By 8 p.m., she'd intubated two patients, argued with a pharmacy about the last available vented masks, and helped a family say goodbye over FaceTime.

She hadn't eaten. She hadn't peed.

She barely noticed.

***

That night, she stood outside the bedroom door with a thermos of soup. She didn't knock immediately. She just listened.

A breath. A cough. A groan.

Still alive.

She knocked once and entered, now fully suited again.

Jim looked worse. His eyes were sunken. His speech was slower. He tried to sit up but winced.

"You don't have to play hero," Nancy said, setting the soup down on the nightstand.

"I just want to see you without this gear on," he said. "Even for a second."

Nancy's throat tightened. "Me too."

He managed a crooked smile. "You always make good soup."

"I didn't make this. It's from the nurse's station microwave."

"Then you picked a good microwave."

She sat on the edge of the bed, careful not to touch anything. "I'm going to bring home a pulse oximeter tomorrow.

We'll track your numbers every hour. If it drops below 90 again, I'm calling an ambulance."

"Not yet."

She didn't answer. She didn't promise. She just sat.

***

At midnight, she wrote in her journal again.

We hold our breath and each other

Behind gloves and glass and rules. This isn't how love was meant to look but it's how we survive.

She closed the journal and set it down beside her bed.

The moonlight slid across the hardwood floor like a silent witness. Outside, sirens wailed. The sound had become constant now, like wind or rain just another part of the soundtrack.

Nancy lay back, eyes open.

Tomorrow, she would fight again.

But tonight just tonight she would let herself feel the weight.

And breathe.

Chapter 4:
The Unthinkable Goodbye

The hospital smelled different now.

Not just bleach and hand sanitizer. Not just Lysol tucked into every corner. There was something older in the air now. Something that didn't come in a bottle. A heaviness. Like dust settling after a building had collapsed. The kind of smell that clings to grief. The scent of absence something that hovered in the fluorescent-lit corridors, in the corners where people once laughed, in the eyes of nurses who no longer had jokes left to tell.

Nancy could feel it in her throat, dry and sore from too many hours under a tight mask. Her face shield fogged gently with each breath, and she blinked past it as she walked the corridor of Mercy West. The linoleum beneath her shoes made a soft squeak. No one looked up. No one had the energy to.

This wasn't the world she trained for.

This wasn't what all those rotations, late-night study groups, or trauma simulations prepared her for. Once, symptoms led to a diagnosis. A diagnosis meant a plan. And a plan meant hope. Now, all they had was oxygen and prayer. Now, "care" meant morphine and whispered goodbyes. It meant holding hands through nitrile gloves. It meant watching a flatline and calling time even before the family picked up on FaceTime.

There were no victories. Only survival. And even that was rationed.

Her shift had barely started. She hadn't even unzipped her bag when Carla caught her at the nurse's station, looking like someone had rung her out and forgotten to hang her back up.

"Eight more intubated overnight," Carla muttered, eyes already scanning a clipboard she probably wouldn't remember five minutes later. "Three code blues before the sun came up. We're out of BiPAPs. Again."

Nancy sighed, pulling her badge over her head. "How many vents left?"

"Five. Two promised to surgery. One is in use for a twenty-four-year-old. No history. Healthy."

"And the last two?"

Carla looked at her like she didn't want to answer. "Locked in storage. Admin says we're conserving inventory."

Nancy's jaw tightened. "So they're just... sitting there?"

"Not our call."

She didn't scream. Didn't throw anything. That would've been a waste of energy. So she swallowed the frustration shoved it down deep, where the rest of the helplessness lived and nodded instead.

"Okay."

That's all she said.

***

The vaccine had arrived two weeks ago.

It came like a whisper at first emails, updates, rumors. Then the posters showed up. Then the QR codes. Then the media headlines: *A Breakthrough. A Light at the End.* And then, just like everything else in the pandemic, it became complicated.

Pfizer was available for frontline workers. Two doses. Maybe a third down the line. Sign-up required. Mild fever expected. No one knew what came after.

In the break room, a laminated flyer was taped to the fridge, curling at the corners. Nancy stared at it without really seeing it. She hadn't signed up. She meant to. Maybe tomorrow.

But how could she think about tomorrow when Jim might not make it through today?

She checked her phone. Nothing.

No message. No update.

Her thumb hovered over the screen.

That morning, his oxygen had dropped to 85. He couldn't sit up on his own. He hadn't touched the soup she left at his bedside. When he breathed, it sounded like paper crumpling. But worst of all he had stopped pretending.

There were no more dry jokes. No witty one-liners about the microwave. No comments about her "hallway glamour." Just silence. Stillness. The kind that came when even hope decided to take a step back.

Dr. Pearson had said what she already knew. Jim's lungs weren't just inflamed. They were deteriorating. One shallow breath at a time. The anti-rejection meds from his transplant once life-saving had now made him defenseless. COVID didn't just invade. It took over.

The only chance now? A double lung transplant.

And even that wasn't really a chance. It was a snowball chance in hell.

Nancy had spent the last two days calling every transplant center in reach.

UCLA. Stanford. UCSF. Sutter. Even small hospitals she had only heard about in passing. She had made a spreadsheet. A running log. Every line was filled in with time stamps, contact names, hopeful beginnings. And then the final column always read the same: "Unavailable."

Too many patients. Not enough donors. Not enough guarantees.

No one said it aloud, but she understood the code. Jim wasn't a priority. He was already compromised. They were gambling on the ones with better odds.

He didn't have time to be on a list. He didn't have the luxury of waiting for a match.

And lungs? They don't grow on trees.

That afternoon, she found herself outside Bay 12.

She didn't know how long she had been standing there.

Inside, a ventilator hissed rhythmically beside a young woman who had come in the night before. Late thirties, maybe. Dark hair. Eyes closed. Already sedated. Nancy didn't know her name. Hadn't read her chart. There wasn't time.

She stared at the blinking monitor.

In. Out. In. Out.

Breath, assisted.

Just like Jim.

Carla stepped beside her, a paper coffee cup in one hand. She didn't say anything right away. Just watched the same monitor.

"You okay?" she finally asked.

Nancy shook her head. "No."

Carla didn't press. She didn't need to.

Some things don't need to be spoken out loud anymore.

***

In the back room, Nancy collapsed into a plastic chair that wobbled slightly under her weight. She pulled out her phone again.

More voicemails. More numbers she already knew by heart. Her fingers hovered. She didn't know who to try anymore.

She opened her journal instead.

The page was blank.

Usually, she could fill it. Even if just fragments. Even if just phrases. But today, no poem came.

No metaphors. No clever comparisons.

Just a single word, scribbled at the top.

Jim

And next to it, a shaky question mark.

She stared at it for a long time.

Her pen hovered. Her hand trembled.

But she couldn't write another word.

Finally, she closed the journal and exhaled through clenched teeth.

Outside, somewhere down the hall, an alarm beeped steadily.

Someone else was coding.

Someone else was slipping.

Nancy stood up. Tightened her ponytail. And walked back toward the noise.

Because that's what you do when your own world is falling apart.

You save someone else's.

Even if it's just for one more breath.

***

Back home, Nancy moved on autopilot. The mask went on. The gloves. The face shield. The gown. But nothing about it felt like armor anymore. Her hands fumbled at the zipper. Her fingers shook while tying the straps. The layers weren't for safety now they felt ceremonial, like dressing for a moment she had no name for. A moment suspended between effort and helplessness.

Inside the bedroom, dimmed lights cast long shadows on the walls. The humidifier buzzed softly. Jim stirred beneath the blankets, his form thinner than it had been just a week ago. His face, pale and drawn, turned toward her as she entered. He opened his eyes, and for a second, they flickered with something familiar.

"There you are," he said, voice barely above a whisper.

She stepped closer, sitting down on the edge of the bed. His skin was damp and cool when she reached for his hand. His breath came quick and shallow, like he had to bargain with his body for every inhale.

"I called three more hospitals today," she said, brushing her fingers along his arm. "There's a facility in Nevada that might consider it. I'm still waiting for someone to call me back."

He nodded faintly. "Nancy... don't burn yourself out chasing miracles."

"I'm not burning out. I'm fighting. For you."

He smiled, barely. "Still the same. You never let go once you decide."

"And you're still trying to talk me out of doing the impossible," she said gently.

He coughed, a raw rattle that shook through his chest. Nancy leaned in, steadying him, one hand on his back. The thermometer beeped a few seconds later 102.4.

Still rising.

"Is there soup?" he asked after a moment.

She reached for the tray beside her. "Tomato basil. Your favorite."

"Homemade?" he asked with a half-smirk.

"Microwaved. But made with love."

"Even better," he murmured. "Everything tastes better when it's from you."

Nancy dipped the spoon and brought it carefully to his lips. He sipped slowly, weakly, pausing between swallows like each mouthful took all the energy he could spare. She didn't rush. She kept her eyes on him, watching the way his jaw moved, the tremble in his hand, the way his lashes fluttered each time he blinked. Every detail mattered now. Every second counted.

Halfway through the bowl, he leaned his head back against the pillows.

"You look tired," he whispered.

She smiled softly. "You're not exactly glowing either."

A thin laugh slipped out of him. "Touché."

Nancy set the spoon down and ran her hand across his forehead, brushing back a strand of sweat-damp hair. "I'm going to find those lungs. I swear to you, Jim. I'll find them."

His eyes drifted shut. "You already gave me one," he said.

Her brows knit in confusion. "What do you mean?"

"The kidney. Months ago. You gave it to me. That's why I made it this far."

Her throat tightened. "That was different."

"No. It wasn't." His voice faded, quiet but sure. "It was life. It bought me time.

And you never once made me feel like I owed you for it."

Nancy swallowed hard, her hand still resting on his chest. She could feel the erratic rhythm beneath her palm.

"I'll stay as long as I can," he murmured, eyes still closed. "But if I go... just know you gave me everything."

Her eyes stung. She leaned forward and pressed her forehead gently to his, mask and all.

"No," she whispered. "It's not your time yet."

He didn't respond. His breathing grew softer, slower.

She sat there long after he fell asleep, her hand still in his, heart caught somewhere between hope and heartbreak. The clock ticked, the humidifier hummed, and in that small, quiet room, she made another silent promise:

This wasn't the end. Not tonight. Not if she could help it.

***

46

At Mercy West, the day had barely begun and already the hospital felt like it was slipping underwater. Every step Nancy took down the corridor felt like she was pushing through resistance. Not panic exactly, but a weight. Like the building itself was bracing for something worse.

A nurse collapsed in the break room mid-shift change. No warning. She'd been holding a saline bag and then just... dropped. They laid her on the couch, checked her vitals, gave her fluids. It wasn't COVID just sheer exhaustion. Four doubles in five days. No time to eat. Barely enough time to breathe.

Downstairs, EMTs rolled in a young woman whose belly announced she was well into her third trimester. Her breaths were short and erratic, like she was gasping through a straw. The baby's heart rate was elevated. She kept gripping her chest and whispering, "I can't catch my breath." She was thirty-two. No prior conditions. They couldn't intubate her yet the risk to the baby was too high but she was teetering.

Room 6 now had a sign taped outside the door that read "No Visitors." One of the attendings Dr. Mateo Lopez was inside, unconscious, heavily sedated, and declining fast. He'd intubated two patients three days ago without a proper N95. The unit had run out again that morning.

Nancy was halfway through logging vitals when Carla appeared beside her with a chart tucked tight to her chest.

"We need to talk," she said, pulling Nancy into the side hall behind the nurses' station.

"What's going on?" Nancy asked.

Carla exhaled. "Ventilators. Admin wants us to start using triage protocols." "Triage?" Nancy repeated. Her voice had stiffened.

"They're drafting an internal algorithm. Age, comorbidities, DNR status, probability of survival based on SOFA scores."

"You mean we're choosing who gets to live."

Carla didn't answer. She didn't need to. Her silence said it all.

Nancy shook her head slowly. "That's not what we do. We treat patients. All of them."

Carla's voice was tight. "We're out of vents, Nancy. Two were pulled from our unit this morning for OR cases. Another was reassigned to the trauma floor. That leaves three. We admitted nine patients today who'll need them within hours."

"We can't just pick and choose based on numbers on a chart."

"I know. But we're being told to prepare for it."

Nancy stood there, her arms folded across her chest, her mind flicking between her ICU board and Jim lying in bed at home, losing more lung function by the hour.

She didn't reply. What could she say? The math didn't care about emotions, and the system didn't care about love. Every ventilator meant a life extended or denied. As Carla walked off to resume rounds, Nancy stood frozen in place, her throat dry, her pulse drumming in her ears. Somewhere in this building, she was being asked to decide fates. And somewhere across town, the person she loved most in the world *was running out of time*.

Later that night, with the floor dimmed and the staff busy transferring a patient to telemetry, Nancy stepped into the back supply closet and closed the door behind her. She dialed Dr. Pearson's direct line with trembling fingers.

"Pearson," he answered, voice thick with fatigue.

"It's Nancy," she said. "I need to ask you something. Off the record."

"I'm listening."

"Is there any center with donor lungs available? Anyone within airlift range? I don't care if the odds are bad. I just need to know if there's a sliver of a chance." He paused. She could hear him typing.

"There's a possibility out of Seattle. A male donor, early thirties. Declared braindead after a motorcycle accident. Blood type A positive. No smoking history."

Nancy's heart caught. "Jim's A positive. That's a match."

"It's not that simple. There's a recipient already lined up. But the lungs aren't viable for him anymore due to size mismatch. So they're considering secondary candidates."

"How far down the list is Jim?"

Pearson's voice softened. "He's not on the list at all. He's not in that system."

"Then get him in. Whatever it takes."

"I can make calls. But even if we push it through, the real challenge is getting him there in time. He's unstable. A pressurized cabin could be too much for his vitals."

"I'll stabilize him. I'll keep him breathing. If there's a way to transport him, I'll find it."

"You'd need a critical care flight team, clearance from admin, and a transplant coordinator to sign off. That's a lot of moving parts."

"But not impossible," she said.

Pearson sighed. "No. Not impossible. Just very, very thin."

"I'm willing to take thin."

"I'll reach out to Seattle and see if they're willing to consider it. But Nancy..."

"I know," she said. "We're out of time."

She ended the call and leaned against the metal shelving. Her fingers were still clenched around the phone, knuckles white. She didn't cry. Not yet. But she knew if Jim didn't get those lungs, it wouldn't be long before she'd be holding his hand for the last time.

And she wasn't ready for that. Not even close.

***

She rushed home.

Streetlights smeared across her windshield like streaks of paint. Empty storefronts flickered by without faces, without sound. The only noise came from the engine and the rattling inside her chest. She gripped the steering wheel so tightly her knuckles blanched, not because she was scared to crash, but because she was terrified of arriving too late.

She couldn't recall how the car stopped or how she made it to the front door. She couldn't remember if she locked it behind her. The only thing she knew was her feet were moving and her hands were shaking and Jim was inside that room, still tethered to a hope that was slipping faster by the minute.

He was asleep. Or something that resembled it. His body was still, but not in peace. His breathing was fragile. The kind that made you hold your own breath, just to listen. The oxygen concentrator gave off its steady hum. Tubes framed his face like strands of thread barely holding him to this world. His lips were cracked. His chest barely rose. Each breath felt like a gamble, a negotiation with something unseen.

Nancy didn't speak. She didn't make noise. She sat beside the bed and reached for her journal with mechanical familiarity. Her pen hovered over the page, but she didn't write. The ink never touched paper. Her eyes kept drifting back to him, measuring the pause between each inhale. The longer the silence, the tighter her throat became.

Time passed like water leaking from a crack. Hours maybe. It was nearly three in the morning when he stirred.

"Nance?"

The sound of her name from his lips felt like sunlight in a locked room.

"I'm here," she answered, her voice softer than a breath.

His eyes fluttered open. Clouded. Tired. But warm. Like he had been waiting for her in a place only he could see. He was trying to speak but then Nancy broke the silence with her news.

"I found a center," she said. "In Seattle. They might have lungs. They're checking compatibility." She smiled with tired soul.

Jim's gaze didn't shift. He stared at the ceiling like he was looking beyond it.

"You just have to keep holding on," she said. "We're closer than we've ever been."

"I'll try," he whispered. "For you."

"I had a dream," Jim whispered, each word slow, deliberate, as if it cost him effort just to speak. "You were wearing that red scarf. From our first winter."

Nancy smiled gently, lips trembling. "The one you said made me look like a cardinal."

His lips curved into a faint smile. "We were in the kitchen. You were barefoot. It was so cold that night... but we held each other close."

Nancy gave a quiet laugh that trembled at the edges. "You were singing some old love song; completely off key."

Jim's gaze softened, steady and full of memory. "Didn't matter. You were laughing. I was holding you. That moment felt right."

She leaned in a little closer, her voice low. "The air was freezing, but being with you... it felt like the whole world melted away."

Nancy reached for his hand. Her latex glove brushed against his skin. She hated it, this barrier between them. Every part of her ached to touch him without plastic in the way, to press her cheek to his chest, to kiss his fingers and feel the warmth for real. But she couldn't. Not with the virus still lingering in the room like a shadow she couldn't shake. So she held his hand the only way she could. Gently. Reverently.

"Want to hear it?" she asked. "The song from that night...on which we later danced?"

Jim gave the faintest nod.

Nancy picked up her phone and scrolled through their old playlist. Her thumb hesitated over the screen before pressing play. The opening notes of *You Are The Reason by Calum Scott* drifted through the room, soft and slow.

"There goes my heart beating

'Cause you are the reason..."

The music clung to the air like perfume, weightless but thick with memory. Jim closed his eyes, and for a moment, he looked younger. Less sick. Like the boy who had spun her around their tiny apartment while soup boiled on the stove.

Nancy stood beside the bed and slowly lifted her arms. Her gloved fingers stretched into the space between them. She began to sway, body fluid and weightless despite the PPE that clung to her skin. She took one step back, then forward, her feet gliding as if across a kitchen floor dusted with flour. The rhythm moved through her gently, not as a performance, but as a gift.

"Remember this part?" she asked, her voice a hush over the music. "I spun so fast, I knocked over the radio."

"You blamed the cat," he murmured, lips curling with the ghost of a laugh.

"You never believed me."

"Not for a second."

The lyrics rippled around them.

"And there goes my mind racing

And you are the reason..."

Nancy stepped closer. She bent low and brushed his knuckles with her forehead. Then, as the chorus began, she lifted his hand to her masked cheek.

"That I'm still breathing

I'm hopeless now..."

His mouth moved, singing along in whispers. A tear slipped from the corner of his eye, trailing down his temple. His voice cracked but didn't break.

"I love you, Nancy," he said. "You're the best thing that ever happened to me."

Her breath caught. "I love you more."

"No," he whispered. "Not possible."

He raised his hand toward her, as if offering a flying kiss, but midway through the motion, his wrist dropped. His fingers fell limp. His eyes lost their light.

His chest did not rise again.

Nancy froze, mid-dance.

The pulse oximeter beeped once. Eighty-three percent.

Then eighty-one.

Seventy-nine.

And silence.

"Jim?"

Her voice was thin. Shaken.

"Jim!" she called again, louder now.

She dropped to her knees at his side, tearing off her gloves with a snap. The mask followed. She pressed her bare hands to his cheeks, cupping his face.

"Jim, breathe. You hear me? Come on."

She tilted his head gently and sealed her lips over his. One breath. Two. She pulled back, checked his chest. Nothing. She placed the heel of her palm to his sternum and began compressions, counting under her breath, trying to match the rhythm that once made them dance.

"One. Two. Three. Four. Come on, Jim."

She was sweating now, tears pouring freely. Her arms shook with the effort.

"Please," she cried, voice cracking. "I need you."

Still nothing.

The music kept playing.

"I'd climb every mountain

And swim every ocean

Just to be with you..."

She slammed her palm once against his chest, helpless. Her other hand pressed against his pulse point. Stillness. No flicker of life.

She collapsed forward, draping herself across him. Her cheek against his shoulder. Her breath hitched against his skin.

"Jim," she whispered. "No. No, not like this. Please. Don't go. Not yet."

She buried her face in his neck. Breathed him in. His scent, faint but still there, clung to her like a second skin.

"There goes my hands shaking

And you are the reason

My heart keeps bleeding

I need you now..."

And then there was only Jim's lifeless body, the empty room, and a silence that broke her heart beyond repair...

"And if I could turn back the clock

I'd make sure the light defeated the dark

I'd spend every hour, of every day

Keeping you safe."

Nancy lay there as the music faded and the dawn began to rise. The light crept through the blinds, painting his face with a soft gold that should have belonged to sleep, not death.

Her body didn't move. Her heart beat without permission. The world, so cruelly normal, spun on.

But her world had stopped.

And somewhere inside her, she was still dancing in that red scarf, barefoot and laughing, held in the arms of a man who had always caught her....

Until now.

***

The first call she made wasn't to Dr. Pearson. It wasn't to Jim's brother. It wasn't even to the hospital.

It was to the kitchen sink.

Nancy turned the faucet on and let it run until steam curled up from the basin and the scalding water bit into her palm. She didn't pull away. She just stood there, letting the heat press into her skin, burning into the places grief couldn't reach.

Then she began to wash.

Each finger, each nail. She scrubbed mechanically, like she had before every shift for the past year. As if by rinsing her hands she could undo what had just happened. But there was no one left to save.

She peeled away the layers of PPE one by one. The gown first. Then the gloves. The face shield. Each item dropped into the trash like armor shed from a soldier who never made it home. The mask was last. It hit the bin with a dull thud.

She walked through the hall barefoot. The light above flickered once, steadied, and held. The hallway felt longer than it had the day before.

Jim's scent still lingered in the bedroom. Faint, familiar, impossible to let go of.

She opened the closet and reached for one of his shirts. The dark gray one with the frayed collar. The one he wore when they made pancakes on Sunday mornings. She slipped it on over her tank top and curled her fingers into the sleeves. It hung loose, soft, and smelled like him.

She padded to the living room couch and curled into its corner, pulling a throw blanket over her legs. The bedroom was too much. The kitchen too hollow. But the couch... the couch was where he had kissed her forehead when she'd fallen asleep watching reruns. It was neutral territory. Familiar. Safe.

She pressed her face into the collar of his shirt and let the smell hold her. It didn't take long before sleep pulled her under not peaceful, but necessary.

***

At dawn, the phone rang. She blinked against the light and reached for it, heart pounding before her brain could catch up.

It was Dr. Pearson.

He listened. Quietly. Then asked, "Do you want me to call the coroner?"

"Yes. Please," she said.

"I'll handle it."

She nodded, her voice barely a whisper. "Thanks, Dr."

They didn't say anything else.

***

She made the next few calls quickly. Tyler Jim's oldest friend answered after the first ring. His voice cracked.

"I'll be there by noon," he said. "We all will."

Owen, Jim's brother, didn't speak for a long time after she told him. When he finally did, he said only, "He loved you more than anything," before promising to arrive before the funeral.

Carla came by without calling, arms wrapped around a brown paper bag.

"I brought soup," she said softly. "I didn't know what else to do."

Nancy accepted it with a quiet nod.

They sat at the table. Carla reached for her hand but didn't quite touch it. The air between them held all the words neither knew how to say.

"Want me to stay the night?" Carla asked.

Nancy shook her head. "No. But thank you."

Carla nodded. She left the soup on the counter, pressed her lips together like she was swallowing every emotion at once, and walked out the door.

***

By early morning, the sky was a soft blue-gray, light creeping in beneath the blinds.

The house stayed still, but no longer felt quiet.

Everyone had promised to be there before noon.

The funeral would begin before the day was halfway done.

Nancy sat up slowly on the couch, still wrapped in Jim's shirt, and held the warmth of him close to her chest.

She didn't feel ready.

But she would stand anyway...

Chapter 5:
Choosing a New Path in Cincinnati

By late morning, the sun pushed its way through a dull gray sky. Not warm. Not hopeful. Just there. Like a witness.

Nancy stood in the hallway, fastening Jim's old watch around her wrist. It slid loosely on her arm, but the weight comforted her. It felt like a final touch. Like something of him was still holding on.

She had dressed in a plain black dress, pulled her hair back in a low knot, and left her face bare. No makeup. No need. Today wasn't about looking presentable. It was about standing still and letting grief have its place.

The funeral was held at Trinity Memorial Chapel on the edge of the city, a small place with white siding and a cracked bell that hadn't rung in years. Jim had once said he preferred simplicity over grand ceremony. Today, he got exactly that.

When she stepped outside, the driveway was already lined with a few parked cars. Not many. Just the people who mattered. Dan, Jim's brother. Charles from the department. Dr. Pearson. A couple of nurses from her floor. One of Jim's old police department's buddies. Each of them masked. Each standing six feet apart. Each holding grief behind fogged-up glasses and lowered eyes.

Across the street, a single patrol car sat under a leafless tree. A young officer stepped out and stood at attention beside it. Jim had trained him once. The boy couldn't have been more than twenty-five. He looked like he was trying not to cry.

Nancy stepped down the porch slowly. She let the moment settle. Let it remind her she was still here.

Dan met her at the bottom of the steps and handed her a folded paper. "You don't have to speak," he said gently.

She shook her head. "I do."

The chapel inside was stripped down and spaced out. No organ music. No floral arrangements. Just a pine casket up front and chairs placed safely apart. A few tissues crumpled quietly in people's laps. The air smelled faintly of sanitizer and old varnish.

Nancy sat in the front row. When the pastor nodded at her, she stood and walked to the small podium. Her mask muffled her breath, but her voice, when she spoke, was clear.

"I don't know how to say goodbye to someone like Jim," she began. "So I won't. I'll just say thank you."

She glanced around. Everyone's eyes were on her. Some glistening. Some red. Some already spilling over.

"Thank you, Jim, for making people feel safe when the world was on fire. Thank you for laughing at the worst jokes. For loving big and soft and without conditions. Thank you for dancing in our kitchen barefoot and pretending you could sing." Her voice caught, but she didn't stop.

"You made the hard days easier just by being in them. You were never the loudest, but you always showed up. You gave your strength away freely. And even when you had almost nothing left, you still tried to smile."

She looked at his casket. Her fingers tightened slightly around the edges of the podium.

"You didn't go with noise. You didn't go with fear. You went with love still in your eyes. You waited for me. And I will never stop being grateful for that." She paused, breathing shallowly.

"You were my home. And now I'll carry you with me everywhere I go."

A hush followed. No one shifted. No one dared.

She stepped down and returned to her seat, folding her hands in her lap as tears finally fell quietly onto her dress.

When the service ended, the few in attendance walked outside as the casket was carried to the waiting hearse. The young officer saluted again. Charles whispered something as he placed a hand on the wood. Dr. Pearson nodded at her, his hand against his heart. Dan wept openly.

Nancy stood by the chapel door, eyes on the sky. She didn't feel the ground under her feet. Just the moment pressing in. She was not undone. Not yet.

The world had not stopped.

But something inside her had turned.

And in that quiet turn, she felt the faintest pull toward what might come next.

***

Carla had offered. So had Dr. Pearson to drive Nancy home. Even Jim's brother Dan stood awkwardly by the curb, keys dangling from his hand, unsure whether to press or pull back.

But Nancy had declined them all.

"I just need time to process," she said gently to Carla, her voice hoarse from the service. "Before I go back to anything routine."

Carla nodded, her eyes kind. "I understand. Just take care of yourself. I'll come by tomorrow, okay?" She touched Nancy's shoulder briefly. "I'll bring fresh fruit. And no soup, I swear."

Nancy smiled at that. A small one. But it stayed on her lips a beat longer than expected.

She walked slowly to her car. Not because she was tired, but because movement felt like a betrayal. A funeral had just ended. Her husband was gone. How could her legs carry her forward like the world hadn't shattered?

The seatbelt clicked into place with a mechanical finality. She sat for a long moment before starting the engine.

Driving home felt unreal. The afternoon was impossibly bright. The streets looked too clean. A pair of teenagers walked out of a 7-Eleven laughing, one licking a melting ice cream cone. A man walked a golden retriever. A toddler on a tricycle chased bubbles along the sidewalk while her father crouched nearby, clapping for her like she had just won a race.

None of it matched what Nancy carried inside her.

Each red light felt too long. Each green one, too fast.

The house came into view with painful familiarity. It was theirs. She had driven up this same street hundreds of times. But today, it felt like approaching a replica. The fern by the porch still wilted in the heat. The welcome mat tilted just a little from where Jim used to straighten it with his foot. It should have comforted her. But it only reminded her of everything he used to touch.

She pulled into the driveway slowly. Gravel crunched under her tires. For a second, she didn't move. Then, with quiet resolve, she stepped out of the car and walked to the door.

Inside, the air was still. The kind of stillness that pressed on your chest and wrapped around your throat.

Nancy kicked off her shoes at the threshold. Not neatly. Just off. She left her purse on the floor by the wall. The black dress clung to her skin in the summer heat. It felt like a costume someone else had put on her.

She walked straight upstairs.

In the bedroom, she didn't hang the dress. She didn't fold it. She stepped out of it slowly and let it fall to the floor. She didn't even glance back at it. Jim used to be the one to pick up her dresses and hang them gently, scolding her with that playful smirk.

"You're a whirlwind, babe," he'd say. "And I'm the guy chasing your paper trail." Now there was no one behind her to fold the chaos into order.

She stood in front of the mirror for a moment, bare, unguarded, her skin flushed from the heat and her chest streaked faintly red where tears had dried. Her own reflection didn't recognize her. There were no signs of strength in her eyes today.

Only weariness. And that weight in her chest that had settled like sand.

She walked into the bathroom and turned on the shower. The water ran lukewarm. No need for heat. The summer air was thick enough. She stepped under it and let it roll over her, not to clean but to ground herself.

She stayed there a while. Letting water glide down her spine, drip from her fingertips. She didn't cry. She didn't move much either. Just stood and breathed in the quiet.

When she finally stepped out, she wrapped herself in a towel and walked to Jim's dresser.

She pulled open the second drawer. Took out the shirt. Not just any shirt. The soft gray one he wore when he wanted to be close. The one he always wore when he wanted her to know without words. He would come up behind her, lean down, and kiss her neck in that shirt. He'd run his hand down her back. He never said it. He didn't have to.

She slipped it on. It fell loose around her, the sleeves brushing her elbows. The scent of his skin was there to hug her and his combination of different perfumes, something only she knew how to name.

She walked to the bed and sat at the edge, the fabric clinging to her thighs.

Her gaze drifted to the bookshelf.

Jim's biography still lay open, a page folded to hold his place. His coffee mug on the nightstand had a ring around the rim, dried. His phone charger still tangled at the side of the bed.

She ran her fingers over the pillow he slept on. Pulled it into her lap. Held it close.

The silence in the room was not peaceful. It was deafening. And it wasn't silence. It was absence. She curled tighter around the pillow.

Nancy had spent her life trying to save people. It had been her purpose, her heartbeat, the rhythm of her every day. She had cracked ribs beneath her palms doing compressions, whispering, *Come back, come back,* into the ears of strangers. Her hands had blistered against defibrillator pads, too focused to notice the sting. She had looked into the eyes of mothers and told them the words no human should ever have to say. She had seen the look of hope vanish. She had carried grief, again and again, and somehow, she had stayed standing.

She had been everything to everyone. Calm in chaos. Strength in panic. Grace in the storm.

But she could not save Jim.

Not with her experience. Not with her instinct. Not with the fierce, all-consuming love that had guided every breath she took in the last weeks of his life.

She had failed the one life that mattered most.

That truth did not scream. It sat heavy in her lungs, made her breath shallow, her chest sore. It hummed behind her eyes, stealing sleep, robbing rest.

And now, she had nothing left to give that world.

The codes. The alarms. The beeping that never stopped. The cold tiles under her shoes at 3 a.m. The exhausted prayers in sterile rooms. The clipped nods exchanged between nurses when one more life slipped through their fingers.

Every hallway at the hospital reminded her of loss. Every room held a memory of someone she had held, or tried to hold, until death pried them free.

Even victory felt borrowed now. Temporary. Fragile. She had become someone who could still function, still stitch wounds and chart vitals but something inside her was no longer answering the call.

What she had once done with power, she now did with weight.

She needed something different now.

Something not about surviving.

***

She didn't know how long she had been sitting there. The quiet had swallowed her whole. One minute it had been late afternoon. The next, the room had grown dark around her, and the glow of the laptop was the only light touching her face.

When she glanced at the clock in the corner of the screen, it read **9:15 PM**.

Nine fifteen.

She blinked. That couldn't be right. The funeral had ended hours ago. Carla had dropped off the banana bread sometime around two. And now it was night.

Eight hours. Gone. As if time had folded in on itself and she had sat right through it.

Nancy exhaled and stood up. Her back cracked as she stretched, the kind of stiffness that came from staying in one place for too long, both physically and mentally. The couch cushion still held the shape of her. The banana bread remained untouched on the counter.

She crossed the room and turned on the television without thinking. The volume was already low, but the headline caught her eye:

MERCY WEST FACING ICU OVERFLOW AS SUMMER CASES SPIKE

The news anchor looked pale beneath the studio lights, reciting numbers that had stopped feeling like numbers a long time ago. ICU beds full. Emergency triage tents reopening.

Nurses pulling double shifts. The overlay showed masked healthcare workers wheeling patients under a hazy orange sky.

Nancy froze. That was her hospital. Her floor. The same unit where she had spent years trying to hold the line.

Her heart clenched. Not out of guilt. But out of exhaustion. It was always the same story.

And then, uninvited but crystal clear, Jim's voice echoed in her memory.

"Nance, whenever you feel stuck, don't fight the wall. Look for the door. You've always known how to find the way forward. You just forget sometimes."

She pressed her palm to her chest as if his voice had physically touched her. That voice wasn't here anymore. He wasn't here. Not to hold her hand. Not to help her figure it out.

But his words had stayed.

She walked back to the desk and sat down again, this time with something different inside her. Not clarity. Not purpose. But a small tug of movement. The kind that makes you lean just slightly toward change.

The laptop screen had gone to sleep. She tapped it and the image returned. A photograph filled the background her and Jim, on their wedding day. He was laughing at something she had whispered, his forehead leaning into hers, his tie slightly askew. She was grinning wide, her veil caught in the wind.

She touched the screen lightly. "What now, Jim?"

Then she opened a new tab and typed in:

"Nursing jobs near St. Louis"

She scrolled mindlessly. Everything felt too familiar. Same hospitals. Same chaos.

Then she typed in something she hadn't dared to search for until now:

"Travel nurse jobs transplant unit Midwest"

A few listings popped up. She skimmed the results until her eye caught one name:

St. James Medical Center – Cincinnati, Ohio

She clicked the link.

The website opened to a clean, crisp homepage. A banner at the top read: *Compassionate Innovation. Life Beyond Survival.* Below it was a photo carousel: a smiling transplant team, a patient ringing a recovery bell, and then there he was.

Dr. Elijah Leigh

His headshot appeared beside a short bio. Director of the Transplant ICU. Twenty-three years in post-op care. She remembered the same face from a **virtual symposium nine months ago**, where she had attended one of his panels. He had spoken not just like a doctor, but like someone who believed in the after. The *what now*. He had said something that stayed with her all this time.

"We don't just fight death. We create beginnings."

Nancy's pulse ticked faster.

She clicked the *Careers* tab.

A listing appeared.

"Immediate Opening – Travel RN, ICU/Transplant – St. James Medical Center"

She didn't think. Her hand moved faster than her thoughts.

Click.

The job description loaded. Right there, at the bottom of the page, was the line she needed.

For inquiries, contact: Dr. Elijah Leigh – leigh.j@stjamescincinnati.org

She hovered over it.

Clicked.

A new email tab popped up.

She stared at the blinking cursor. The "To" field was already filled in with leigh.j@stjamescincinnati.org. Below that, the subject line box waited blankly.

She typed:

Travel Nurse Application

Then deleted it.

Too dry.

She tried again:

Inquiry About ICU Position

Then deleted that too.

She stared at the empty line and whispered, "Just write like a person."

Her fingers moved again.

Looking for New Ground

She didn't delete it this time.

In the message box, she typed a greeting.

Dear Dr. Leigh,

And then stopped. Her mind spun. Too many thoughts crowding the same space.

The first draft came out rushed and shaky.

We met last year during a symposium. I think you mentioned the role of emotional pacing in transplant care. I'm a nurse. I've worked trauma for 15 years. I'm tired. I want to change. Please let me know if there's an opening.

She cringed and hit *Select All*, then *Delete*.

Too raw.

She tried again.

I'm writing to express interest in the travel nurse position at St. James Medical Center. I have extensive experience in high-acuity trauma and critical care settings, including ventilator management, rapid response, and code leadership. I am deeply committed to clinical excellence and...

She stopped. Highlighted half the paragraph. Deleted.

Too polished. Too robotic.

Her fingers hovered.

Jim's voice floated through her again. That memory of him saying, "You're not just skilled, Nance. You're human. That's your difference."

So she took a breath. And wrote it like she meant it.

***

Dear Dr. Leigh,

We met briefly during the organ transplant symposium last fall. You spoke on the philosophy of post-op care and said something that has stayed with me ever since *We don't just fight death. We create beginnings.*

I've been a trauma nurse for over fifteen years, most recently at Mercy West in St. Louis. I've worked in ICUs, ERs, surgical recovery floors. I've led codes, trained new hires, and held hands in too many final moments.

But lately, something in me has changed. I've lost someone I love deeply; my husband, Jim. And in the wake of that, I've realized I want my work to be about more than keeping people from dying. I want to be somewhere that gives them a new chance to live.

I saw the travel nurse opening on your site and felt pulled to reach out. My background includes advanced cardiac support, ventilator care, and transplant recovery experience. But more than that, I still believe in patients. In second chances. In hope.

I've attached my resume and credentials. If the position is still open, I would be honored to speak with you.

Warmly,

Nancy Brooks,

Trauma & Critical Care Nurse

St. Louis, Missouri <u>nancy.brooks@gmail.com</u>

(314) 555-0429

***

Nancy read it twice. Then again.

Her finger hovered over the mousepad. She didn't click "Send" yet.

She leaned back in the chair, exhaled deeply, and looked at the photo on her wallpaper again Jim in his wedding suit, winking at her like he knew something she didn't.

"I'm trying," she whispered.

Then she clicked.

Send.

The message whooshed out into the quiet room.

She stared at the screen for a long moment. The cursor blinked like a heartbeat.

Nancy didn't feel whole. She didn't feel healed.

But she felt honest.

And for now, that was enough.

She stood up slowly, closed the laptop, and walked toward the kitchen to finally cut herself a slice of banana bread.

Outside, the streetlights had come on. The city continued, unaware that something small had shifted.

Nancy Brooks had taken her first real step toward something new.

Chapter 6:
Covid changed Everything Everywhere

The sun was already high when Nancy woke.

Not gently. Not with ease. But with the kind of dull awareness that came after too much crying and too little sleep. Her body refused to shift at first, cocooned in the thick quiet of a house that no longer echoed. She stared at the ceiling. The fan above rotated in lazy circles, pulling warm air that barely moved. Jim's shirt clung to her, stretched out and soft with years of wear. The fabric smelled faintly of his cologne and something older, something that felt like memory.

Her phone buzzed on the nightstand, screen lit with dozens of notifications. Missed calls. Voicemails. Messages that came in through the night and early morning condolences from people who meant well but hadn't shown up. Others from colleagues trying to say the right thing. A few from old friends she hadn't spoken to in months, all beginning with "I just heard." She didn't open them. Not yet.

Instead, she let her feet touch the floor, each step down the stairs like moving through mud. The kitchen felt like neutral ground. Sunlight filtered through the sheer curtain, casting soft stripes across the tile. The banana bread sat half-wrapped on the counter. Nancy reached for a mug Jim's mug. The one with the chipped handle he never let her throw away and filled it with black coffee. No sugar. No milk. It was bitter and grounding. She drank it like it had a job to do.

Some part of her thought the world might have changed after yesterday. That maybe time would pause to mark the space left by Jim. But the silence was not reverent. It was indifferent. The house didn't hum with grief. It just didn't hum at all.

She sat at the kitchen table, laptop open in front of her, the same browser still pulled up from last night. No email from Dr. Leigh. That was expected. Nothing moved quickly in medicine unless it was an emergency.

She scrolled past inbox alerts and local headlines until one story caught her eye.

Organ Supply Crisis: Pandemic's Hidden Toll The headline shouldn't have stopped her, but it did.

She clicked.

The article was long. Dense with data and government briefings, but she read every word. Her hand tightened around the coffee mug as the statistics piled up. Donor rates had plummeted. Waitlists had exploded. Recovery teams were getting benched in high-risk areas. Cold ischemia times were climbing. Surgeons were turning away organs they would have once accepted. And every rejected match meant someone else waited longer. Or didn't survive the wait at all.

There was a line in the middle that made her physically lean back from the screen:

"Organs are dying with their donors, not because of medical unsuitability, but because the system can't keep up." Nancy set the mug down.

It clinked too loudly against the counter.

This wasn't a theory anymore. This was reality. Her reality. She thought of all the patients she had seen over the past year whose lives had drifted out of reach not because they weren't salvageable but because the structure meant to catch them had holes too wide to patch.

There was the young woman who had finally received a match for a new lung only for the transplant to be delayed twelve hours due to a staffing issue in post-op. She didn't live to see the morning.

There was the man who coded in the hallway after waiting nine hours in a non-COVID wing that was too understaffed to catch the drop in his vitals.

There was the eighteen-year-old with failing kidneys whose mother called Nancy at 2 a.m., begging for a timeline that didn't exist.

Each one still lived somewhere in Nancy's memory. Not as cases. But as voices. As hands she had held. As final words spoken through masks and suction tubes.

It was no longer just about sickness.

It was about logistics.

Timing.

Chance.

The pandemic had turned organ donation into a race against an invisible clock. One where the rules kept changing and nobody really knew where the finish line was anymore.

Nancy stood up and paced the room.

Her mind pulled her back to the night she had last talked with Jim about the transplant world. It was late. She had been venting about delayed OR turnover times and his response, as always, had been calm.

"You're fighting for lives that haven't even happened yet," he told her. "That's not failure, Nance. That's hope with long odds."

She didn't reply that night. She had just climbed into bed beside him, laid her head on his shoulder, and closed her eyes.

Now those words felt heavier. More like prophecy than comfort.

She returned to her seat. Her hands hovered over the keyboard again. Not for a new application. Just to search.

She typed in **"UNOS shortage 2020 trends"** and then, **"Organ donation during pandemic"**. Each result was worse than the last. And it was all verified. Documented. Calculated. The demand was growing. The supply was vanishing. The windows were closing faster than they opened.

Nancy exhaled slowly and leaned back in her chair.

This wasn't just a bad year. It was a turning point.

A shift in how they would define success from now on.

You didn't get to win anymore just by showing up. You had to outpace the collapse. You had to reinvent your role in it.

For a nurse like her, that meant leaving behind the places where you could only slow the dying.

It meant going where people still had a fighting chance to live.

Her eyes drifted again to the open email tab. Still no reply.

But the seed had been planted. And it was rooted now in something larger than grief.

This wasn't just about saving others.

It was about saving herself from a profession that, left unchanged, might break her spirit before it broke her body.

She stood up. Moved to the sink. The house was quiet again, but something had shifted.

***

Nancy stood and moved to the window. Across the street, a mail carrier dropped a few letters into the box with a quick flick of the wrist. Life was still ticking forward, she thought. The gears hadn't stopped. The mail came. Trash got collected. Dogs still barked at nothing. But behind so many of those doors, something had shifted. Death had stopped being rare. It had become rhythm. Familiar. Quietly absorbed into the fabric of daily life.

And with it, the organ pool had started to dry up not because people weren't dying, but because they were dying in the wrong places, at the wrong times, without the right systems in place. Dying alone, in overwhelmed hospitals, where the necessary boxes weren't checked fast enough to preserve the gift inside them.

Her phone buzzed again.

This time, it wasn't another sympathy message. It was Jim's brother.

She stared at the screen for a second before answering.

"Hey, Dan," she said softly.

His voice was rough on the other end. "I didn't want to text. Just wanted to hear your voice."

"Thanks."

A short silence followed.

"I've been going over some of Jim's old academy photos," he said. "Found that one where you and I are both giving him grief about his awful buzz cut."

Nancy smiled faintly. "That was a bad cut."

"You said he looked like a Q-tip that got caught in a fan."

She exhaled a small laugh. "He took it like a champ."

Dan's tone softened. "He always did." There was a longer pause now.

"You hanging in there?" he asked.

Nancy walked back toward the kitchen table. "Some moments are worse than others. But I'm okay. I think I'm… shifting gears. Trying to figure out where I can be of use."

"You're always of use, Nancy. You were his anchor. You were all of ours during the worst of it."

She lowered herself into the chair. "I couldn't save him."

"That's not on you. You saved him every day for eighteen extra months. Don't forget that."

Her eyes blurred but didn't spill. "I just keep thinking if this had happened a year earlier, he wouldn't have even made the transplant list. He would've been one more loss buried under Covid stats. That reality keeps hitting me."

Dan didn't speak at first. When he did, his voice was steadier than she expected.

"You know, I used to joke that Jim got all the stubborn in the family. But I think it was just that he found someone who matched it."

She ran her thumb along the rim of the coffee mug. "I'm trying to do something with it now. There's an opening on a transplant team in Cincinnati. It's not finalized, but… I might be moving."

There was a beat of silence.

Then Dan said, "Jim would be proud."

She swallowed. "That matters."

"It should."

Another pause. Then Dan added, more quietly, "Call if you need anything. Not just for errands or condolences. I mean for real. The stuff people don't offer help with."

Nancy's throat tightened. "Thank you, Dan. Really."

After they hung up, she sat for a moment, grounded by the conversation in a way she hadn't expected. Grief hadn't lifted, but something else had arrived in its place. Resolve. A quiet flame lit from shared memory and silent support.

She returned to the kitchen table, pulled out her notepad, and flipped to a clean page. At the top, she wrote:

Covid's Effect on the Transplant Cycle

It wasn't a research paper. It wasn't a report. Just a nurse's shorthand, her own way of making sense.

- Fewer ventilated patients stabilized long enough to donate

- ICU overflows leading to delayed referrals

- Family consent harder to obtain under visitation bans

- Transplant teams pulled into Covid wards

- OR availability dropped drastically

- Hearts lost. Livers too slow. Kidneys expired in cold storage

It read like a list of preventable tragedies.

She paused. Added one more line:

- So many chances died with them

Nancy didn't cry. She hadn't for a few days now. But her hands trembled slightly as she set the pen down.

She thought of Jim again not just as her husband, but as a patient. A recipient. A survivor. He had made it to transplant in time. Barely. She still remembered that window the five hours between coding and the call. The razor's edge they had lived on. The surgery that bought them eighteen more months.

If Covid had hit back then, he wouldn't have stood a chance.

Not because the donor wouldn't have existed.

But because the system would have failed him.

Her laptop chimed.

She glanced down.

1 New Email: Dr. Elijah Leigh

She froze.

Then opened it...

Subject: Re: Looking for New Ground

Dear Nancy,

Thank you for your email. I remember your name from the virtual symposium we spoke briefly in the Q&A chat. I'm very sorry to hear about your loss, and I admire your willingness to write so openly in the wake of it. That kind of honesty matters here.

We do have an urgent opening on the ICU transplant team, and I believe your experience would be an asset, especially in this climate. Our unit is stable for now, but the demand is growing faster than we can train for. We've lost three nurses to burnout this year alone.

If you're available for a preliminary phone conversation, I'd be happy to speak this week.

Warmly,

Dr. Elijah Leigh

Medical Director – ICU Transplant Unit St. James Medical Center, Cincinnati

***

Nancy reread it three times.

Not because the words were unclear. Not because she doubted her qualifications. But because something in her still struggled to accept the idea that there was a "next." That something could follow this grief and not feel like a betrayal.

She let the cursor hover for a beat.

Then she clicked *Reply.*

Her fingers moved slowly at first, choosing each word with care.

Dear Dr. Leigh,

Thank you for getting back to me. Yes, I remember our exchange at the symposium. I appreciated your candor then and I appreciate it now even more.

I would be honored to speak. I'm available anytime, whichever works best for your schedule.

With respect,

Warmly,

Nancy Brooks,

Trauma & Critical Care Nurse

St. Louis, Missouri nancy.brooks@gmail.com **(314) 555-0429**

She hit send.

The message zipped away into cyberspace. No fanfare. No drumroll. Just a soft whoosh and the quiet click of moving forward.

Nancy leaned back in her chair.

She glanced around the kitchen. Jim's badge still hung from the hook beside the door. His soup bowl sat on the counter, untouched since the morning he got sick. There were reminders of him in every corner of the house, but instead of closing in, they felt like markers on a trail she was still walking.

Her phone buzzed.

Another text from a friend checking in.

Her inbox and voicemail had overflowed with condolences. People she hadn't heard from in years, college classmates, former coworkers, distant cousins, had surfaced texts and prayers. She appreciated it, but the outpouring had felt like rain against glass. It made sound, but it didn't really reach her.

Now, though, this email from Dr. Leigh; that felt *different*.

It wasn't sympathy. It was action.

She turned and walked slowly to the bookshelf.

It was packed tight; spines creased, corners softened by time. She ran her fingers across them absently. Fiction, medical texts, a few memoirs, one of Jim's old police force guides still wedged sideways near the top. She reached for a collection of poetry, one she'd never managed to finish, but paused halfway through pulling it out.

Her phone rang.

Carla.

Nancy let the book fall back into place and picked up.

"Hey," she said, voice low but calm.

"Hey," Carla replied gently. "I didn't want to bother you… I just wanted to check in. How are you today?"

Nancy exhaled through her nose and looked around the living room. "I'm… okay. Still in one piece." "Banana bread still on the counter?"

"Half, yes, untouched."

They both let out a soft laugh.

Then Nancy took a breath. "Actually… there's something I should tell you."

"What is it?"

"I'm leaving," she said. "Not forever. But I applied for a travel nurse position. ICU transplant unit. Cincinnati. It's at St. James Medical Center."

There was a pause.

"You *what*?"

"I sent the email last night. Got a reply this morning. It's moving fast. They want to talk this week."

Carla was silent for a second longer than usual.

Nancy filled the space. "It's not a whim. I've been thinking about it. For weeks, really. Even before Jim passed. I just… didn't want to admit it to myself. But everything feels different now. And I can't stay in this house, in this city, waiting to feel like myself again. I need something that matters. Something that gives instead of just… reminding."

Another beat of silence. Then:

"Is it about him?" Carla asked. "Or is it about you?"

"It's about both," Nancy said quietly. "But mostly me. I need to believe I can still do this. Not just survive *do* something. Make it count. And if Jim had the strength to hold on through everything, I can have the strength to start again."

Carla's voice cracked just slightly. "You really mean it."

"I do."

"I'll be there in an hour."

Nancy smiled. "You don't have to…"

"I know. I want to."

And true to her word, Carla was knocking on the door fifty-three minutes later.

Nancy opened it and barely got out a greeting before Carla pulled her into a hug. Tight. Unapologetic.

"I still remember the day you moved into this place," Carla said, voice thick. "You didn't even know where the breaker box was. Jim spent a whole afternoon labeling every switch."

Nancy laughed softly against her shoulder. "He labeled the toaster."

"I know."

Carla pulled back and looked at her, really looked. "You're doing the right thing, Nancy. I know it hurts. But I also know you. And you don't run. You rise."

Nancy's eyes burned, but she didn't look away. She reached out and pulled Carla close again, this time with both arms around her.

"You were there when I got here," she whispered. "And you're here as I go. That means something."

Carla pressed her face into Nancy's shoulder. "I'll miss you." The hug didn't break easily.

Even when they pulled apart, Carla kept Nancy's hand in hers, fingers laced like she wasn't quite ready to let go. Her eyes were still misty, her breath unsteady.

"Can I… come with you?" she asked, nodding toward the hallway. "To the room, I mean. Help you set aside a few things? Just the stuff you won't pack yet."

Nancy gave a soft smile. "Of course."

They walked slowly, past the stairs, down the short hallway that led to the bedroom. The door was half-shut. The room still smelled faintly of lavender and aftershave. Nancy's pace slowed for a moment, just outside the threshold. Carla noticed.

"You've been wearing his shirt," Carla said quietly.

Nancy looked down. It hung loosely over her jeans, sleeves pushed halfway to her elbows. "I haven't taken it off since the funeral."

Carla stepped in first. Her eyes swept the room the rumpled sheets, the book on the nightstand still open to the last page Jim had read, the pulse oximeter cord coiled neatly but unused. Her gaze stopped at the framed photo beside the lamp: Jim in uniform, smiling at something just off camera.

"Oh Jim," she whispered, her voice breaking, "you left too early."

She sat down hard on the edge of the bed. Her shoulders trembled.

Nancy walked over slowly, sat beside her, and didn't say a word. She didn't need to.

A few seconds passed, then Carla leaned against her, pressing her forehead to Nancy's shoulder.

"I thought I was okay," she said. "But it just hit me again. Seeing this room. Seeing you in his shirt. It's like… he could walk in any second."

"I know," Nancy whispered. "I keep hearing the front door creak. My brain still thinks it's him."

They didn't move.

Eventually, they slid to the floor, backs against the bed, shoulders brushing. No packing happened. Not yet. Instead, they talked. About everything. About nothing. They shared stories they'd never told before, things that made them laugh too hard and then cry just as hard. The hours stretched and softened. At some point, Carla reached for the blanket draped over the foot of the bed and pulled it around them both.

They drifted off that way, side by side on the floor like two girls hiding from a storm.

Then Carla's phone buzzed sharply against the hardwood.

She jerked awake, blinking. The screen lit up with a name and number she knew too well. She answered in a hushed voice, careful not to wake Nancy, who remained curled under the blanket, her breath deep and steady.

"Carla speaking." A pause.

"Yeah… right now? Okay. I'll be there in twenty."

Her voice softened. "Tell them to hold the line. I'm on my way."

She ended the call and looked down at Nancy, still asleep in Jim's shirt, her face turned toward the space where he used to lie.

Carla stood quietly, brushing the hair from her own face, and took a slow breath. She grabbed a pen from the nightstand drawer and a scrap of notebook paper tucked beside Nancy's journal.

Dear Nancy,

Duty calls, as it always does for people like us. I got pulled for an emergency shift they're short again, and I couldn't say no. I didn't want to leave like this, not without saying goodbye, but you were sleeping so peacefully for the first time in days. I didn't have the heart to wake you.

Tonight, sitting in that room with you, I remembered something I think I forgot: how deep love can go. How loss doesn't flatten it it only stretches it wider. You're living proof of that.

Watching you fight for Jim, then grieve for him without collapsing completely it's something I'll carry for a long, long time.

I know this decision you've made to go to start again in

Cincinnati it wasn't easy. It takes guts to walk forward when half of you is still clinging to yesterday. But I believe in you. And more than that, I'm proud of you.

Take only what you need. Leave the rest. And if you ever find yourself needing home again, you know where to find me.

Hold fast to your purpose. It's bigger than the loss.

Love you always, **Carla.**

Carla folded the note gently and slid it under Nancy's hand. She lingered just a moment, brushing her palm against her friend's knuckles.

Then she picked up her keys, grabbed her bag from the hallway chair, and stepped quietly out into the night back into the current of urgency that never really stops flowing.

***

The following week came early.

Nancy sat in her car outside the hospital, staring up at the pale sky above Cincinnati. A different sky. A different city. But the same weight in her chest.

Her call with Dr. Leigh had gone well. Direct. Professional. But human. He had asked her one question near the end that stuck with her.

"Are you ready for this kind of pressure again?"

She had paused, then answered, "No. But I'm willing to step into it anyway."

Now she sat parked in the staff lot of St. James Medical Center, her badge clipped to a new lanyard, her scrubs freshly laundered. Her bag held a stethoscope, two pens, a protein bar, and a small folded photo of Jim that she hadn't decided where to place yet.

Inside, the hospital was cooler. Brighter. The scent of disinfectant carried a citrus bite. Nurses moved briskly behind the front desk, faces familiar only by their eyes. Behind double doors at the end of the hallway, lives were balancing on machines and Nancy had arrived to help catch what could still be saved.

By 9 a.m., she had met the team. A mix of burnouts and believers. Young and old. Some new to transplant, some hardened by it.

By 10, she was scrubbing in for a liver transplant. A donor twenty-nine, male, trauma accident, brain death confirmed, no Covid complications had come in at midnight. The liver matched perfectly with a woman in recovery who'd waited 214 days. Her kidneys were failing. Her heart was tired.

If this surgery worked, she might see Christmas.

Nancy stood at the edge of the sterile field as Dr. Leigh glanced up at her from behind his mask.

"You ready?" he asked.

Nancy nodded.

"Let's begin," he said.

The lights above them bloomed to full brightness. Instruments clinked. The silence of concentration settled in.

Three hours passed like seconds.

At 1:27 p.m., the liver was in.

At 1:41, blood flow returned.

At 1:43, the organ blushed pink.

It worked.

Not just science. Not just timing. But something else.

Nancy exhaled as she watched the numbers stabilize on the monitor. She felt her shoulders drop, just slightly, for the first time in months.

Back in the hallway, she washed her hands slowly and stepped outside the surgical suite.

A nurse came jogging down the corridor.

"There's another one coming in. Possible donor, age forty-five, just coded in the ER. Intubated. Brain bleed. No pulse on arrival, but organ team's en route."

Nancy's eyes snapped to the nurse.

"How soon?"

"Ambulance ETA six minutes. We may have a match. Dr. Leigh's checking with UNOS."

Nancy's pulse quickened.

Two in one day.

Two lives saved.

Or maybe more.

And just like that, the rhythm returned. Not the rhythm of chaos or failure, but the rhythm of hope. Fast. Urgent. Real.

Nancy turned toward the ICU.

There was no time to dwell. The world didn't stop. Not for grief. Not for fear.

And not for Covid.

Inside those hospital walls, the rules had changed.

But so had the stakes.

Organs were rare. Time was shorter. Every match was a miracle.

And Nancy Brooks had just stepped back into the fight.

Chapter 7:
Behind the White Doors of St. James

Life, Nancy often thought, moved like seasons you never got to vote on. One day you'd wake to warmth and light, and just as you started to settle into it, everything turned. Spring might come while you still felt frozen inside, and summer would slip through your fingers before you ever had the chance to breathe it in. And when someone you loved took their last breath, the world didn't stop, it just rolled on, pretending nothing had changed. Seasons moved on. And you? You just tried to keep up, dragging your heart behind like a coat too heavy for the weather.

She was thinking this while scrolling through photos on her phone, one leg tucked under her as she sat near the vending machine. A soft beanie covered her half-dried hair from the earlier shower she barely remembered taking. The breakroom light buzzed faintly overhead, more yellow than white, casting a tired tint across the hospital-blue walls.

Her thumb hovered over a photo of Jim. His birthday. He had a paper crown crooked on his head, and he was grinning at a half-melted cake with the kind of unbothered joy that made strangers smile back. They had just talked about moving. Just started saying "when" instead of "if." He wanted a backyard. Maybe a small dog. He wanted something that felt permanent.

Nancy exhaled quietly, eyes stinging. She closed the photo, dropped the phone on the counter beside her coffee, and turned toward the sandwich she'd barely touched.

The door swung open.

Evelyn entered like she always did; brisk, focused, never needing permission to take up space. Her dark hair was wound into a low bun, a few flyaway catching static in the air. She wore forest green scrubs with an ID badge clipped low, a lab coat slung over one shoulder, and compression socks that had little lightning bolts on them, of all things. Her jaw was tight. Her hands clutched a printout like it was going to bleed.

Nancy didn't look up right away. She already knew from Evelyn's posture that something had gone sideways.

"You're off lunch," Evelyn said flatly, stopping in front of her.

Nancy peeled back the sandwich wrapper, one slow inch at a time. "Barely started."

Evelyn didn't crack a smile. "We just lost one man. Forty-two. Walk-in. Or rather; drop-in."

Nancy raised her eyes. "What! How? COVID?"

"Yeah, COVID it was. Collapsed before the desk. Paramedics said he had a weak pulse in the rig, but by the time they unloaded him, it was gone."

Nancy shifted upright. "How long did they try?"

"Fifteen minutes. Trauma bay tried for another ten. Flatlined through both. Called it just past six-thirty."

Evelyn handed over the sheet. "And his kidneys are clean. Creatinine 1.1. BP was holding right up until the collapse. No history of renal failure. No diabetes. Lungs are shot, but the renal system? Stable."

Nancy scanned the page quickly. His name was Ethan Cole. Forty-two. No listed comorbidities outside of mild

hypertension. She noticed the name of his next of kin. *Sofia C...*
Spouse.

"He was married," Nancy murmured.

"Yeah," Evelyn said softly. "She came in with him. Waited out in the hallway while they tried to bring him back. Then... she signed the papers. Crying the whole time."

Nancy's breath hitched, her eyes narrowing in suspicion. She blinked; once, then again...like the words had scrambled her thoughts. "Signed the papers?" she echoed, voice tight. "What papers?"

Evelyn pressed her lips into a thin line and spoke carefully, almost like she wasn't sure if she should say it. "Consent... umm... he was registered. An organ donor...Kidney."

Nancy's chest tightened. "Organ donor?" she said, like the words didn't belong in the room yet.

"And there's a match," Evelyn added quietly.

Nancy's brow pinched. "Who?"

"Room 314. Delilah."

That name hit like a quiet knock.

"Seriously?" Nancy asked, straightening. "She just cleared UNOS."

Evelyn nodded. "Last Thursday. Blood type O. No antibodies flagged. Tissue match is clean."

Nancy exhaled slowly, piecing it together. "She's been waiting since... what, March?"

"End of February, actually. She's been here so long, I almost forgot she's not technically admitted full-time."

"She's the one with the daughter in Houston, right?"

"Yeah. Facetimes her every night, if the Wi-Fi holds up."

Nancy leaned back against the counter. "How's she doing today?"

"Stable. A little foggy after her session this morning, but responsive. She asked if we were stalling when Leigh told her there might be a donor. Said she didn't want another false alarm."

Nancy didn't blame her. False hope was a hard bruise to keep poking.

"She knows it's a COVID case?" Nancy asked.

Evelyn gave a small nod. "Leigh's walking her through it. Risks, everything. She didn't hesitate. Said she doesn't have time to wait for perfect."

Nancy nodded slowly, mind spinning through protocol. "Has Leigh been paged?"

"He's talking to Delilah now."

"And the board?"

Evelyn gave a half-shrug, half-scowl. "Stuck. They want a second PCR confirmation. Another round of risk evaluation. There's a new memo this week about COVID-positive donors. They're tightening the approvals again."

Nancy sighed through her nose. "How long since time of death?"

"Thirty-five minutes into cold ischemia."

Nancy then picked her phone up and gave papers back to Evelyn. "That gives us what? An hour? Ninety minutes if we're pushing it?"

Evelyn nodded. "Maybe."

"Where's the body?"

"Trauma bay. Fridge."

Nancy didn't answer. She was already moving for the door.

***

The trauma bay was quiet, but not calm. It felt like the breath held after a punch, tight, braced, suspended in time. Monitors blinked silently, IV stands stood like motionless sentinels, and even the overhead lights seemed dimmer, as if they too were holding back. It was the kind of stillness that didn't feel peaceful; it felt loaded, like the walls themselves were listening, waiting for someone to speak, to declare what came next... or to confirm what everyone already feared.

Nancy stepped through the last curtain.

The trauma bay always carried a kind of weight that didn't come from the machines or the gurneys. It was the pause after everything had already been done. No more running. No more shouting. Just stillness. Just what remained.

The body lay zipped up on the gurney, a white sheet pulled neatly over what had once been a man. Beside it, a red organ transport cooler sat sealed on its tray, humming faintly, like it still had a job to finish.

She stayed a moment longer than she needed to see the dead body... the sterile lights catching on the zipper and the brushed steel. There was nothing dramatic about death in the trauma bay no alarms, no shouting. Just the stillness. A dry, hollow quiet that slipped in when the soul slipped out.

The last time Nancy had seen a body like this...tagged, zipped, and silent; it was Jim. Her husband. Her best friend. The man who once danced around their tiny living room holding her old college sweatshirt like it was a baby blanket. The man with whom she lived the intimate moments...*Love* was always the important part of her life... and now...it felt *blurred*.

Now it's Ethan Cole's body. Someone's husband... Maybe the kind of man who wore his wedding ring without thinking about it, who sent text messages like "be home soon" and meant every word. Probably had a favorite chair, a chipped mug he never replaced, a habit of humming old songs under his breath. Maybe he fixed things around the house with too much tape. Maybe he danced with his wife in the kitchen... Maybe he just held her hand every night like it was a quiet promise.

And if he was a father; Nancy pressed a hand to her stomach without thinking...those kids would be waking up soon. Maybe they were still asleep, their world still intact for just a few more minutes. Maybe they would ask where he was. Maybe no one would have the words yet.

And now he was still.

She thought of his wife. Sofia.

Nancy hadn't seen her, but the name stayed with her. It had a softness to it. She imagined a woman walking out of the hospital doors with tears...with silence clinging to her like fog. A woman who had just signed papers no one should ever have to sign. A woman who would be called brave, when all she really wanted was one more morning to make coffee for someone who wasn't coming back.

Nancy had lived that walk.

She had stood where Sofia stood now, holding nothing but memories... and the weight of goodbye still fresh in her chest. In this moment, she maybe sorting through his things, maybe picking out what he'd wear one last time. Preparing for the memorial, or just trying to hold herself together long enough to face it. And when she came back to claim the body… would she still be the same woman who had signed those papers through tears? Or would the weight of it all have already begun to change her, in ways she wouldn't notice until later?

Nancy's thoughts wandered. Had Sofia loved him the way she had loved Jim? Not just the everyday kind; the dinners, the texts, the shared routines but the kind that lives deep in your chest. The kind that doesn't leave, even when the person does. The kind that shows up in silence, in memories, in the way you still set two plates at the table. A quiet, ordinary forever.

Maybe they had their own version of it. Maybe they argued about bills or whose turn it was to take the car in for an oil change. Maybe they laughed over terrible takeout and kissed with toothbrushes still in their mouths. Or maybe they had unresolved fights, long silences, complicated pasts. Maybe Sofia would carry guilt, or regret, or relief. Nancy didn't know.

How cruel it is when the person you love leaves, the world does not pause to grieve with you. It just moves on. Fast and indifferent. And you are left trying to catch up with something you never wanted to chase. She didn't cry now. That part of her grief had already passed through like a storm. What was left was the quiet after. The learning to live again. The mornings she got out of bed because someone needed her to. The meals she ate without tasting. The patients she saved while a part of her stayed somewhere behind with Jim.

Sofia didn't know it yet, but this was the start of that same learning. One day she would stop waiting for him to walk through the door. One day she would realize she had gotten through a whole day without speaking his name. And she would hate herself a little for it. But eventually, life would start to move again...well that was what Carla told Nancy but she did not agree much.

But then she hoped, for the woman's sake, that love had been there. Fully. Honestly. That Sofia and even herself... had something to hold on to now that the rest had fallen away. Nancy hoped that when it did, it wouldn't feel like betrayal anyone of them...

Her thoughts were broken by the low buzz of footsteps entering the bay. Firm. Purposeful.

Dr. Romero stepped into the bay, his coat half-buttoned, clipboard tucked under one arm. His face was calm, but the set of his jaw gave him away. He was a transplant surgeon, usually methodical, rarely rattled. But right now, he looked like someone doing math in his head with numbers he didn't want to believe.

"Hi, Dr. Romero. Status...Any news from the board?"

He didn't look at her at first. His eyes were fixed on the red cooler by the gurney, as if waiting for it to speak.

He shook his head. "The board's quiet. Not even a callback. Legal hasn't signed off. They want the second PCR before anyone touches a scalpel."

Nancy gave a small, tired nod. "Right. The new memo. Evelyn mentioned it earlier. They're playing safe. Nothing moves without double clearance now."

She met his eyes. "And you agree with them... because that's protocol, right, sir?"

Romero finally turned to face her. His expression wasn't angry, just worn down. "They're scared. Of everything."

"Scared of what, exactly?"

He sighed. "Making the wrong call. Getting dragged in the press. Lawsuits. Losing credentials. The ethics committee still hasn't let go of what happened to Dr. Mallick last spring. Remember? That was highlighted on the news for a longer time...Harvested a liver from a COVID-positive donor before the second test cleared. Kid made it. But the surgeon's license didn't."

Nancy folded her arms. "So we punish success now?"

Romero gave a tired half-shrug. "That's the climate. Hospital's walking on glass."

Nancy looked over at the covered form. "And Dr. Leigh?"

Romero checked his phone, the screen lighting up briefly with a message. He didn't say anything at first, just stared at it with a look that was part exhaustion, part decision.

Nancy caught the shift in his face. "What is it?"

He slipped the phone back into his coat. "Leigh just texted. If the board doesn't clear it in the next few minutes, he's doing it anyway."

Nancy's eyes widened. "What?"

"He said the labs are solid. Perfusion's clean. Match is airtight. Delilah's ready. He's not willing to wait and let this window close."

She stepped closer, lowering her voice. "But we're still waiting on the second PCR. The new memo says both tests have to be clear."

Romero nodded once. "He knows. He just doesn't care. He thinks saving her life is worth the risk."

Nancy shook her head slowly. "But if something goes wrong if the board decides to make an example of someone what about the license? The review panels? We were trained to follow protocol for a reason. To protect the patient. Ourselves. The whole system."

Romero's voice was steady, but there was a flicker of weariness behind it. "As I mentioned Nancy, Mallick followed his gut last year. Took an organ from a flagged donor. Saved the recipient, yeah, but the hospital came down on him hard. Full ethics probe. Lost his license in three states...And Dr. Leigh..."

"And Leigh...?" Nancy asked.

Romero met her gaze. "Nothing. Not even a write-up. He bent protocol last fall. Similar case. Same risk. Saved a guy who was days away from organ failure. The review board let it slide."

Nancy looked at him, stunned. "How? Why?"

Romero's mouth pulled into a tight line. "Because it's Leigh. He's not just a surgeon. He's the transplant face they show donors during fundraisers. Ivy League trained. Squeaky clean file. He could operate blindfolded and still get invited to speak at conferences."

Her voice dropped. "So they let him bend the rules because he's good PR?"

He didn't answer the question directly. Just said, "He told me if I go in with him, I won't take the fall."

Nancy went quiet. Something about it felt heavier than just hospital politics. It was the kind of moral math that kept her up at night. Some people were worth protecting. Some rules only applied to the ones without a spotlight.

She folded her arms. "And you trust that?"

Romero didn't answer. Just rubbed the back of his neck like it ached. "Delilah is a match. You know that. And she's not getting another shot. But we're thirty-eight minutes into cold ischemia and nobody upstairs wants to be the one to authorize it."

Evelyn stood near the doorway, arms crossed, clipboard pressed against her chest. Romero turned slightly toward her.

"Family was here?" he asked, voice quieter than before.

Evelyn nodded. "His wife. Sofia. Mid-thirties, maybe. She walked in like she'd already mourned him before stepping through the doors. Calm. Steady. You could see it on her face like the weight had already been carried."

"What did she say?" Romero asked.

"She only asked one thing," Evelyn replied. "'Will it really help someone?' I told her there's a woman upstairs Delilah who could be off dialysis by sunrise. She just nodded and said her husband told her once, if anything ever happened to him suddenly, to make it count. Then she signed everything and left."

"She didn't even hesitate?" Romero said softly.

Evelyn shook her head. "Not once."

Nancy glanced down at the sealed cooler. The timer was ticking in her mind. They were running dangerously close to losing viability.

"How much time left?" she asked.

"Forty minutes, maybe less," Romero said.

Nancy's phone buzzed. She glanced at it, expecting another protocol delay. But it was a text from Dr. Leigh.

Come to my office. Don't mention it to anyone. Need to speak. Urgent.

She excused herself quietly and made her way down the hallway. Her mind raced with questions. Leigh wasn't the type to text without reason.

She reached his door, knocked once.

"Come in," Leigh said.

He stood near the window, his back half-turned, the sunlight catching the faint gray in his hair. He didn't look like the head of transplant in that moment. He looked... tired. Weathered. Human.

"I need your help," he said without turning.

Nancy stepped in. "Of course, Dr. Leigh. What's going on?"

He finally turned and gestured toward the chair across from him. "Sit. Please."

She did.

"You know how it feels to lose someone," he began. "Your husband. Jim."

Nancy blinked. The mention caught her off guard. She nodded once, warily.

Leigh continued, his voice lower now. "I lost my wife to cancer a few years ago. And then... COVID. Took my son. Quick. No time to process. One week he was cooking dinner, the next I was signing papers."

Nancy sat still, unsure why he was telling her all of this... and what to say.

His voice cracked on the last sentence.

He took a breath, as if pushing himself forward. "Delilah....umm...she's my son's girlfriend. They weren't on good terms when he died. Neither was I. But she's the mother of my grandchildren."

Nancy's eyes widened slightly. Trying to process everything.

"I promised my wife, on her deathbed, that I would take care of what's left of our family," he said. "And I failed with my son. I can't undo that. But this...this morning...when a man walked in lifeless but with functioning organs... that's not coincidence, Nancy. That's something I can't ignore. That's...that's the miracle I was waiting for..."

Nancy swallowed, heart suddenly heavy.

"I'm really sorry for your loss, Doctor. There's no greater wealth than having your loved ones alive...just being able to watch them breathe, grow, stay healthy. Losing someone you love… it's not something you just get over. It changes the shape of everything. One day they're here, and the next, the world keeps going like nothing happened, but you don't. You carry it with you. Quietly. Every day."

"You get it Nancy...This is the whole truth I don't want to stand with everyday..." He said.

Leigh sighed. "That's why I want you in the operating room..."

"Oh...so...you want me to assist?" Nancy's throat felt dry.

"I need you to," he said. "Romero will be there too. But this is Delilah. I need someone in the room who understands loss. Someone who won't flinch when the rules get blurry."

Nancy stood slowly. "Dr. Leigh... with all due respect... I this could cost everything. My license. My future. The ethics board is already breathing down everyone's neck."

He nodded. "I know. And I'm telling you, nothing will happen to your license. I'll make sure of it."

She hesitated. "You said the same to Mallick?"

Leigh's face darkened slightly. "No. I didn't."

"Why not?"

"I didn't have that kind of pull back then. And honestly, I didn't think it would escalate the way it did. But this time, I've already cleared the internal track. Just not the board. And they're... slow. We don't have that luxury."

Nancy stared at him, unsure where her fear ended and her responsibility began.

"You're asking me to put faith in a system that didn't protect Mallick," she said.

"I'm asking you to trust me," Leigh said. "Not the system. Me. Help me save her. This isn't about politics. It's about doing what we're here to do save lives."

She didn't speak for a few seconds. Her thoughts swirled with images of Jim. Of the day she lost him. Of every minute she wished someone had gone further to save him.

She nodded once. "Yes. I'll assist."

Leigh let out a breath. "Thank you."

But just as she reached the door, Nancy paused. She turned back, voice even. "You didn't promise Mallick. But you're promising me. Why?"

Leigh held her gaze. "Some things I can't tell you, Nancy. But I need your skillset in that OR. And I need your trust."

She looked at him for a long second, then gave a slow nod and closed the door behind her.

Back in the hallway, she leaned against the cool wall, breath shallow. For the first time in weeks, she wasn't sure if she was stepping toward something right or away from something safe.

Nancy stepped into the prep area quietly, the air humming with low fluorescent buzz and the metallic scent of antiseptic. Dr. Romero stood at the counter, reviewing something on the surgical board. He hadn't noticed her yet.

She cleared her throat, just loud enough.

Romero turned, surprised. "Nancy? What are you doing here?"

She gave a small, unreadable smile. "I'm gonna join you. And Dr. Leigh, of course."

His expression shifted concern replacing surprise. "Nancy, no. You're still early in your career. Don't take this risk. Why would you..."

"I don't have time to answer that," she said quickly, cutting him off. "But trust is my choice. And if Leigh wants me in there..."

She paused, glanced down at the floor, then back up. "I don't know, Dr. Romero. I think I've lost the ability to make clear decisions. So in this moment, whatever direction my heart followed, my mind did too."

Romero didn't reply right away. Just stared at her, trying to read the emotion behind her calm face.

"So let's not talk about it," she added gently. "Let's just go save someone."

Romero gave a slow, reluctant nod.

They didn't say another word as they walked toward the scrub station. Nancy tied her hair back, reached for the sterile gown. The water ran cold at first, then warmer. The rhythm of scrubbing in filled the silence between them.

Across the room, the transplant tray was being prepped. Labeled instruments lined up like quiet promises. The red cooler waited, its hum now louder in her ears.

Nancy glanced once at Romero.

He met her eyes and nodded again.

They were in this now. *Together.*

***

The operating room had a stillness that was both clinical and sacred. Lights overhead glared white-hot, humming faintly above the sterile trays and the patient prepped on the table.

Delilah lay under the sheets, unconscious, her body prepped from chin to mid-thigh in antiseptic drapes. The anesthesiologist had already administered a **combination of propofol and fentanyl**, enough to keep her under smoothly and pain-free. A **rocuronium drip** ensured muscle relaxation, allowing her body to lie still completely trusting the team around her.

Nancy stood at the sink, scrubbing her hands in long, practiced strokes. Romero was next to her, quieter than usual. They didn't speak as they dried and gloved up, just exchanged a look before stepping into the OR.

The kidney had arrived in a triple-sealed cooler, packed in **preservation solution** and kept at optimal temperature in sterile saline ice. It had been perfused once more in the transplant prep bay, flushed with **UW (University of Wisconsin) solution** to ensure clean margins and ready flow.

Nancy gently lifted the kidney from the sterile tray. It was smaller than people imagined light brown and smooth, like something half-alive and half-still dreaming. She placed it on the surgical drape while a perfusionist confirmed the arterial line once again.

"Vitals steady?" Leigh asked as he walked in, already gloved and gowned. His eyes didn't miss a detail. There was no tension in his voice, just precision.

"Heart rate sixty-five. BP holding at ninety over fifty-eight. O2 at ninety-eight percent," the anesthesiologist replied from the head of the table.

Romero stood to Leigh's left. Nancy took position to his right.

"Incision," Leigh said.

The clock on the wall read 2:23 p.m.

The first incision was made along the lower right quadrant of Delilah's abdomen. They worked cleanly through subcutaneous fat, then muscle. A faint buzz of cautery followed each movement, cauterizing vessels to limit blood loss. When Leigh reached the **iliac fossa**, he paused.

"Romero, clamp," he said. Romero was already handing it over.

They visualized the **external iliac artery and vein**, identifying the anastomosis site the point where Delilah's bloodstream would be connected to the donor kidney.

Nancy had done this dozens of times before, but this one felt different. Maybe because it wasn't just about skill anymore. It was about a man who'd never woken up that morning, and a woman who still could.

"Kidney," Leigh said, glancing at Nancy.

She handed it over.

With precision, Leigh began attaching the **renal artery and vein to the iliac vessels** using fine 6-0 Prolene sutures. It was delicate work each stitch mattered. Oxygenated blood would soon flow through this organ if they got it right.

They worked in silence, each movement rehearsed and purposeful. The final suture tied off, and then came the moment everyone held their breath for.

"Release the clamps," Leigh said.

The vessels opened. Blood flowed.

The kidney flushed pink.

"She's perfusing," Romero whispered. A hint of awe in his voice.

They watched, waited. Within minutes, the kidney began producing **urine** a stream that trickled into the clear catheter line.

Leigh gave a nod that almost passed for a smile. "She's working."

By 4:10 p.m., the organ was fully secured, the surgical site flushed and closed in layers. The final sutures were in place by **4:26 p.m.** A neat, clean line replaced what had been raw opportunity just two hours ago.

As the monitors beeped steady and Delilah remained under sedation, the team finally allowed themselves to breathe.

Leigh stepped back, peeling off his gloves. "This one mattered," he said, quiet but clear.

Nancy looked down at the closed incision. She didn't answer, but she felt it too.

Romero wiped his forehead with the back of his arm. "So... now we wait."

"For her to wake up," Nancy said, stepping away from the table.

"No," Leigh replied, looking at both of them. "For them to find out."

And with that, he walked out.

And just like that, protocol was no longer in charge.

They were.

***

Two days had passed since the transplant. Two days of silence.

No alert. No warning. No inquiry from the board.

No disciplinary memo. No emergency meeting.

Nothing.

The lack of fallout felt louder than any siren. Nancy had been in this system long enough to know that when something felt too quiet, it usually meant something was being kept quiet.

She couldn't shake it. Something didn't sit right.

With that thought running through her mind like static, she walked over to the admin desk and signed off on Delilah's discharge paperwork. The forms were still warm from the printer as she held them, almost too aware of what they symbolized. A life saved. A risk taken. A silence bought.

Nancy made her way down the hall toward Dr. Leigh's office.

Just before she raised her hand to knock, she heard it.

A low laugh. Confident. Cruel.

Then a second voice came through the speaker, thick and edged with street slang.

"Doctor, the boys at the docks are impressed. You packaged that kidney like a pro. They said it looked cleaner than the ones we move from overseas. No bruising, no trace. Our buyers in Dubai already cleared the payment."

Nancy's entire body stilled.

Leigh answered with a calmness that felt inhuman.

"That is why you hired me. Your field teams hack. I refine. I give the market a product that never raises alarms. I handle the hospital side. You handle the money."

The man laughed.

"And that nurse. The one who helped you. How did you get her under you like that? She looks like the type who would report anything suspicious."

Leigh's chuckle was low and poisonous.

"You give people a story they want to believe. Humans are emotional tools. Get them at the right angle and they will build your house for you."

The man asked, "Still. She agreed too fast. What did you feed her?"

Leigh's voice shifted into mockery.

"I gave her a tragedy. I told her I lost my wife and son. I told her Delilah was my son's girlfriend and the mother of my imaginary grandchildren. I made her believe she was helping a family stay whole. She is grieving her dead husband. She swallowed every word."

Nancy's knees weakened. Her pulse hammered in her ears.

Leigh continued, sharper now.

"She thinks we bypassed the ethics board because we were desperate. No. We bypassed it because the donor was perfect. Fresh. Unreported. A clean pull for the black market. And she helped me stitch it in with her own hands."

The man whistled, impressed.

"Heartless, Doctor. I like it. The ring will too. Your name is becoming a brand for our buyers."

Leigh replied with chilling pride.

"This was always going to work. Now I will wait for my fruit."

The man laughed again, wicked and satisfied.

"You will get it. The shipment is already on the move. The cash transfer will hit your offshore account by midnight."

A soft beep ended the call.

Silence swallowed the hall.

Nancy stared forward, frozen.

She was not confused.

She was not mistaken.

She had heard everything.

Her phone slipped from her hand and cracked against the tile like a gunshot.

Inside, silence.

Nancy pressed her hand over her mouth, eyes squeezed shut, willing herself to vanish. She crouched to pick up her phone.

The office door creaked open just as she was bending down. She stood up quickly, heart pounding.

First, she saw the shoes. Black. Shiny. Steady.

Then the voice sweet like syrup masking something bitter.

"Nancy," Leigh said, stepping out. "Were you eavesdropping, honey?"

She stepped back instinctively. "No, sir. I...I came to get the discharge..."

His hand shot out and clamped onto her upper arm. Too tight.

She winced. "Dr., you're hurting me."

"Shhhh," he whispered, but it didn't feel like quiet. It felt like a threat.

Then came the change. His mask slipped. His grip tightened.

"Listen to me, little hero," he hissed. "You speak a word just one to anyone about what you *think* you heard? I'll make sure your license is the first thing shredded. One silence, a thousand benefits. Are we clear?"

Nancy didn't respond right away. She was trembling but held her stare.

"So this is how Dr. Mallick lost his license," she said, voice barely audible.

Leigh's smile curved, cruel and slick. "Oh, you're so smart, Nancy. I knew I was right to have you in there with me. That mind of yours it'll go far. Now, remember that smart mouth is exactly what will get you *buried* if you ever turn it against me. One word. That's all it takes. Next time, it'll be *you*."

Her pulse roared in her ears. "Yes," she whispered. "Yes, Dr. Leigh."

He let go, snatched the paperwork from her hand, and stepped back inside, closing the door without looking back.

Nancy stood frozen. Then her legs finally moved.

She didn't even realize she was crying until she was in the women's restroom, locked in a stall. The paperwork still crumpled in one hand, her phone clutched in the other.

She sat on the closed lid of the toilet, put her hands to her face, and let it out.

The sobs came quiet at first, but deeper. Shakier.

She thought about Carla. But not how could she explain this?

She thought about Jim's brother. No. No words would come out right.

So she turned to the only person she wanted to hear.

Jim.

She scrolled through WhatsApp, past old photos, old threads, until she found the voice note. One he'd sent her during the chaos of the first COVID wave. Back when hope was a rationed thing and she was barely sleeping.

She hit play.

"Hey, babe. I know you're neck-deep in it, but remember, you're the best nurse I've ever met. Not just 'cause you know your stuff 'cause you care. That's your edge. That's your fight. Stay safe. I love you."

The sound of his voice cracked something deeper inside her.

She cried harder. She didn't know if the tears were for Jim, or for Delilah, or for the pieces of herself she was starting to lose.

Her eyes closed.

Would Jim still be alive if someone had bent the rules for him?

Is this what doing the right thing felt like now quiet, dark, and full of guilt?

Was this the new normal?

There was no answer.

Just her breath and a mind running marathon.

Chapter 8:
St. James: Too Clean to Be True!

Five days had passed.

Five long, brittle days since the transplant board had gone quiet.

No Zoom links. No case reviews. No memos floating through inboxes in the early morning hours. Not even a red-marked decision logged into the secure portal. Just silence. The kind that hums under fluorescent lights and lingers in hallway glances. The kind that makes your stomach twist because *something* should have come by now, but didn't.

Yet, somehow, the transplants never slowed.

If anything, they increased.

And on the surface, it looked like a win.

Survival rates were up. Recovery times shortened. Patients who'd been stuck on dialysis or tied to ICU vents were walking out within days.

Every morning brought fresh numbers to the main board...charts that would've once triggered celebration. But Nancy didn't celebrate. She couldn't.

Because she knew what was fueling it.

COVID hadn't stopped claiming lives. Not in their city. Not in the country. But now, those deaths were showing up faster in the transplant wing than they were in ICU. Healthy organs were arriving like clockwork. No delays. No bureaucratic gridlock. No grieving families sobbing in the lobby. Just organs. Almost clean. Almost perfect.

Too perfect.

She noticed it first when reviewing intake logs; case after case of post-COVID fatalities with the same vague phrasing: "respiratory failure, negative PCR pending." These were supposed to be red-flagged for double-confirmation, sometimes even shelved pending ethics committee review.

But they weren't shelved.

They were processed.

And used.

Nancy kept her face neutral. Her voice steady. She asked no questions that would suggest she knew more than she should. Especially not about the Delilah's organ transplant.

Because that was the day she learned what Dr. Leigh was truly capable of.

And what silence could cost.

She hadn't told anyone...not Romero, not Evelyn...about Leigh's threat in his office. About the grip on her arm, the deadpan cruelty in his warning, the sickly-smooth way he'd turned it all into a compliment.

"You're smart, Nancy. That's why I want you with me. One silence, a thousand benefits."

She heard those words in her dreams now. Every time she scrubbed in, they echoed off the tiled walls like a second set of footsteps.

Dr. Romero had casually mentioned Dr. Malick yesterday.

Said his license had finally been pulled last month.

The official story was "multiple protocol violations." But Nancy knew the real reason.

Mallick had pushed too hard. Questioned too many of Leigh's closed-door calls. He'd filed a quiet report with the medical ethics committee, just enough to trigger an internal review.

He thought they'd back him.

Instead, Leigh buried him.

A week later, Mallick was off the rotation. Then off the schedule. Then erased.

They said it was disciplinary action.

Nancy knew it was a warning.

She still remembered the look on his face the last time they crossed paths in the hallway like a man who'd walked into a fire thinking he'd come out a hero and was still waiting for the burn to fade.

Nancy wasn't about to make the same mistake.

So she kept her mouth shut. Even when it trembled to open.

She smiled through staff briefings. Gave neutral nods during post-op rounds. Played the part. Played it well.

Because silence wasn't just a choice anymore; it was protection.

Protection for her license. For the patients she still might save. And for the memory of Jim, who died waiting for a lung that never came.

If she spoke now…

If she exposed Leigh…

Would she still be able to help *anyone*?

She didn't know.

But she knew what happened to people who tried.

Mallick was gone.

And Nancy?

She wasn't ready to be next.

***

It was Evelyn who spoke first, breaking the uneasy silence that had settled between them.

They stood at the OR logboard, barely a foot apart, yet each wrapped in her own thoughts. The corridor behind them buzzed with distant footsteps and overhead pages, but here, in front of the board, it felt quiet. Still. Their coffee cups sat abandoned on a nearby ledge, the steam long gone. A film of cold had crept into the rims, unnoticed until now.

"We've done seven transplant cases in three days," Evelyn said, her voice a low murmur as she spun a pen between her fingers. She didn't look at Nancy. Her eyes were fixed on the columns of patient names and procedures scrawled in dry-erase marker. "That's not normal. Is it?"

Nancy didn't answer right away. She stared at the same board, trying to make sense of the numbers and names as if they might explain themselves under the right gaze. Her tone, when she finally spoke, was steady. Flat. "We've had surges before."

Evelyn gave a slow nod, almost to herself, but her grip on the pen tightened. "Yeah, but even the wildest surges leave a mess. Scrambled labs. Backlogged tests. Nurses running on fumes. This? This is too clean. It's like someone ironed out the chaos."

Nancy tilted her head slightly, letting her eyes move down the list again. "You're saying it's too smooth?"

"I'm saying it feels scripted," Evelyn replied, her voice sharpening just a touch. "The match confirmations come in before I finish reviewing the chart. Prep teams show up like they've been standing by. The sterilization crew is already in motion before I get paged. It's like they're working from a clock I haven't seen."

That landed. Nancy's fingers curled slightly at her sides, and her gaze lingered on one name near the top of the board. The patient had been wheeled in less than twenty minutes after the donor was cleared. She'd chalked it up to efficiency. But Evelyn had a point...efficiency still had seams. This felt sewn shut.

"Is anyone else talking about it?" she asked quietly.

Evelyn didn't respond right away. Her pen stopped spinning. "Romero said something yesterday. Just in passing. He noticed some weird timing on the transfer reports. Stuff not syncing. Tiny things, but... off."

And there it was. A hollow drop in Nancy's chest. Like a single knock echoing down an empty corridor.

Romero had seen it too.

She said nothing, but her breath slowed. A beat passed. Then another. She looked back at the board and saw something different this time. Not a list of names. Not just numbers.

A pattern.

And it was starting to speak.

***

By the time the wall clock blinked past noon, Nancy found Romero exactly where she expected him; slouched in the corner of the breakroom, surrounded by a scatter of open files, radiology prints, and two half-drunk energy drinks. The blinds were pulled halfway down, casting dusty slits of light across the table, and the faint hum of the vending machine filled the silence.

Romero didn't look up right away. He was hunched over a clipboard, jotting something with a blue pen in his left hand while his right flipped through a donor intake packet. When he finally glanced up, he looked like he hadn't blinked in half an hour.

"You ever try writing with both hands at once?" he asked, voice dry and frayed around the edges.

Nancy set her coffee down on the counter. "Not unless I'm trying to impress a toddler."

He didn't smile. Just tapped his knuckle against two open charts on the table, their top pages aligned like evidence exhibits. "This one's a donor file from the West Wing. Signed off at 9:12 AM by Julian Hughes. Intern. Neat handwriting." He slid the second folder forward. "Twelve minutes later, this one rolls in. ER patient, different case. Same intern, same pen strokes. But this time it's a different shift. According to staffing, Hughes wasn't even scheduled until ten."

Nancy stepped closer, her eyes scanning both signatures. Identical. Same angled tilt in the 'J.' Same overly round loops in the 'g.' Too perfect to ignore. She crossed her arms.

"Maybe he batch-entered them after the fact," she offered, though her voice lacked conviction. "Late-night uploads? Sometimes they don't log the entry time, just the approval."

"That's what I thought," Romero said, leaning back in his chair, the metal legs creaking beneath him. "It was the best guess I could come up with. But it doesn't line up. West Wing doesn't handle ER overflow. And Hughes isn't certified for transplant evaluations yet. So why's his name on both?"

Nancy didn't answer. She just stared at the papers. Something in her chest tightened...a coil pulling inward.

Romero looked at her again, his eyes scanning her face like he was searching for a different conclusion. Something that would let him dismiss this as a clerical hiccup or some routine tech glitch.

She gave him nothing. Just a small nod. "You'll check more?"

He was already flipping open a third file. "Started at 7 this morning."

Nancy forced a faint smile, but her chest felt like hollow glass. She could hear her heartbeat in her ears...steady, but distant. Something wasn't right. And now it wasn't just a hunch. It was logged. Signed. Dated.

It was real.

***

By 2:12 AM, the last of the night staff had either drifted off to rounds or dozed into half-sleeps in the breakroom. The hallway lights were dimmed. The station monitors ran quietly. Nancy sat at her desk, still in scrubs, still technically on shift but now she was waiting.

She wasn't charting anymore. Not really. Her screen displayed an open patient file, but her eyes weren't on it. They were on the admin bay, and the man slouched in the far corner of it **Mr. Kolt**, the Medical Records Supervisor. Middle-aged, sharp when alert, but terrible at pacing himself during night shifts. He had started dozing just after midnight, jolting awake every few minutes, muttering something about backlogs, then slipping off again.

Now, his head had dropped fully to his shoulder. One arm dangled over the chair-rest. The other still clutched his tablet, screen dimmed. His chest rose and fell in a slow, rhythmic way that told her it wasn't a light nap anymore.

Nancy stood quietly, her pulse ticking louder in her ears than the wall clock. She smoothed the front of her coat and walked toward the admin bay like she had every right to be there.

She kept her pace calm. Unhurried.

His jacket was draped on the back of his chair, half-folded beneath him. She reached for the inside pocket, fingers tense, ready to retreat if he stirred.

He didn't.

But the key pass wasn't in the pocket.

Nancy's breath hitched.

She checked the outer chest pocket. Empty. She crouched slightly, angling her fingers toward the hip pouch of the jacket.

There.

Her fingertips brushed cold plastic.

The passkey.

She slid it free with slow, steady care, then stepped back, heart thudding. Still, he didn't move.

She slipped out of the admin bay, careful not to let her shoes squeak on the tile.

The **Medical Records Archive Room** was buried in the far end of the administrative wing. A dead hallway past Radiology, behind a locked utility corridor most staff never walked through. It was one of those places people forgot existed until a lawyer asked for a signature or an auditor called in an old chart.

Nancy reached the end of the corridor and stopped in front of a heavy steel door. A small white plaque read:

RECORDS ARCHIVE – AUTHORIZED ACCESS ONLY

Below it, the scanner blinked red. She held up the card.

It paused. Then blinked green. The lock clicked.

She slipped inside, quietly closing the door behind her.

The room smelled like old paper and sterilized air. It was cooler than the rest of the floor. Silent. Floor-to-ceiling cabinets lined the walls, each one labeled by category operative histories, discharge logs, fatality reports.

She pulled on a fresh pair of gloves from the storage tray near the door.

Nancy wasn't just here to snoop. She had come for something specific.

Earlier that week, she'd overheard Dr. Leigh talking to a nurse by the coffee cart. It had been an offhand comment he was annoyed about "Cabinet 9 being reorganized," and joked that "nothing ever stays where it's supposed to."

She hadn't thought much of it at the time.

Now, it felt like a trail of breadcrumbs.

She moved to the far left side of the room.

Cabinet 9: Transplant Records

She opened the drawer slowly. Inside were thick folders yellow-labeled, alphabetized by procedure date. She picked three from the last 72 hours and carried them to the central prep table.

Procedure: Liver Transplant Logged: 5:47 AM, three days ago Donor ID: DB-6542 Male. Age 45. Trauma Bay 2 Organ Serial: LV-98211

Everything looked routine. Signed. Logged. Verified.

She flipped to the next page; the physical tag form scanned in with the body. This was the original tag meant to stay with the donor from the moment of death through organ retrieval.

Body ID: FN-8861 Female. Age 36. East Wing Organ Serial: LV-98211

Nancy's eyes froze.

Same serial number.

Same liver.

But not the same body.

She checked again...Donor ID DB-6542 was a male from Trauma. The tag, however, belonged to a female patient from the East Wing. Yet both records were attached to the same transplant case, and both showed the **same unique organ serial number: LV-98211**.

One liver.

Two identities.

That wasn't a typo. That wasn't a staff mix-up.

That meant the organ that had been transplanted into a patient three days ago came from someone other than the person the hospital claimed it did.

There was no documentation explaining the switch. No emergency override. No replacement form. Nothing.

Either someone had gone back and rewritten the file to match a donor who looked better on paper, Or the liver had been taken from someone who was never meant to be a donor at all.

Her mouth went dry.

This wasn't just bad paperwork.

This liver had **two paper trails** and only one of them could be true.

Then **a sound.**

Footsteps.

Soft. Close. Right behind her.

Before she could react, a hand landed on her shoulder.

Nancy jerked upright with a sharp breath and swatted the hand away, spinning around.

Evelyn.

Her eyes wide. Both hands raised in mock surrender.

"What the fuck are you doing here?" Nancy whispered, furious and stunned all at once.

Evelyn stepped back, glancing toward the hallway. "Shhhh. Are you crazy? Someone might come in, bro. And I should be asking you the same thing."

Nancy's pulse thundered in her neck. "You followed me?"

"I came to get the key," Evelyn whispered, nodding toward Nancy's pocket. "Didn't know I'd find the door already open."

They stared at each other for a moment. The quiet of the room pressed in.

Nancy finally broke the stare, exhaling hard and turning back to the table. "You want to see something?"

Evelyn stepped closer, glancing down at the folder Nancy flipped back open.

Nancy pointed at the pages. "Donor ID says the liver came from a 45-year-old male. But the body tag? It's from a 36-year-old female. Same liver. Same case. Same serial number."

Evelyn frowned. "That's not possible. They triple-check those tags."

"I know."

They stood there in silence, eyes locked on the file. No scribbles. No edits. It looked... perfect.

Too perfect.

"You think it's a one-off?" Evelyn finally asked.

"Maybe," Nancy said while thinking about Dr. Leigh's warning... "Maybe not."

Evelyn nodded slowly, unsure what to say.

Nancy shut the folder and slid it back under the others, her gloved fingers lingering for a second too long.

"I think it's probably just a clerical error...hmmm it is," she said quietly, her tone shifting. Less sharp now. Controlled. "I came in to look at a file I thought might be connected to one of Jim's relatives."

She forced a small, dismissive shrug and avoided Evelyn's eyes. "Curious mind, that's all. I stumbled on this by accident. It's nothing. Just... never mind."

Evelyn watched her, lips parted slightly, as if weighing whether to believe her or not.

But Nancy didn't give her room to push.

Evelyn hesitated. "You'll tell me if you find something?"

Nancy gave her a tight nod. "Regarding this error? Yeah. Sure."

But in heart she knows she wouldn't...

***

By the next morning, Romero had three more discrepancies.

"These are all organ logs from the last 96 hours," he said, spreading them on the table. "And every single one has something off. Not just ID mismatches timestamp overlaps, unsigned recipient notes, double scans logged under one patient."

Nancy looked at him with a well-practiced mask of concern. "You think it's one of the interns?"

"I think someone's bypassing the process," he said. "And not by accident."

Nancy hesitated, leaning back. "What does Evelyn say?"

"She thinks it's too aligned to be random. But she hasn't seen these."

Nancy picked up one file and slowly turned the pages, eyes scanning like she was learning this for the first time.

"You think it's Leigh?" she asked softly.

Romero didn't answer.

He just said, "This doesn't feel like a slip-up."

***

By noon, Nancy was back in the file room.

129

This time, she wore surgical gloves. Not for hygiene she'd already sanitized her hands twice before entering but to keep fingerprints off the pages. Her coat was buttoned, a notepad folded snug in the inner pocket. She moved with quiet urgency, steps sharp, efficient. Not rushed. Just... decisive. Like someone who knew exactly what she was looking for.

And someone who wished, with every breath, that she didn't.

The mismatches were stacking.

Five.

Then eight.

Each file she opened was a layer deeper into something she didn't want to name. Body ID tags that didn't line up with donor reports. Serial numbers assigned to more than one recipient. Gender switches. Wing transfers that hadn't been logged. By the time she hit the tenth discrepancy, her stomach was in full revolt. A cold twist coiled tight beneath her ribs, the kind that made her press the back of her hand to her mouth and breathe through her nose just to keep it down.

But she said nothing.

Not to anyone.

When Evelyn glanced at her across the station later that day, brow raised in quiet question, Nancy just nodded like she hadn't been anywhere unusual. She softened her tone. Matched concern with curiosity. Asked questions back.

Romero caught her near Radiology and mentioned a missing timestamp. She replied with another question. Played along like she hadn't already seen more than she could make sense of.

And then, as the shift wound toward evening, Leigh passed her in the hallway.

It was brief. A four-second window. No clipboard. No entourage. Just him. Alone. Hands in the pockets of his white coat, that smooth, unreadable calm on his face.

He didn't stop.

He didn't speak.

He just nodded once, slow and deliberate, like nothing was wrong.

But her ears rang the second he was gone. Her blood had started pounding somewhere around her collarbone, and now it echoed behind her temples like storm waves on concrete.

She couldn't breathe properly until she reached the stairwell.

***

That night, Nancy sat in her car long after her shift had ended.

The parking lot was nearly deserted, just a few staff cars and the glow of streetlights reflecting off the damp asphalt. Her badge lay on the dashboard, face-up, like it was watching her. Her hands gripped the steering wheel so tightly her knuckles had gone white, but she didn't notice.

She stared straight ahead. Engine off. Windows up.

Her phone rested in the passenger seat, screen dim until she picked it up.

She scrolled to Jim's name. His voice note.

Her thumb hovered over the play button.

But she didn't press it.

Not yet.

***

Two days later, the mistake arrived in a sealed steel box.

The transplant tray was delivered to the ICU, logged under Dr. Robert's name scheduled for a liver case later that evening. Evelyn had signed for it casually, flipping through the chart while finishing her coffee. She popped the lid on the tray and froze.

Inside was a kidney.

She double-checked the tag. **Robert. Liver case.** But this this wasn't even close.

Frowning, she scanned the donor ID at the station terminal.

The screen blinked red.

INVALID. NO MATCH.

She stared. Then tried again.

Same result.

That donor didn't exist in the system.

Across the hall, Nancy had just exited a supply closet when she heard Evelyn call out. "Nancy hey, can you look at this real quick?"

Nancy walked over calmly, masking the twist in her gut the moment she saw the tray.

Kidney.

She didn't even need to see the scan. She already knew.

Wrong organ. Wrong patient. Wrong surgeon.

Her last sliver of denial disappeared.

"What do you think?" Evelyn asked. "Is this some routing error?"

Nancy kept her face blank. "Probably. Central's been juggling case loads all week."

"Still, a kidney showing up in a liver case? That's... major."

"I'll take it back," Nancy said, already reaching for the tray. "Faster than waiting for someone from logistics to respond."

Evelyn hesitated. "Shouldn't we call it in?"

Before she could finish, a voice broke in behind them. Calm. Controlled.

"Did a tray just get delivered?"

Nancy's stomach dropped.

Dr. Elijah Leigh.

He walked in from the south hallway, sleeves rolled to the elbow, tie slightly loosened. He stopped when he saw the tray, then gave a little frown. Concerned. Curious. Perfectly timed.

"Oh," he said. "That's... not right."

He stepped closer and peered into the box. "This is supposed to be a liver. This is clearly renal."

He looked at Evelyn, then Nancy. His expression was textbook confusion no trace of blame.

"That donor ID doesn't even ping in the system," Evelyn said.

Leigh blinked. "Seriously? Let me see."

Nancy stood motionless as he leaned in and read the label. He even gave a soft whistle. "Well, that's a mess. Could be a clerical glitch. Could be Central routed the wrong specimen."

He turned to Nancy with a sympathetic smile.

"You're already heading that way, right? Good. Take it down, get them to cross-check the delivery record, and have them notify me when they've sorted it."

He looked toward a junior nurse passing by. "Let Prep know to hold all trays until I confirm today's deliveries. No more surprises, please."

Then, turning back to the two of them, he offered a dry chuckle. "This is what happens when too many hands touch the chain. I read a piece the other day about how medical supply chains in high-volume hospitals can become backdoors for all sorts of... creative recordkeeping."

His gaze briefly flicked to Nancy.

"You'd be shocked how many black market cases start just like this. One wrong label. One missing tag. And poof no way to trace the donor."

Evelyn crossed her arms. "Yeah...dramatic."

Leigh smiled. "Maybe. Or maybe I've just read too many case studies. Either way, it's why we follow protocol." He turned back to Nancy, his voice softer now measured. "Right?"

Nancy felt the words land like a needle under her skin. There was nothing accidental about his timing. Or that smile. Or the comment about traceability.

She met his eyes for only a second.

Then broke away.

"I need the restroom," she muttered, already turning.

She didn't wait for permission. She carried the tray with her, her jaw clenched so tight she could hear the blood in her ears.

When she reached the end of the corridor, she didn't turn toward the restroom.

She just kept walking. Away from the ICU. Away from Evelyn. Away from **him.**

Because Leigh wasn't trying to fix a system.

He was controlling it.

And he was reminding her, in front of everyone, that if she stepped out of line

He could erase her just as easily as a mislabeled donor.

***

Nancy's phone buzzed just after 9 AM.

Romero: *Can we talk? Outside the hospital. Café Coral. Ten minutes.*

She stared at the message, rereading it twice before responding with a single:

On my way.

She didn't ask what it was about.

She already felt it wasn't good.

Ten minutes later, she pulled into the narrow parking lot just off Westwood Avenue. Café Coral sat tucked beneath a rust-red awning, a few blocks from the St. James Medical campus. She spotted him right away Romero, already seated by the window.

But he didn't look like himself.

This wasn't the sharp, clean-cut day-shift doctor she was used to. This was someone who had been awake too long, someone whose shirt had creases and whose face had given up pretending to hide stress. His hair was slightly uncombed, and there was a half-empty cup of coffee already on the table.

She stepped inside and walked over. He looked up, tired eyes meeting hers.

"Hey," he said, motioning to the chair across from him. "Thanks for coming."

Nancy sat down slowly. "What's going on?"

Romero didn't waste time. He slid a file across the table overstuffed, messy, flagged with notes.

"I've been up all night," he said. "And Nancy, what I've been finding… it's frightening. If this is real and I believe it is it's going to dirty everything connected to that hospital."

Nancy didn't touch the folder. "Romero…"

"No, just listen for a second," he said, flipping it open. "This is not just poor recordkeeping. This is surgery logs that don't align with actual OR usage. This is post-op files signed by doctors who weren't even on the floor that day. This is a kidney that shows up under a donor ID, and two days later, that same ID is used again for a liver. Same number, same name, two organs."

"It could be technical."

"Stop," he cut in. "No IT system reuses organ serial numbers across separate anatomical structures. That's not a software bug. That's a fabrication."

Nancy took a deep breath, held it in her lungs. "Even if you're right… even if all this is happening, it's not our business.

We're not compliance. We're not ethics board. You are a surgeon; I am a trauma nurse. We're cogs in the wheel, not the ones steering it."

Romero blinked at her, stunned. "You're really going to say that?"

"Yes," she snapped. "Because this thing whatever it is if it's as deep as you think, speaking up gets us all destroyed. Careers gone. Licenses gone.... and..."

Romero's tone sharpened. "You think silence protects us?"

"I think it's all we have!"

He leaned in, voice firm but shaking. "Nancy, if tomorrow this story blows open if one donor family starts asking questions, if one journalist connects one fake name we are all in it. You, me, Evelyn, everyone who has touched a scalpel or a checklist at St. James in the last six months. Every single person in the operating chain is exposed."

"Only if you make noise!"

"And only if we stay silent long enough for someone else to pin it on us! I will talk to Leigh and..."

Nancy stood, her chair screeching back. "Don't take his name!"

Romero stood too, startled. "What?"

She looked away. Her voice cracked. "Nothing. Doesn't matter. Dr. stay out of his business!"

He leaned in slowly, hands flat on the table now. "Nancy… what do you mean *his* business?"

She froze.

Romero's voice dropped. "What did Leigh say to you?"

Nancy didn't answer.

Romero stared at her. "Tell me."

"Just leave it alone."

"Nancy," he said more firmly, "tell me."

She whispered, "Well! he told me if I flagged another donor discrepancy… he'd suspend me. That I'd lose my license. That he'd destroy me quietly, and no one would lift a finger."

Romero looked gutted.

Nancy lowered herself back into the chair, whispering now. "In my whole career, I've done everything by the book. Never let a patient slip through. Never missed a protocol. My husband… he used to call me Iron Lady. Because I never blinked under pressure. But if he saw what I've kept quiet about… what I've let myself be part of… he'd be ashamed of me."

Romero softened, but his voice was still strong. "He wouldn't be ashamed. He'd tell you to do the right thing."

Nancy covered her face with her hands. "But I'm scared. Don't you get that? If we take Leigh down, we don't survive it."

Romero let out a slow, pained breath. "You think I'm not scared? But fear is a luxury, Nancy. It's not just about us anymore. If we don't say anything, this cycle keeps going. More falsified donors. More organs with no names. More patients trusting a system that's being twisted from the inside."

She didn't look up.

Romero continued. "You remember my wife? Lilly?"

Nancy nodded faintly.

"She used to say the easiest way to be complicit was to stay quiet just long enough to stop noticing. She taught me that. She taught me to think with conscience, not fear."

He slid the folder back toward her.

"She'd be disgusted with me if I ignored this. And so would Jim with you."

Nancy flinched.

Romero lowered his voice. "But together, we're not powerless. Together, we can gather the right files. Build the timeline. Get it in front of someone who *can't* ignore it."

Nancy looked at him, eyes glassy.

"And if we don't?" she asked.

Romero didn't blink. "Then we wait for our names to show up on a subpoena. Or worse, a headline."

Silence.

Then Nancy reached forward. Placed her hand on the folder. Her voice, when it came, was barely a whisper.

"…Where do we start?"

Romero let out a breath he hadn't realized he'd been holding.

"Start with Leigh's last approved donor log," he said. "And don't delete your messages anymore."

Chapter 9:
Black Market Organs

The air inside St. James Medical Center had turned strange again.

It wasn't COVID this time. That storm had passed, mostly. But its shadow lingered like smoke in the walls. The masks stayed, worn more out of habit than need. Temperature guns still blinked at every entrance, and glass dividers remained bolted between patients and their families silent reminders of how fragile the system had become. Fear had faded into something quieter, heavier. Fatigue had settled into the staff's bones, but this wasn't the kind of silence born from exhaustion.

This was the kind that came from too many people learning too much, too fast, and deciding to say nothing.

Nancy felt it the moment she stepped off the elevator. The hallway looked the same polished tiles, fluorescent lights, carts parked neatly beside medication rooms but it didn't sound the same. The usual murmur of morning staff, the shuffle of sneakers, the beeping of IV monitors, all felt... muted. Even the white noise of the building had pulled back.

Her steps echoed longer than they should have. Nurses who normally nodded or cracked jokes with her kept their heads down. Conversations that started before she arrived stopped as she passed. There were no code calls, no alarms, no disasters just a feeling that something beneath the surface had shifted.

She clutched her clipboard tighter, her thumb tapping lightly against the edge. Her badge brushed her hip with each step. Everything looked right. Nothing felt right.

She found Romero in the staff locker room. The door creaked as she opened it, but he didn't move. He sat on the edge of the bench, elbows planted on his knees, staring at the floor like he'd been sitting there for hours. His scrubs were wrinkled. His face was drawn, jaw tight.

He didn't look up when she entered. He just raised his hand and held out a folder.

There was no greeting. No words. Just the silent weight of what he was giving her.

Nancy took it, slowly, and flipped it open.

Inside were three transplant forms, each more damning than the last. The dates were fresh. The donor names were recycled. The signatures were digital clearly copied and pasted from an old record.

She scanned the form again, then met Romero's eyes.

"This one's been dead four months."

Nancy didn't look up as she said it. Her eyes stayed fixed on the donor chart in her hand, the way a surgeon studies a scan for something the surface doesn't show. She tapped the date of death with her thumb, just once, to make sure Romero saw it too.

Romero crossed his arms, his jaw clenched tight. "Same intern signed off again."

Nancy finally looked up.

"He left the program last week," Romero added. "Didn't even complete his infectious disease rotation. Packed up his locker, deactivated his badge, and just vanished."

Nancy flipped to the second page, scanning the timestamped OR logs. "Liver resection at 2:07 a.m., kidneys before 4. No tissue compatibility file. No match confirmation through UNOS. No immunosuppressant prep listed in post-op."

"Nothing went through EPIC," Romero said. "No pre-op orders. No labs. Just entries backdated into Cerner after the fact. All scrubbed clean on the surface."

She turned toward the bank of lockers behind them, searching for something that wasn't there. This wasn't new. The inconsistencies had been compounding for weeks. It started with cases that moved too fast, approvals that bypassed transplant review boards, and a few undocumented organs arriving without notice. She had chalked it up to stress. Covid had altered protocols. But this... this was something deeper.

She folded the folder closed with a kind of care that belonged to something dangerous, not fragile. "This isn't one bad call," she said. "It's systemic. They're using ghost donors."

Romero leaned against the wall, eyes narrowing. "It's criminal."

"If we report this now, it dies before it hits the server," Nancy replied. "The audit team will wipe it clean. And it won't just be Leigh."

"You think he's working with admin?"

Nancy didn't respond.

Romero shook his head, voice low. "Someone in Scheduling has to be in on it. There's no way OR3 gets prepped, staffed, and sterilized twice in one night without a paper trail unless someone's controlling the flags inside the system."

"They're using shell profiles," Nancy said. "Recycled EMR data from previous patients, maybe some pulled from deceased donor lists before they're officially entered into the federal transplant registry."

Romero let out a quiet breath. "So nothing pings as new. Everything looks familiar to the system, just off by a digit or two."

"And they're forging surgical consents," Nancy added. "The signatures on these forms are clipped. No stroke variation. Scanned from a single file and pasted across multiple charts. Whoever's doing this isn't just cutting corners. They're scripting the whole operation from the backend."

She looked back down at the folder. Three surgeries, all performed in under 36 hours. No verified donor matches. No ICD-10 surgical codes logged correctly. And every recipient's post-op file had been altered within the same five-minute window the morning after.

Romero's voice hardened. "They're laundering organs."

Nancy looked at him. "If we go to the board now, we get protocol. Not truth. And definitely not accountability."

Romero stepped closer, lowering his voice. "You really think Leigh is the only name behind this?"

She stared at the laminated whiteboard near the exit. A single transplant team name was circled twice on that day's roster. The same team that always worked the overnight shifts when no one else was watching.

She didn't answer his question.

She didn't have to.

The deeper they went, the clearer it became. This wasn't a string of isolated decisions. This was a designed bypass. A silent, coded rerouting of human lives. And it had been built to survive undetected.

The truth was no longer buried.

It had been programmed to vanish.

***

Romero's office was dim, lit only by a tired reading lamp perched on a cluttered bookshelf. The blinds had been drawn tight since the afternoon. Outside, the hospital pulsed with fluorescent urgency, but in here, time had paused. Nancy was curled up in the worn recliner near the filing cabinet, still in her surgical gown. One arm rested across her midsection, the other dangled at her side. Her head leaned against the wall, hair loose, face slack with exhaustion. Romero sat at his desk, hunched forward, neck stiff, eyes scanning across his monitor. Encrypted folders, lines of code, patient files he had stopped seeing the words an hour ago. His fingers clicked through the screen purely out of habit.

A soft creak snapped him back to the room.

Then another sound. Sharper. Metal brushing metal.

He turned, his spine straightening.

The door opened slowly.

A figure stood in the threshold. Masked. Dressed in dark scrubs. One hand trembling slightly. The other held something that caught the lamplight a slim surgical blade.

Romero rose from his chair so fast the wheels spun backward.

"Who are you?" he barked, already stepping in front of Nancy.

Nancy stirred, then jerked awake at the sound of his voice. Her eyes widened, snapping between Romero and the intruder. Her chest tightened, breath catching.

The figure raised their hand slowly, not in threat, but in plea.

"Shhh... please. I need to talk. But first what do you know about Dr. Leigh?"

It was a woman's voice. Shaky. But there was a crackling urgency beneath it. Controlled chaos on the edge of unraveling.

Romero's voice was firm. "Put the blade down."

"I'm not here to hurt anyone," she said quickly. She stepped forward, lowered the knife onto the metal tray table beside the door. "I just... I didn't know how else to do this. I couldn't be seen coming here. I couldn't risk being dismissed. I needed you both to listen."

Nancy was on her feet now, arms tense at her sides, eyes narrowing.

"Take off the mask."

The woman peeled it away slowly.

It was Laila Shah.

The intern.

Romero let out a heavy breath. "You could've knocked."

Laila gave a dry, broken smile. "You would've locked the door."

Nancy stepped forward, studying her. Pale skin. Hair undone. Dark circles under her eyes. Her hands wouldn't stop shaking. This was not someone just nervous. This was someone unraveling under pressure that had nowhere else to go.

"I heard you both talking," Laila said, stepping to the center of the room. "Last week. In the café. You were talking about Leigh. The black market. You didn't say it in so many words, but I heard enough. I've been trying to come forward for weeks. I just didn't know who to trust. And then I heard you."

Nancy's voice was steady. "Why us?"

"Because you're not part of it."

She reached into her scrub pocket, pulled out a flash drive, and placed it on Romero's desk like it was a live wire. Her fingers brushed the surface like she was afraid it might disappear.

Romero stared at it. "What's on here?"

"Everything," Laila whispered. "Names. Footage. Forged clearances. Unauthorized removals. Payouts. Emails. I've been collecting it since the day I walked into this place."

Nancy's expression didn't change. "You've only been here two months."

"My story didn't start at St. James."

She walked to the window and sat heavily in the chair beside it. Her body folded into itself like she hadn't exhaled in days. Her voice dropped.

"I'm Dr. Mallick's girlfriend."

She looked at them both, her eyes beginning to water.

"I'm pregnant."

Romero's lips parted slightly, but no words came. Nancy's breath stilled.

"He worked under Leigh. He admired him. Wanted to be like him. Until he saw what was really happening. The forged match records. The post-mortem approvals. He questioned one case a liver transplant that came through without clearance. He refused to sign off."

Her voice hitched.

"Three days later, they suspended him. Claimed he violated procedure. The board didn't even blink. His career was over before he could defend himself."

Nancy stepped closer, heart sinking.

"He called me that night," Laila continued, wiping her face. "Said he felt like a failure. Said he had nothing left. Not his name. Not his work. Not even the future he promised me. He couldn't bear the shame."

She took a shaky breath.

"And then he vanished."

Romero moved around the desk, standing across from her now.

"I joined this hospital to find out what happened. I thought I could play it smart. Quiet. But then... Leigh noticed me. He reeled me in. Started trusting me. Late calls. Special assignments. I played the fool. I acted like I didn't know anything about Mallick. I let him believe I was new. Impressionable."

Nancy's tone was clipped. "You got close to him."

Laila nodded. "Too close. I became his mistress."

Romero's brows twitched, but he stayed silent.

"I delivered organ shipments. Drove patients between labs. Logged things into fake databases. I was in the room when surgeries were scheduled without match approvals. I never asked questions. I let him use me."

Nancy's voice was low. "But you kept records."

"Yes," Laila said. "Every single detail. On private servers. Then I backed them up onto this drive."

She pointed at it.

"But he doesn't know I'm Mallick's girlfriend. Not yet. He will. He always finds out. And when he does... I won't survive it."

Nancy stared at her. "You could've run already."

"I wanted to do one thing right," Laila said, sobbing again. "I want someone to clear Mallick's name. I want to destroy the system that chewed him up."

She turned her head toward the desk.

"There's more. The money trail goes past Leigh. There's a man. A CEO based overseas. Leigh doesn't operate alone. This hospital gets wired millions every quarter. No explanation. No oversight. Mallick traced one of the accounts. Right before he disappeared."

Romero leaned forward. "The board?"

"They're either blind or bought. Leigh answers to no one in here. But he's not the top. He's the butcher. Someone else owns the knife."

Nancy finally stepped toward the desk, her eyes on the flash drive.

"You said this has proof?"

Laila nodded. "I hope it's enough. I won't be here tomorrow. My flight leaves early. I need to disappear. Just... promise me you won't let my name come out."

Romero picked up the drive carefully, as if it were glass.

"You're risking everything," Nancy said.

"I already lost everything," Laila whispered. "At least now, I can lose it for something that matters."

She turned and walked to the door, wiping her eyes.

She looked back one last time.

"Thank you. For listening."

Then she was gone.

Romero turned off the desk light. The room dimmed to near black.

He plugged in the drive.

Lines of data scrolled across the screen.

Footage of undocumented patients. Anonymous donors. No OR charts. Coolers labeled only with color codes. Video feeds showing gurneys being wheeled in through back hallways. Transfer logs signed under fake names. Payout ledgers. Foreign account numbers.

Nancy sat down slowly, hand to her mouth.

"This isn't negligence," she said. "It's a criminal ring. They're selling organs like supplies."

Romero spoke without looking away.

"This is organized trafficking. And we're sitting on the files."

Nancy's voice was quiet. "She gave up everything for this."

Romero didn't answer.

Because they both knew

if they moved wrong now, they'd lose everything too.

And maybe more.

***

The ICU bay smelled like lemon disinfectant and leftover adrenaline. Evelyn stood at the foot of Bed 12, chart in hand, listening to the soft wheeze of a recovering COVID patient. The man was stable, mildly dehydrated, and watching the ceiling like it owed him an apology.

Behind her, a familiar voice piped up.

"Is it just me, or do these gowns make us look like rejected extras from a sci-fi reboot?"

Evelyn turned to see Nancy dragging her feet into the unit, surgical gown half-tied, badge swinging against her hip. Her eyes were red, her bun looked like it had been in a wind tunnel, and the coffee in her hand was definitely not her first.

"You look like you fought sleep and lost," Evelyn said.

Nancy yawned and waved her off. "I'm here, aren't I? Technically alive."

"You're also technically late."

"I'm redefining punctuality," Nancy said, holding up her coffee like it was a peace offering. "It's an art form."

Evelyn raised a brow. "Rough night?"

Nancy gave a vague shrug. "Let's just say... secrets, silence, and no good lighting."

Evelyn leaned forward, suddenly curious. "Secrets? Like what kind of secrets?"

Nancy's lips curled into a sly smile. "The kind involving a fake coma, an exploding catheter, and a woman who can't pronounce 'scalpel' without threatening someone."

Evelyn blinked. "Wait. Are you talking about *The Protocol is Lying*?"

Nancy nodded and took a sip. "Absolutely. You think I'm sharing real-life drama before coffee?"

Evelyn let out a loud laugh. "You had me. For a second, I thought you were about to confess to some underground hospital mafia."

"I might, depending on how bad this coffee is."

They both chuckled and walked toward the nurse station, their steps in sync. The morning buzz hadn't fully kicked in yet, and the monitors beeped in a low, sleepy rhythm.

"I finished episode six last night," Evelyn said. "That show is insane."

"Episode four wrecked me," Nancy replied. "The guy fakes a coma for seven years just to skip jury duty and nobody notices?"

"And his wife keeps feeding him pudding and reading him *Wuthering Heights* out loud like he's going to thank her one day."

Nancy laughed. "That woman deserves an award. Or therapy."

Evelyn nudged her. "Both. That nurse with the eyebrow ring? Icon."

Nancy nodded. "The moment she leaned in and whispered 'I know you're faking it, I just don't care'? Chills."

"Honestly, I respect her emotional boundaries."

They slipped into the break room and poured two fresh mugs of hospital-grade coffee.

"To unhinged plot twists and questionable ethics," Evelyn said, raising her cup.

"To caffeine-fueled coping mechanisms," Nancy replied.

They clinked their mugs and sat by the window, sunlight barely crawling through the blinds, but it was enough. For now, this moment belonged to coffee, TV conspiracies, and the comfort of someone who knew when to laugh with you; even when everything else was on fire.

***

Romero sat on the edge of his desk, the flash drive plugged into his laptop. Files flickered across the screen: videos, logs, altered donor IDs, account traces, screenshots of unsigned approvals. Nancy stood nearby, arms crossed, staring at the evidence that no longer needed interpretation.

"We can't keep this to ourselves anymore," she said.

"I know."

Romero leaned forward, typing a few lines into a secure viewer. "We'll have to email it. But not just anyone. Not the hospital board. They'll bury it. We need an outside agency."

Nancy nodded slowly. "What about the DOJ's Bioethics and Medical Oversight division? I remember they handled the St. Cloud transplant fraud."

"They'll need full evidence," Romero replied. "And a trigger. Something that forces immediate attention."

"They'll also need this to come in clean. No red flags, no sloppy headers, no chance of metadata pointing back to her."

Romero looked up. "You're talking about Laila."

"I'm talking about protecting someone who already gave up too much," Nancy said firmly. "We send this, but her name stays out of it. No personal logs. No intern badge screenshots. No metadata with timestamps from her station."

Romero nodded. "I can encrypt the footage, strip all the properties, reroute the IP through multiple relays. But we need a burner account for the tip."

"I'll make one now," Nancy said, pulling out her phone.

Romero continued prepping the email. They labeled the subject line: *URGENT: Unlawful Transplant Practices – Confidential Whistleblower Evidence*. Attached every document and video they had, with a note that said: "Immediate investigation requested. Patients' lives and human rights compromised. Donor records falsified. Evidence contained herein."

Nancy hit send.

Then she stared at the screen.

"Do you think this changes anything?" she asked.

Romero didn't answer right away. "I think it stops more damage."

***

The news vans were already circling by the time Nancy pulled into the hospital lot. It was just after 8 a.m. when the first wave of reporters began filming. Their voices echoed across the lawn, competing with the hum of generators and the clicks of long-lens cameras. Yellow barricade tape rippled at the edge of the garden. Paramedics stood in a silent half-circle near the hedges, guarding what none of them wanted to say out loud.

Someone had jumped.

From the fifth-floor fire exit.

Right into the garden Evelyn once called the "quiet corner" of the hospital.

Nancy stood frozen, halfway between her car and the ER door, unable to move. For a moment, she thought it couldn't be true. That someone had misunderstood. But then she heard it. The name.

A broken voice from the east side of the lawn.

"No... Evelyn!"

Nancy's blood ran cold.

She stepped forward on instinct, moving slowly through the crowd of nurses and techs who had started gathering. A few feet ahead, two security guards were trying to block the view of the body. A white tarp covered most of it now. One shoe had fallen off and lay beside the flowerbed, its laces soaked in morning dew.

Romero arrived at her side just as a nurse sobbed, "She left a note. In the driver's seat. Said she couldn't carry the weight anymore."

Nancy stared straight ahead, blinking like she couldn't quite process it. "I just talked to her... yesterday."

Romero glanced at her, voice barely steady. "What?"

"She was checking a COVID patient in Pod C. I came in late, looked like hell. She teased me for it. Said I had zombie eyes."

A bitter laugh caught in Nancy's throat. "We joked about that stupid TV show, the one with the coroner who can talk to ghosts. She asked me if I was keeping secrets like the main character. I told her it was just a show. That I wasn't hiding anything."

Nancy turned to him now, eyes wide with disbelief.

"She smiled. That tired, real smile. And said, 'Good. Secrets like that mess people up.'"

Romero looked away, jaw clenching. The morning light hit his face just enough to show how tired he really was.

Nancy's voice dropped. "She was talking about herself."

Behind them, a Channel 9 van was already live. The reporter's voice cut through the breeze.

"Tragedy struck this morning at St. James Medical Center when a longtime staff member was found dead just outside the east wing garden. Preliminary reports suggest suicide. The hospital has yet to release an official statement."

Romero watched the tarp being zipped. He flinched.

More staff had gathered now. Some covered their mouths. Others cried openly. A few stood in stunned silence, hands pressed to their pagers like they didn't know what else to hold on to.

Nancy whispered, "Evelyn didn't just break. She collapsed under everything we didn't say out loud."

Nancy covered her mouth with one hand, eyes rimmed red. "now she's gone. Because none of us asked her how she was really doing..."

They stood together, shoulder to shoulder, as the ambulance doors closed with a hollow clunk.

A nurse nearby wept into another's shoulder. Someone from housekeeping crossed themselves and whispered a prayer. A resident stared blankly at the tarp, mouthing the word "Why" over and over.

Nancy glanced back at the yellow tape, then at the reporters, and finally at Romero.

"Whatever happens next... we don't let her be forgotten."

Romero nodded once, his voice hoarse. "She deserved better. We all did."

And as the crowd thinned, as morning rounds resumed and patients were wheeled past with sedatives and saline, the garden remained still.

A place once used for coffee breaks and quiet walks had become something else.

A memorial without a plaque.

A wound that would not close.

But the horror didn't stop there.

Inside, just past the emergency wing, another body lay covered near Bay 2. Monitors around the room were still on, flashing unread vitals. The nurse at the desk looked stunned.

"She coded ten minutes ago," the nurse said. "They didn't even get to bag her."

Nancy pulled the sheet back slowly.

Laila.

Her face was too still, her skin too cold.

Romero's hand touched her shoulder.

Nancy whispered, "This wasn't a coincidence. This was cleanup."

She backed away, shaken, breathing hard as the hospital hallway grew louder sirens outside, footsteps echoing from all corners, voices rising.

In the corridor, two young nurses walked past, whispering in disbelief.

"Leigh and Evelyn? No way. I thought she was straight arrow."

"Yeah but... two dead in one morning?"

A resident from Pulmonary passed by with a bag of PPE, muttering to a colleague, "They sealed the trauma OR, grabbed all the ICU interns, and even took the transplant techs. Something big has gone down."

"They said someone tipped them off," the other replied. "I heard it was Dr. Romero."

Nancy looked at Romero sharply. He was already sweating, back tense.

Then came the knock.

A tall man in a black coat stepped into the ICU corridor, flashing credentials that weren't hospital issued.

"Dr. Romero?" he asked calmly.

Romero turned.

"You'll need to come with us."

Nancy stepped forward. "Where are you taking him?"

The man didn't flinch. "Department of Justice. We have a few questions."

Romero gave her a quick look.

Stay calm. Stay quiet.

And then he walked away.

Nancy stood rooted to the floor, the sound of ambulance sirens in the distance, reporters pressing against the gates outside, and the memory of Laila's broken voice in her head.

This wasn't the end.

It was just the reckoning.

Chapter 10:
The Tip That Started It All

Room B12 felt more like a fallout bunker than a federal office. Concrete walls. No clock. One surveillance camera blinking red in the ceiling's corner. The air was cold enough to sting.

Dr. Romero sat at the steel table, back straight but jaw clenched. Across from him, Agents Moore and Carter reviewed a thick file, their faces unreadable. His attorney, Diana Keats, sat to his left, heels crossed, legal pad open, pen already in motion.

Agent Moore spoke first.

"Dr. Romero, as you've been informed, this is a voluntary interview. But you are considered a person of interest in an ongoing federal investigation involving unlawful organ procurement, falsified death records, and obstruction of national transplant protocols under the NTS Act."

Romero nodded slowly. "Understood."

"We'll begin with your direct involvement. You were on shift during at least six transplant procedures now under audit. Each involved organs transferred under emergency pandemic exceptions, bypassing standard UNOS registry verification. Were you aware of that?"

Romero answered calmly. "I wasn't aware they bypassed UNOS. My role as a trauma surgeon begins and ends at the OR. I review vitals, consult with the procurement team, and oversee the transplant. I don't monitor what happens after the patient is wheeled out."

Agent Carter tapped a photo from the folder and slid it across the table. "Do you recognize this cooler?"

Romero barely glanced. "They're standard issue. Hundreds like it pass through every month."

"This one was used for a directed donation that was never logged in the federal tracking system. Your electronic signature is on the handoff form."

Diana leaned in. "My client has routinely signed off on standardized consent forms provided by the transplant coordinator. If those forms were misrepresented or tampered with, that's a separate matter."

Moore didn't blink. "The problem is, doctor, those sign-offs greenlighted the removal of organs from COVID-positive patients who did not meet the updated clinical clearance guidelines."

Romero's expression darkened. "Are you suggesting I performed illegal extractions?"

"No," Carter said coolly, "we're saying the chain of custody broke down, and your credentials appear repeatedly at the breakpoints."

Moore placed three timestamped surveillance stills on the table Laila near the back exit, a vehicle marked "medical courier," and Romero walking through a staff corridor.

"Same night. You were there. You passed that cooler."

"I was on post-op. I went to the scrub-out station."

"You didn't question the backdoor transport?"

"We're told not to interfere with logistics. If I challenged every cooler in a hallway, I'd never leave the OR."

Moore leaned forward. "Evelyn Meyers' badge was scanned minutes before the transport. She approved the donor paperwork. You're telling us that's coincidence?"

Romero stayed silent for a moment. Then: "I'm saying if Evelyn authorized it, she believed it was legal. She was meticulous. If something changed, it wasn't because she suddenly turned corrupt."

Moore's tone sharpened. "She committed suicide... You still think she was clean?"

"I think she was hunted."

That hung in the air.

Agent Carter shifted, flipping open a new file. "Dr. Romero, a tip was submitted to the DOJ anonymously. It contained patient lists, donor mismatches, unsigned approvals, and GPS logs of private couriers rerouting organs off-registry. That email came from a device inside St. James. It pinged your login, the admin lounge WiFi, and a timestamp matching your shift."

Diana's pen stopped mid-sentence.

Romero let out a breath. "I sent it."

Both agents paused.

"I masked the source," Romero continued. "I didn't want it traced to Nancy. Or to me, if things backfired. We were trying to keep our jobs long enough to get real evidence. That flash drive from Nurse Shah that was the break. She gave me everything."

"You're saying Laila Shah was the source of the files?" Carter asked.

Romero nodded. "She worked directly under Leigh. She brought me the logs, access codes, donor chain errors, even DMV routing info. She said we'd only have one shot to expose it all."

Moore exchanged a glance with his partner.

"I sent the email," Romero repeated. "It wasn't sabotage. It was a warning. And from what I've seen in this room, it was a warning you needed."

There was a heavy silence. The agents reviewed the printed evidence again, then Moore finally asked, "Was Ms. Brooks involved?"

Romero looked up sharply.

"She didn't know at first. But yes eventually. She saw inconsistencies in the transplant orders. Missing signatures, incompatible matches being rushed. We didn't understand the scale of it until Laila... until she turned up dead."

Carter's voice lowered. "What about Dr. Mallick?"

Romero blinked. "Mallick? Leigh got his license suspended. I assumed it was over a procedure error."

Carter nodded slowly. "Mallick submitted a complaint about organ routing two months before his suspension."

Romero exhaled. "So he tried too."

"Dr. Romero," Moore said, "Leigh is now unaccounted for. We have a federal search out. His office was cleared before dawn. No digital trail. No backup devices. Just one burner account used to reroute internal files to an unknown cloud repository."

Romero didn't respond. Just leaned back and stared at the table.

Finally, Moore closed the folder. "We're moving Ms. Brooks now. She'll be questioned next. After that, both of you will be escorted to Oversight for official briefing."

Diana asked, "Are you charging him?"

"Not at this time," Moore said. "But neither of you are permitted to leave the state. Until the case is closed, you remain under federal observation."

Romero nodded.

As the door opened, he turned once toward the mirrored glass just in time to catch a glimpse of Nancy being escorted through the hallway.

He knew what came next.

And he was done staying quiet.

***

Nancy Brooks sat stiffly in Room C03. Her lawyer, Julia Mendel, sat beside her, sharp-eyed and silent, her tablet synced to every document the agents might reference.

Across the table, Agents Lowell and Singh placed two identical folders down.

"Ms. Brooks, thank you for coming voluntarily. As you've been informed, you're being questioned as a witness and a possible accessory in the ongoing investigation tied to black-market organ distribution, violations of the National Transplant Safety Act, and at least two deaths connected to St. James Medical Center."

Nancy folded her hands together. "I'm here to answer everything honestly."

Agent Lowell opened the first folder. "According to internal hospital logs, you were present during the July 3rd transplant of a lung from an unverified donor. That same night, a patient died on Table 2. What can you tell us about that?"

"I flagged the match," Nancy replied. "The donor bloodwork didn't line up with what we had on file. The procurement tech told me they had override approval from Dr. Leigh."

Agent Singh frowned. "Did you request documentation?"

"Yes. I never received it. I raised concerns, but the surgery proceeded while I was dealing with the patient in Bay 1."

Lowell flipped the page. "So you believe someone intentionally went around the system?"

"I believe someone was using the pandemic as cover to bypass safeguards. Transplants were happening faster than records could be verified. Leigh's name was everywhere, but no one questioned him."

Singh looked up. "Why didn't you escalate it further?"

"I did. Internally. No one responded. Leigh had authority. Everyone else had fear."

There was a pause. Agent Singh then placed three stills on the table: Nancy with Romero near the trauma bay; Nancy logging into the admin system at 11:47 p.m.; and a timestamped chart review on a flagged donor file later marked as "approved."

"You accessed donor logs after hours," Lowell said. "Why?"

Nancy kept her voice steady. "Because we'd already lost a patient to a mismatched liver. No one reported it. I needed to know if it was a pattern."

Singh tilted her head. "You found something, didn't you?"

"Yes," Nancy said. "I found multiple logs with missing consent forms, two unmatched blood types that were never flagged, and at least three cases where the procurement route was edited after the transplant."

Lowell pressed further. "And you never reported this outside the hospital?"

Nancy hesitated. Then: "No."

Singh leaned forward. "Did someone...umm threatened you or you simply..."

"Dr. Leigh..."

Nancy said with a gulp. "But...Romero...umm we both later dig in and found..."

Lowell interrupted, "We know Ms. Brooks...Dr. already enlightened us on your schemes of work...Umm...tell me...Nurse Shah was investigating this on her own?"

"Yes...She didn't trust the system. She wanted to protect herself in case everything came crashing down..."

Agent Singh opened a new file. "Well. We traced the anonymous tip to a St. James administrative device. That email triggered our involvement. Do you know who sent it?"

Nancy looked at her attorney, who shook her head.

"No comment."

Lowell paused, then asked, "Well...Dr. already agreed he did. Never mind. Were you aware that this made you complicit in a federal breach if the evidence turned out to be manipulated?"

"I didn't think about the legal outcome," she said quietly. "I thought about the patients. The ones still alive."

A long silence followed.

Then Singh said, "Ms. Brooks, we have reason to believe that what happened to Laila Shah was not accidental. Her death appears to have been staged.... Did you ever see anyone threaten her or she mentioned?"

Nancy swallowed hard. "Not just she died...Her baby ..." Nancy took a deep breath.

"We know that Ms. Brooks."

"Umm, okay and no comments."

Singh's jaw tightened. "Dr. Leigh has disappeared. His office has been cleared. Internal audit logs show that his badge was used to override at least four patient status tags. And until this morning, he was still approving transplants through an offshore EHR platform."

Nancy sat back, stunned. "So he ran."

Lowell gave a slow nod. "And he took enough with him to shut down your entire department."

The door opened. Agent Carter stepped in, whispered something to Lowell, then nodded to Nancy.

"We're transferring you to Oversight," he said. "Dr. Romero is there now. You'll both be briefed by our joint task force."

Nancy stood slowly, her knees stiff.

She turned to her lawyer. "This isn't over, is it?"

Julia's voice was calm. "No. But you've made yourself clear. That helps."

***

Romero, Nancy, their lawyers, and four agents gathered in the glass-walled Oversight Room.

Agent Moore addressed them both. "You are not under arrest. However, neither of you are permitted to leave the state until this investigation reaches a resolution. You'll be required to remain available for questioning. Your credentials will remain suspended until further review."

Nancy asked, "What about the hospital?"

Moore looked grim. "We are not sealing St. James yet, but the evidence suggests we should. Until that decision is made, you are both expected to uphold procedural integrity and report any further findings."

As he turned to leave, Nancy called after him. "What about Evelyn?"

Moore paused at the door. "Her silence wasn't guilt. It was leverage. We believe someone cornered her. And we believe that someone was Leigh."

Romero looked at Nancy. She didn't speak. But her eyes told him everything.

The reckoning had found them both. And it wasn't finished yet.

***

The parking lot behind the Federal Health & Ethics Division felt eerily quiet despite the chaos that had unfolded inside. Dusk settled over the building, painting long shadows across the cracked pavement. Nancy stood beside Romero, both still in their scrubs, their bodies tense, eyes scanning for answers that hadn't come.

Their lawyers Julia Mendel and Diana Keats flanked them like sentinels.

Julia crossed her arms, voice low but firm. "From this moment on, both of you are to avoid discussing this case with anyone. No press. No friends. Not even staff unless you're subpoenaed."

Diana nodded. "And if someone from the hospital or media reaches out, your only response is 'no comment.' One wrong word, one misinterpreted sentence, and you'll both be pulled back in under obstruction charges."

Nancy looked at Romero, uncertain.

Julia continued. "There's no solid evidence to clear either of you yet. The DOJ hasn't ruled you out. So whatever you think you know stop digging. Until we say otherwise."

Romero shifted, jaw clenched. "But what if...."

"No what-ifs," Diana said. "Not now. You're both under observation. Surveillance, possibly tapped phones. This is not the time for heroics."

Nancy's eyes dropped to the asphalt. The wind blew cold across her skin.

As the lawyers walked ahead toward their cars, Romero stayed back. He leaned toward her, voice barely a whisper.

"Keep your head down," he said. "Until we know more."

***

Nancy sat motionless on the edge of her couch, a half-folded blanket slipping from her shoulders. The glow of the television bathed the room in cold blue light, flickering headlines flashing across the screen like warning signs in the dark. No sound, just silence and the hum of her own breath.

On screen, Evelyn's photo appeared once more. Her smile too soft, too unsuspecting hung there like a ghost. Then came a live image of the sealed trauma wing at St. James. Floodlights. Police tape. A makeshift memorial where someone had lit candles and left a hand-drawn poster: *Justice for the Silenced.*

Nancy reached for the remote and raised the volume just as the anchor's voice dipped into something graver.

"In a new development, six families have come forward with shocking claims. Their loved ones were discharged postmortem without critical organs. No consent paperwork. No explanations. While the hospital denies misconduct, internal leaks suggest an expanding black market scandal. Sources say the Department of Justice is now reviewing transplant records dating back several months..."

Her heart thudded once hard like it wanted out of her chest. She grabbed her phone and typed with trembling fingers.

Nancy: *Did you see the segment just now?*

It took a moment.

Then the screen lit up.

Romero: *Yeah. It's worse than we thought.*

She dropped the phone in her lap, folded her arms, and leaned back against the couch. The anchor's voice droned on in the background, but her mind had already drifted.

To Jim.

To their quiet mornings. The way he always insisted on brewing the coffee even though she drank tea. His lazy Saturday smiles. The nights they stayed up reading, sharing the blanket on the sofa she was now sitting on his place still marked by the worn-out cushion.

And that one time he tried to cook.

He'd waved a spatula like a sword and declared himself *"King of the Kitchen."* It ended with the dish towel on fire and both of them laughing breathless on the floor. That memory like all the others carved a hollow ache in her chest.

His voice surfaced in her mind, clear as a bell.

"You're the tough one, Nancy. You fix everyone else. Just don't forget to breathe."

Her eyes stung.

Nancy stood in the quiet stillness of her living room, her arms crossed, fingers curled tight around her sleeves. The air felt heavier now. Her mind was racing but her body ached with fatigue. She turned the TV off. Enough noise. Enough headlines.

She picked up her phone again.

Nancy: *What symptoms?*

Romero didn't reply immediately.

She sat back down, pulled the blanket tighter.

Then came the buzz.

Romero: *Low-grade fever. Light cough. Some chills. Didn't sleep well.*

She frowned.

Nancy: *Could be the beginning. Check your temp every few hours. You have a pulse oximeter, right?*

Romero: *Yeah. Oxygen is stable. 97. Not panicking yet.*

She stared at the screen, thinking.

Nancy: *You need to rest. No hospital shifts. No board calls. Nothing.*

Another buzz.

Romero: *Already cancelled everything. Not taking any risks.*

Then, another message came through a second later.

Romero: *You should stay home too. Yesterday was too much. Interrogations. Evelyn. Laila. Just... rest today. I'll handle anything urgent that comes up.*

Her thumb hovered.

She could almost hear his voice in those words firm, but tired. Like the doctor in him was fighting to stay in charge while the human behind it was starting to break down.

Nancy: *You sure?*

Romero: *Yeah. Don't push yourself. We need to think clearly. There's more coming I feel it.*

Nancy closed her eyes and pressed the phone to her chest.

The texts weren't just instructions. They were protection. A shield, even if temporary. Romero was trying to carry more than his own pain and she knew it.

Another buzz.

Romero: *Get some tea. Turn off the news. You're not saving anyone today. You're just surviving.*

Her eyes welled up. Not with grief this time, but with something more fragile.

Gratitude.

Then, finally, a last message:

Romero: *I'll check in later. Don't open the door unless it's me or Julia.*

Nancy smiled faintly through the tired ache and typed:

Nancy: *Same goes for you. Stay in. Stay safe. And if your oxygen dips, you call me.*

She placed the phone down gently beside her. The apartment was still again.

But not for long.

Something was about to knock again.

And this time, it wouldn't be a text.

***

Evening crept in without sound. The golden wash of the setting sun had long faded, replaced by the dull flicker of streetlights outside Nancy's window. The shadows in her apartment grew longer, bending across the floor like fingers reaching for something they couldn't hold.

She stood in the kitchen, glass in hand, but hadn't taken a sip. Her thoughts were too loud. Every headline from the day echoed through her six families, missing organs, no consent. Evelyn. Laila. The DOJ's cold eyes in that interrogation room. Jim's voice still lingering in her head like a breath she couldn't release.

The clock ticked.

The heater hissed.

And then three soft knocks.

She turned.

Silence returned.

No footsteps in the hall. No shuffle. Just a single, manila envelope lying neatly against the base of her door.

Nancy's heart stuttered.

She crossed the room slowly, each step echoing louder in her chest than on the wooden floor. The envelope had no return address. Just her name, centered on a white label in all-caps type. Clean. Precise. Chosen.

She crouched and picked it up.

It was heavier than it looked dense, deliberate. Not something casually dropped off. The seal was intact, but slightly frayed at the corners, like it had changed hands too many times.

She opened it with a butter knife, careful not to tear anything.

Inside was a thick stack of papers hospital transplant logs. Nancy's fingers trembled as she flipped through them.

Thirty-two procedures. All from the past four months. All organs harvested from COVID-designated donors. All signed off by one man.

Dr. Elijah Leigh.

She stared at the signature. Page after page, the same name. But none of these were in the official hospital database. These had been hidden. Off the record. Off the radar.

The final page was paper-clipped to a yellow Post-it.

No signature.

No handwriting.

Just a single typed line in bold block letters:

"You were never supposed to find these."

Nancy's breath caught in her throat.

She backed away from the envelope like it might explode. Her mind flooded with questions.

Who left this? How did they know where to find her? And what else was missing?

Her hand moved instinctively to her phone but stopped mid-reach.

No. Not yet.

She stared down at the documents spread across her coffee table, the yellow Post-it like a quiet scream.

This wasn't a warning.

It was a message.

A line had been crossed. And whoever sent it knew she was close too close to something they'd buried deep.

Nancy slowly sat down, the envelope still half-open beside her.

Her fingers curled tight around the edge of the table.

This wasn't the end.

It was the start of the hunt.

Chapter 11:
The Silence is Cracking

The first rays of morning peeled across the city skyline, streaking the hospital's tinted glass windows in shades of cold silver. Nancy pulled into the parking structure, the engine ticking after she shut it off. The silence inside her car felt oddly sacred. She sat for a moment, both hands still on the steering wheel, forehead resting lightly on her wrist.

Another day, she whispered to herself. Or maybe just the next chapter in whatever this nightmare had become.

Inside, St. James Hospital buzzed faintly to life, though something about the building's energy felt off. The entrance scanner gave its usual reluctant beep, and the mechanical click of the glass door opened to a lobby that was far too still.

No clipped heels on tile. No cafeteria smells wafting up the corridors. Just a sleepy nurse at reception sipping lukewarm coffee, scrolling absentmindedly through her phone. She gave Nancy a half-glance, then looked away.

Nancy adjusted her mask and walked in. Her phone buzzed as she passed radiology.

"Two patients just intubated. Rapid deterioration. Need trauma review ASAP."

She stopped briefly to type a response.

"On my way."

Then she hesitated. Something had been eating at her all morning, a shadow that followed her home and back again.

She opened her messages and quickly typed to Romero:

Nancy: Morning. How are you feeling? You resting?

Also... I got something. An envelope. Brown, anonymous. Thirty-two transplant logs. All signed by Leigh. None of them are in the official system. I don't know who's playing with me, but I'm scared.

Her fingers hovered over the screen. She hit send and stared at it, as if waiting for the phone to buzz back would somehow make it all feel safer.

No reply came.

The ICU doors stood open ahead. Machines beeped in staccato rhythm, and muffled voices slipped out into the hallway. She tucked her phone into her pocket and walked in.

The ICU had always been a dance between order and chaos. Today, it felt more like a battlefield.

Nurses moved fast but without panic, their motions sharp, deliberate. A resident wheeled a vent cart past her, muttering to a colleague. Alarms chirped from three different beds. The lights were bright, too bright, washing everything in a sterile glow that hurt Nancy's eyes.

She walked toward Bay 4, where a middle-aged man mid-fifties, maybe lay motionless beneath the cascade of wires and tubes. His chart read *COVID positive, oxygen saturation dropping despite BiPAP, moved to full intubation at 4:47 AM.*

Nancy skimmed the vitals on the monitor. His lungs were barely exchanging air. His chest rose and fell in mechanical rhythm. A prone chart was taped to the bed's railing, and someone had already ordered a transplant consult.

A junior doctor noticed her and stepped closer.

"We started corticosteroids and remdesivir, but he tanked in less than an hour. We're prepping ECMO as backup. ID wants to push for a transplant option if he survives the next six hours."

Nancy's throat tightened. ECMO meant desperate. Transplant consult meant dying. Neither felt right so soon after arrival.

"Is there a match already?" she asked, her voice low.

The junior doctor looked unsure. "Not yet. But Trauma flagged him high-priority. We're watching for an eligible donor. His blood type is common."

Nancy nodded and moved to Bay 7. Another patient. This one, a young woman. Early twenties. Her frame small beneath the hospital blankets, but her face bruised from repeated intubation attempts.

Diagnosis: *COVID pneumonia. Progression to ARDS. Oxygen sat at 73% despite full support.*

Nancy leaned over the chart and scanned it again.

"She was healthy," a nurse said softly behind her. "Ran marathons. This hit her hard. They brought her in just last night."

Nancy's chest ached. They were seeing this too often now. Late-stage COVID, crashing fast. And every time someone whispered the word "transplant," it no longer rang of hope it sounded like a trap.

She finished reviewing the scans, noting the progression, and stepped away.

"I'll finish notes from the conference room," she told them. "Keep her stable. Page me if anything shifts."

The nurses nodded.

Nancy walked back down the ICU hall, this time slower. Something was gnawing at her, and it wasn't just the patients. It was the weight of that envelope in her bag. Thirty-two names. Thirty-two organs. All signed off by Leigh. None of them officially reported.

And now, two more patients on death's edge.

She stepped into the stairwell and shut the door behind her. For a moment, she leaned her back against the wall and just breathed.

She reached into her coat pocket and pulled out the envelope again. The pages inside felt heavier today.

Romero still hadn't replied.

And that silence was beginning to feel dangerous.

***

Nancy sat alone on the weather-worn bench outside the ICU's private garden, arms crossed tightly against the morning chill. The sun filtered weakly through gray clouds, casting long shadows over the tiled courtyard and the stone Virgin Mary that stood near the hedge wall. The air smelled faintly of hospital-grade disinfectant, mingled with the scent of overwatered grass. Her breath steamed in the cold. Everything about this place felt sterile except for what was now burning a hole in her hands.

She reached into her shoulder bag with slow, deliberate movements, as if even her body understood the weight of what she was carrying. The envelope was creased at the corners, the paper now slightly worn from the number of times she had unfolded it, read it, then shoved it back down again like a secret she couldn't bear to keep but wasn't ready to face.

The flap stuck slightly as she peeled it back.

One by one, she lifted the transplant logs again. Thirty-two case sheets, almost indistinguishable from one another. Each entry was meticulously typed, clean margins, uniform format. Patient codes she didn't recognize. Organ descriptions. Destination lines.

And always...always the same signature at the bottom:

Dr. Elijah Leigh.

She scanned the sheet for familiar internal codes: no hospital IDs, no patient chart numbers, no transplant board approvals, no insurance documentation.

Nothing that would tie these to legal procedure.

Just the raw data of a deal. Neat. Quiet. Hidden.

She set the stack down on her lap and reached for the page at the bottom. It wasn't formatted like the others.

It was an invoice.

Her brow furrowed as her eyes traced the heading:

INVOICE #7821

Western Heights Recovery Center – Procurement Account

One (1) Human Heart – **$50,000**

One (1) Adult Liver – **$30,000**

Two (2) Kidneys – **$40,000**

Bundle Package (Includes: Dermal Tissue, Cornea Pair, Partial Lung Segment) – **$60,000**

Total: $180,000 USD

Payment confirmed via offshore transfer. Clearance: Priority Handling.

Nancy stared at it for a full minute. Her jaw clenched. The words were typed in plain font. No embellishment. No medical jargon. Just the business of it.

A human body, broken down like warehouse inventory.

She read it again. Then again. Her breath grew shallow.

She thought about the bodies that passed through the ICU the ones that didn't make it. She thought about consent forms, protocols, family approvals, the entire machinery of ethics that had been drilled into her since med school.

And here it was; dismantled.

Organ procurement as profit.

Nancy's fingers trembled as she reached for her phone, but she didn't text. Not yet. She stared back down at the name on the invoice:

Western Heights Recovery Center.

Something about it scraped her memory. Not from patient charts or rounds, but from something far more ominous. She dug into the recesses of her mind until she remembered; **a federal tip-off report.** She'd skimmed it months ago, about a facility rumored to be operating as a shell company for a mob-run healthcare laundering scheme. A place where terminal patients were kept on life support until the paperwork caught up with the money. A place where organs were moved faster than death certificates.

It had been shut down or so the public had been told.

And now it appeared on this invoice. With Dr. Leigh's name tied directly to it.

Nancy's stomach turned. Her throat burned with quiet nausea.

She flipped the page over.

There, scribbled in smudged blue ink on the back, was a single line:

This is one. There are more.

No signature. No initials. Just the sharp edge of a warning.

She scanned the surrounding garden instinctively. Was someone watching her? Was she being followed?

It was easy to feel paranoid when the truth felt like fiction.

She carefully folded the papers back into the envelope and pressed it against her chest, her grip tightening. Her heartbeat thumped against it like a ticking clock.

She thought of Romero; no reply yet.

Maybe the fever had knocked him out. Or maybe the silence meant something else.

Nancy opened her phone. Her thumb hovered over his name.

What if I'm not the only one holding this?

What if someone else already paid the price for knowing too much?

She closed the screen and stuffed her phone into her coat pocket.

The bench creaked slightly as she stood. She didn't know where to go next...not yet...but she knew one thing for sure:

This wasn't over.

Someone had built a system designed to stay hidden. To feed off hospitals like hers. Off patients like hers. Off the silence of people like her.

And now, the silence was cracking.

The envelope was no longer just a warning.

It was an invitation.

A line had been drawn. And Nancy had just crossed it.

***

Nancy sat on the edge of her sofa, her phone balanced on one knee, TV remote in the other. Her apartment was dim, curtains drawn halfway, morning light struggling to find its way in. The news anchor's voice crackled through the flat-screen as a red banner flashed across the bottom of the screen:

BREAKING: ST. JAMES MEDICAL CENTER SEALED FEDERAL INVESTIGATION UNDERWAY

The screen cut to a live feed. Outside St. James, yellow caution tape fluttered in the breeze, wound tight around the main entrance. News vans lined the block, satellite dishes pointed skyward. A cluster of microphones faced a portable DOJ podium where three men in dark suits stood two from the Department of Justice, one from the UNOS Compliance Bureau. Behind them, a blue backdrop bore the golden seal of the DOJ.

The lead speaker, Assistant U.S. Attorney Jacob Grisham, stepped forward, his voice low and firm.

"Good morning. At 6:22 AM today, federal agents executed a temporary shutdown order on St. James Medical Center, citing violations of federal transplant protocol and suspected criminal misconduct related to unregistered organ transfers. The scope of this investigation has broadened significantly in the last 48 hours."

Flashes fired from the press pit. Reporters stirred. Hands shot up.

Reporter 1 (CBS): "Can you confirm if this is connected to illegal transplant activity or patient trafficking?"

Grisham: "Yes. We have confirmed multiple instances where transplant procedures were conducted without proper registration in the UNOS database. These actions bypassed ethical oversight and legal safeguards. Our investigation indicates a pattern of systemic malpractice."

Nancy leaned forward, her heart thumping.

Reporter 2 (Reuters): "Is Dr. Elijah Leigh in custody?"

Grisham paused, then leaned closer to the microphone.

"No. Dr. Leigh is not in custody. He failed to report to the hospital this morning and did not respond to formal inquiries. We have issued a federal alert and notified law enforcement agencies across state lines. He is now officially considered a suspect."

Reporter 3 (NBC): "Can you explain how this network was first discovered?"

Grisham gestured to Agent Keller, who stepped up, flipping a notepad open in his palm.

"We received an anonymous package three days ago. It contained signed transplant logs, a financial ledger with itemized payments for human organs, and shipping details tied to a third-party facility known as Western Heights Recovery Center. That facility has long been under quiet scrutiny for alleged mob involvement and laundering medical funds."

Nancy sat rigid. Her eyes flicked to the brown envelope still on her coffee table. It was the same.

Reporter 4 (Vice News): "What exactly did the invoice show?"

Keller: "Pricing breakdowns for organs $50,000 for a heart, $30,000 for a liver, $20,000 per kidney, and bulk rates for bundled tissue packages including corneas and dermal tissue. The invoices were stamped as 'paid' via offshore accounts. We traced at least five transactions matching that template. All signed by Dr. Leigh."

Reporter 5 (Bloomberg): "Are you saying Leigh personally profited from these sales?"

Keller exchanged a glance with Grisham.

Grisham: "We're saying there is overwhelming financial data suggesting Dr. Leigh authorized procedures that were compensated through private, unregulated means. These payments were disguised using medical coding systems and filtered through shell entities."

Reporter 6 (LA Times): "How could something like this happen undetected inside a licensed transplant center?"

Keller: "That's exactly what we're asking. This wasn't one lapse. It was systematic. It leveraged the chaos of the pandemic. During a time when hospitals were overwhelmed, oversight became lax. Leigh and possibly others; took advantage of that chaos."

Reporter 7 (NPR): "Who are these 'others'? Are more arrests coming?"

Grisham's tone shifted. Firmer.

"We are closely monitoring two individuals who may have enabled or knowingly overlooked key parts of the operation. We're not releasing names at this stage, but we are pursuing multiple subpoenas."

Nancy's grip tightened on her blanket.

Reporter 8 (The Guardian): "What's being done for the families of the donors and recipients? If these were illegal, are their procedures being investigated?"

UNOS Official: "Yes. We are conducting a full audit. Every donor and recipient on file during the last six months at St. James is under review. Families who believe something was mishandled should reach out to our crisis response team. We'll also be coordinating with medical ethicists and grief counselors."

Reporter 9 (AP): "Can you confirm if the hospital itself will face criminal charges?"

Grisham nodded.

"St. James Medical Center's administrative board is under federal review. All organ transplant operations there are suspended pending the outcome of this case. If institutional complicity is found, charges will be filed."

Reporter 10 (Politico): "And what about Western Heights Recovery Center? Are they part of this investigation?"

Keller: "Yes. We are working in cooperation with Nevada authorities. Several documents tie the two facilities together through untraceable middlemen and suspect couriers. One courier is already in custody. We'll be releasing his identity once charges are filed."

The podium buzzed with murmurs.

Nancy stared at the screen. It wasn't just one or two bad calls. This was massive.

Reporter 11 (CNN): "So you're saying someone tipped you off. Can you tell us who?"

Grisham: "No. We received the documents anonymously. But that single envelope was enough to validate months of internal suspicion. And it confirmed what some whistleblowers had hinted at but couldn't prove."

Reporter 12 (The Times): "Was there any internal staff member aiding your investigation?"

Keller hesitated.

"Not initially. But we now believe someone inside the hospital knew what was going on and may have anonymously sent the evidence."

Nancy's heart skipped. She hadn't sent hers. Someone else had. Someone else inside St. James.

Reporter 13 (PBS): "Are there any indications that patients were harmed or denied organs due to this black market interference?"

Keller: "Yes. That's part of the deeper tragedy. We have reports of qualified patients being passed over in favor of foreign recipients or private buyers. That's what makes this a violation not only of federal law but of basic human decency."

Silence fell for a second too long.

Grisham stepped forward once more.

"I want to make this clear. This is not the end of the investigation. This is the beginning. More subpoenas. More interviews. And more truth to uncover. We won't stop until every name in that chain is held accountable."

The press conference ended with a final statement from UNOS:

"Lives were traded like currency. And we intend to bring justice."

The screen faded to footage of St. James' doors being sealed shut. Two interns escorted into a black SUV. Staff members standing on the curb with packed duffel bags, confused and silent.

Nancy's phone buzzed. Still no word from Romero.

She stared at the screen, the words echoing in her apartment.

Someone else had that envelope.

And that someone had just dropped it straight into the fire.

***

The apartment was quiet, cloaked in the stillness that follows a storm. Outside, the streetlamps cast long shadows across the pavement, their orange light softening the edges of the night. Nancy sat curled on the couch, legs tucked beneath her, a blanket draped loosely around her shoulders. The glow from the muted TV flickered across the room, casting flashes of headlines **ST. JAMES SEALED** across the far wall like ghosts of the day she couldn't shake.

She hadn't moved in hours. Not since the press conference ended. Not since Romero's silence stretched into another worrying night.

Then came the knock.

Not urgent. Not frantic. Just... steady. Soft. Three quiet taps.

Nancy flinched. Her first instinct was caution. No one knew her address. Or at least, no one from St. James.

She rose, barefoot on the hardwood floor, her body still tense from everything she'd heard that morning. She peered through the peephole then gasped and swung the door open.

"Carla?"

Standing in the hallway, holding a small travel bag in one hand and a box of takeout in the other, was Carla Whitaker her best friend from Mercy West. Her wild curls were slightly damp from the mist outside, cheeks flushed from travel, her smile uncertain but glowing.

"In the flesh," Carla whispered. "You gonna just stare or let me in before I start crying like a movie character?"

Nancy didn't say anything at first. She just stepped forward and wrapped her arms around her, burying her face in Carla's shoulder. The blanket slipped to the floor. And for a long moment, they stood in the doorway like that two women who hadn't shared a room in nearly a year, now clinging to each other like the world had cracked open.

"You came all the way from St. Louis?" Nancy finally managed, her voice thick.

Carla pulled back, brushing a tear from the corner of Nancy's eye with the pad of her thumb. "Of course I did, you idiot! I saw the news and I panicked. I called you, like, ten times. But I figured if you weren't answering, you probably needed someone to just show up."

Nancy laughed softly, her nose still red, voice rasping from the tension of the last few days. "I'm sorry. I didn't have the words. I didn't even have the air."

"I know," Carla said gently, stepping inside. "That's why I brought dumplings."

She held up the takeout box like it was a peace treaty.

Nancy shut the door behind her, the click echoing in the quiet. "You remembered."

"You used to eat these with that awful grape soda every time you had a shift longer than sixteen hours," Carla said, settling the bag on the kitchen counter. "Tell me you're at least eating now."

Nancy shrugged. "I'm trying."

Carla looked around the apartment, eyes scanning the modest living room, the potted plant by the window, the books stacked on the coffee table.

"This place is beautiful," she said, turning back with a warm smile. "It's so you. Simple. Quiet. Thoughtful."

"Thanks," Nancy said, her voice catching.

Carla dropped onto the couch, patting the seat beside her. "Now sit your ass down and tell me what the hell happened. And no skipping. I want everything. The tears. The breakdowns. The conspiracies. But only after we eat."

Nancy sat beside her, the weight in her chest loosening just a little. She reached for a dumpling, took a bite, and exhaled slowly.

"I really missed you," she said.

Carla leaned her head on Nancy's shoulder.

"I missed you more than I knew."

The city murmured outside. But inside that small apartment, in the dim glow of overhead lights and a half-muted television, two old friends sat together...one finally exhaling, the other holding the space where healing could begin.

***

Chapter 12:
Truth in Transit

Nancy woke up on the couch, still wrapped in the blanket Carla had tucked over her the night before. The TV was still on muted now but the news ticker at the bottom of the screen scrolled relentlessly.

"Hospital CEO breaks silence on St. James scandal press statement coming at noon."

She blinked against the morning light cutting through the blinds. Carla had already slipped out to grab groceries. On the coffee table, a small note:

"You were talking in your sleep. I figured you needed rest more than coffee. Back soon C."

Nancy sat up, rubbing her eyes, trying to ground herself. The past 72 hours had dismantled everything she thought she knew about the transplant system and about the people who ran it.

But if there was anything worse than the silence that had surrounded these illegal surgeries, it was what came next.

Noise.

By noon, every major network cut to the same livestream.

"LIVE: CEO of St. James Medical Center Addresses Allegations."

Nancy reached for the remote and unmuted. The screen filled with the familiar white pillars of St. James. A podium was set up at the entrance, banners behind it flapping in the wind:

"In Crisis, We Act."

The hospital's new PR slogan.

And there he was **Daniel Reaves**, CEO of St. James. His grey hair looked carefully combed, his tie conservative, his face strained with just enough emotion to look sincere.

"During the peak of the COVID-19 emergency," he began, "St. James was forced to make difficult decisions. Lives were at stake. Ventilators were scarce. Transplant candidates were dying on waitlists every day. In light of these challenges, certain life-saving actions were taken under emergency provisions."

Nancy stared at the screen, lips pressed thin.

He's making it sound noble.

"Every decision made was to minimize loss of life," Reaves continued. "While we acknowledge there may have been documentation gaps, we stand by our team's dedication and sacrifice during an unprecedented public health crisis."

The crowd stirred.

Reporter 1: "Did St. James bypass UNOS matching systems to perform transplants?"

Reaves: "In several emergency cases, yes. The standard UNOS timelines were not aligning with the urgency on the ground. The team did what was necessary."

Reporter 2: "So you admit unauthorized transplants were done?"

Reaves: "I admit emergency interventions were made under extreme conditions. That's different from criminal intent."

Reporter 3: "What oversight, if any, was involved during these decisions?"

Reaves: "Internal reviews were conducted on a case-by-case basis. But again, we were managing chaos. The hospital was operating beyond capacity."

Nancy leaned forward. He was spinning the disaster into a badge of honor.

Reporter 4: "Is Dr. Elijah Leigh under investigation by the hospital?"

A beat of hesitation.

"Dr. Leigh is no longer with St. James. We have cooperated fully with federal investigators. We are not withholding any documentation or access."

Reporter 5: "Was Dr. Leigh acting on his own, or were these decisions approved by higher-ups?"

Reaves: "The hospital has no evidence of an internal conspiracy. Any misconduct by Dr. Leigh will be handled by the DOJ. He acted outside the approved ethical boundaries of our institution."

Nancy could feel her blood heating. She'd seen the documents. Leigh wasn't rogue he was protected.

Reporter 6: "What about the invoices tied to Western Heights Recovery Center?"

Reaves: "We have no formal partnership or communication with that institution. If such documents exist, we have not yet verified their origin."

Reporter 7: "Has the hospital's transplant committee been suspended?"

Reaves: "We have initiated a temporary pause on transplant procedures and launched a full internal audit. I assure you, transparency and accountability are our guiding principles moving forward."

Nancy scoffed at the word *transparency*.

Reporter 8: "How many undocumented transplants were performed during the height of COVID at St. James?"

Reaves: "The Department of Health is still reconciling those numbers. We believe the figure is under two dozen though we acknowledge paperwork may not reflect the total scope."

Reporter 9: "Are any of those transplants linked to missing donor or DMV data?"

Reaves: "We have not been informed of any confirmed data tampering. If donor records were altered, we will work closely with the state to understand how that occurred."

Nancy's stomach dropped. That was the question. That was the missing piece.

Reporter 10: "What's the hospital's message to families of deceased donors whose loved ones may have been used in these undocumented transplants?"

Reaves' voice softened, slightly rehearsed.

"We are devastated by the impact this has had on families. If there were administrative lapses, we will make it right. But I stand by the humanity of our team during a once-in-a-century crisis."

Reporter 11: "Do you personally accept responsibility?"

A long pause. He looked directly into the camera.

"I accept responsibility for leading an institution that served thousands during a national emergency. And I accept the consequences of the decisions made under my watch."

Nancy dropped the remote. She leaned back against the couch cushions, pulse thumping.

He meant every word. Just not the way people would hear them.

To the public, he was a man holding the line.

To Nancy, he was an expert at misdirection.

And the scariest part he wasn't lying. Not exactly.

Just enough truth to bury everything else.

***

The apartment was quiet again.

Carla had gone to take a walk, probably to give Nancy space. After days of chaos, a press conference that had spun lies into virtue, and a morning spent pacing through rooms too quiet for comfort, Nancy found herself standing by the window, arms folded, staring at the world outside.

There was a stillness in the street below. Just a few cars, a delivery bike, someone watering their plants two floors down. It was the kind of normal that didn't match what was happening in her head.

She kept thinking about the press conference. About Reaves' voice, so smooth and calculated. About the way the reporters had stopped pressing after a few rehearsed responses. About the quiet nods behind him the subtle alignment of authority and power, sealing the narrative like a cap on a syringe.

And suddenly, her thoughts shifted.

Jim.

She saw him again, lying in their bed, eyes half-shut, pale and slipping away. Her fingers gripped the windowsill. What if one of those undocumented organs had reached him in time? What if someone had bent the system for *him*?

Would she have said no?

Would she have questioned the ethics of a heart arriving anonymously if it meant holding on to him for even one more year?

The answer clung to her ribs.

No. She wouldn't have.

She would have thanked whoever brought it, signed whatever waiver they shoved under her nose, and never asked how or where it came from.

The thought made her dizzy.

She turned away from the glass and sank onto the couch, face in her hands. It was Carla's voice that had planted the seed today. They'd been curled up under the blanket, wine on the table, exhaustion settling in.

Carla had said, softly, "If they're going to gaslight the world, Nance, then maybe... maybe you play along just long enough to light a match from the inside. They already think you're one of them. Use it."

At the time, Nancy had brushed it off. But now, hours later, those words looped in her head like a thread she couldn't unspool.

She sat up and looked toward the kitchen, where Carla had left her laptop open on the table.

She stood.

Walked over.

Paused.

Then sat down and rested her fingers on the keyboard.

There was no blueprint. No template for this.

Just rage, grief, and knowledge.

She opened a blank document. Titled it.

EORP: Emergency Organ Reform Protocol

Not just a name. Not a slogan. A proposal. A counter-narrative. A seed for change tucked inside the very system trying to devour itself.

She began typing methodically, decisively. Her heartbeat evened out with each line.

- **A secondary verification system for organ match approvals** No more one-signature transplants. Two independent validations. No exceptions.

- **Mandated reporting for third-party facility transfers** If a body left the building, it needed to be documented, logged, and made traceable.

- **Background audits for transplant surgeons working under emergency waivers** No more hiding behind crisis clauses. Even in emergencies, transparency was non-negotiable.

- **Automatic flagging for any unscheduled OR usage** No more midnight surgeries. No more undocumented procedures slipping past tired eyes.

By the time she reached the last bullet point, the sky outside had gone from gold to grey to indigo. The city was quiet again.

Twelve pages.

Not perfect. But strong.

And true.

She read it once, made minor edits, then did what every part of her body resisted.

She hit *send*.

To the hospital board and CEO.

She didn't expect applause.

She didn't even expect a reply.

But someone had to put it on record. Someone had to show that *not everyone* inside that institution was silent, or scared, or paid off.

If they were going to rewrite history…

Then Nancy Brooks had just carved her footnote at the bottom of the page.

***

Response from the Board

The reply came faster than she expected. Barely two hours had passed since she hit send.

Her inbox pinged.

Subject: **EORP Proposal** From: **Board Communications** To: **Nancy Brooks**

Nancy opened it without hesitation, though her pulse quickened with something between hope and suspicion.

Nancy,

We recognize your concern and the effort you've put into drafting this proposal. However, in light of ongoing investigations, we believe it would be premature to entertain system-wide policy shifts at this time.

Furthermore, certain elements of your reform exceed hospital authority and require federal oversight.

Respectfully,

St. James Medical Center Board of Directors

That was it.

Four cold lines. No signature. No thanks. No follow-up.

She stared at the screen, rereading the sentence that stung the most:

"Premature to entertain system-wide policy shifts..."

Nancy slowly leaned back in her chair, her arms crossed, eyes locked on the message like it might rewrite itself.

Translation?

We're not touching this. Not now. Maybe not ever.

She closed the laptop lid with more force than necessary and exhaled.

Of course they wouldn't act. Not while the news cycle was still spinning, not while the DOJ was still combing through evidence. The board wasn't built for reform. It was built for containment. Optics. Preservation. They wouldn't back a staff nurse *even one with ICU credentials and transplant clearance* if it meant owning up to systemic negligence.

To them, she was expendable.

But the worst part wasn't their dismissal.

***

Anonymous Message – GPS Logs

The next evening, a new message lit up her inbox.

Subject: *You missed something*

Sender: <u>anonymous.secure@protonmail.com</u>

Attachment: *GPS_log_extract2020.stjames.csv*

She stared at it for a long time. Her cursor hovered over the subject line, hesitation prickling down her spine like a static charge. The email had no body text. No name. No signature. Just a file.

Her finger tapped the trackpad once. Then again.

Click.

The spreadsheet opened with a clunky, outdated interface. Dozens of rows. Hundreds of entries. Each one labeled with strings of numbers and acronyms: GPS coordinates, timestamps, vehicle IDs, driver codes. It looked like a simple logistics file until she noticed the source column.

Every line was tagged with a *St. James dispatch reference.* Except… none of these entries existed in the hospital's internal dispatch logs. She had checked those herself twice.

Her pulse quickened. She copied the coordinates into a mapping app and hit enter.

The pins populated instantly.

Each one led to the **rear access gate** behind St. James. Not the main delivery dock. Not the emergency ramp. The **service gate** where old linens were picked up, waste bins were rolled out, and food delivery trucks sometimes offloaded overnight.

And from there?

The routes split like veins.

Some headed east, crossing the state line into Indiana. Others veered south toward privately run clinics with minimal oversight. A few landed near surgical centers that had popped up during the pandemic to "ease overflow."

Nancy felt her stomach twist.

They were **sneaking organs out the back door.**

Not in some desperate one-time act during COVID panic. Not under some misunderstood emergency clause. This was **coordinated.** Routine. Structured.

A **supply chain.**

She sat frozen, the glow of her laptop lighting the room in cold blue.

It had worked.

For months.

Unnoticed. Unchecked. Unreported.

Nancy closed the laptop slowly, like folding shut the lid of a coffin. The apartment felt too still. Too clean. Carla's gentle breathing drifted from the guest room, and outside, a dog barked in the distance. Somewhere down the block, a motion sensor light flickered on.

Inside her, something solidified.

The hospital didn't survive COVID because of heroic medicine or desperate innovation.

It had survived because **someone turned it into a trade post** a marketplace wearing the skin of a medical institution.

And now, she had the proof.

Nancy couldn't sleep that night.

She lay awake on the living room couch, watching the ceiling shift from midnight to gray as the hours passed. The **coordinates replayed in her mind like sirens**. She could see them. 3:00 AM. 4:17 AM. 5:06 AM. Always in the dead of night. Always flanking a transplant that had no paperwork.

Who drove those vans?

Who opened the gates?

Who else knew?

Sometime after 6, she got up and opened the file again. Not to confirm what she had seen but to hunt it. To **trace the pattern** like a detective stalking a signature in blood.

Line by line, she scanned.

Then one plate number stopped her cold.

NJX-8173.

A white food service van.

She'd seen it before **countless times** parked casually behind the cafeteria wing while she rushed in for coffee or checked vitals before a double shift. It was always there. She never questioned it.

Why would she?

It was just part of the background.

Except… the logs didn't lie.

That van never clocked in through the hospital's main gate. Never showed up in the kitchen. Never logged a delivery time.

It wasn't there for food.

Her hand covered her mouth, the realization hitting like ice in her lungs.

They had used **hospital supply routes to traffic organs.**

Every hallway she'd trusted. Every corridor she'd run through during codes. Every system she thought was built to protect lives… had been **reengineered to move inventory.**

Inventory.

Not patients.

Not hope.

Not medicine.

Merchandise.

Nancy stared at the screen until her eyes blurred. She wasn't just angry. She wasn't even shocked anymore.

Nancy blinked hard as another memory rose from the fog.

Weeks ago.

Night shift. ICU 3.

She had been called in to confirm a patient's time of death. A 36-year-old stroke victim. Donor card signed. Family had already consented. It was supposed to be routine, just another protocol in a long line of tragedies during the height of COVID.

She remembered walking out of the patient's room into the quiet corridor, flipping through the chart, preparing to log vitals and official notes.

That's when she'd seen it.

Two men in scrubs wheeling a blue cooler past the elevator bay.

Taped shut.

They hadn't said a word. She'd barely looked up, offered a tired nod, and went back to her notes.

She had assumed it was a routine organ transport. Probably lungs or a liver. Happens all the time.

But now, in the sharp light of what she knew, the memory twisted.

What if that wasn't a legitimate handoff?

What if it wasn't part of any official record?

What if that was one of *them*?

Nancy's skin chilled. She hadn't remembered their faces. Not their posture. Not even the color of their badges.

Just that blue cooler.

That was all that had stayed with her.

And maybe it stayed because something in her, even then, knew it didn't belong.

***

The next morning, Nancy hadn't moved from the floor. Her dining room had transformed into a crime board. GPS logs, floor plans, printed emails, and scribbled notes covered every surface. Routes drawn in red. Times highlighted in yellow. It wasn't chaos it was a system being exposed.

Carla entered with two steaming coffees and a bag of bagels. She stopped in the doorway, eyebrows rising.

"Did you sleep?"

Nancy looked up with tired eyes. "No."

Carla placed the coffees down, crouched beside her, and followed Nancy's hand as she pointed to the screen.

"Here. Look at these three vans. Same route. Same time block. Always between 2 and 4 AM."

Carla scrolled through the GPS file silently. She didn't speak for a full minute.

Then, quietly, "This isn't random. These were scheduled runs. Like delivery routes."

Nancy nodded, barely able to swallow. "Leigh wasn't acting alone. He was running a black market operation using the hospital's infrastructure. This wasn't one bad call during chaos. It was a business model."

Carla looked down, eyes narrowing. "So no one saw this?"

"No one saw the whole picture. Maybe pieces. But those who did Laila. Evelyn..."

Romero, still missing.

Nancy didn't finish the sentence. She didn't need to.

Carla reached for her hand and gave it a quiet squeeze.

They both looked at the map again. There were three new GPS logs time-stamped *after* the DOJ had launched their investigation. The transports hadn't stopped.

Someone was still running the pipeline.

And no one had caught them.

***

That evening, the lights in the apartment were dim. Carla sat curled at one end of the couch with a blanket over her legs and a mug of tea cradled in both hands. Nancy was hunched at the coffee table, laptop open, files arranged in rows.

"What exactly are you looking for?" Carla asked gently, her voice breaking the silence.

Nancy's fingers didn't stop scrolling. "There's a gap. A missing link in the route."

The map on her screen lit up with a trail of blinking pings GPS tracks from one of the unregistered medical vans. It moved from the ICU wing to the West Wing, then veered off sharply.

Carla leaned closer.

"That doesn't lead to an exit," she said.

Nancy zoomed in.

"It's not on any blueprint we were given. But that spot right there…" She pointed. "That's the back of the Physical Therapy wing. I remember it. There's a corridor most staff don't use. It's locked during off-hours."

Carla frowned. "So how was the van getting access?"

Nancy tapped a file open a floor plan she'd saved during orientation. She traced the hallway behind PT. At the very end, in small print: **Emergency Egress Access.** No cameras. No entry logs.

Carla set her tea down. "They created a second system."

Nancy nodded slowly. "A second hospital within the hospital."

One that operated in silence. In shadows. That never made it into the public records.

She pulled up another GPS route. Same exit. Same stop. Three different vans. Always the same destination an abandoned facility now under investigation.

Nancy whispered, "They were trafficking organs behind our backs. Right under our feet."

Carla let out a slow breath, her voice barely above a whisper. "No wonder they shut your proposal down. It would've cracked the whole thing open."

Nancy closed the laptop and rose to her feet.

Her eyes moved across the floor plans, the GPS logs, and the envelope still sitting on the table.

"They've turned our hospital into a labyrinth," she said quietly. "And the worst part? They're twisting something that could actually save lives. If done ethically, this system could help reduce wait times and bring real hope to patients who don't have time to wait...Just like Jim..." She finally spoke her heart out.

Chapter 13:
Permission to Reform

Carla had returned home earlier that morning, but not before handing Nancy one final thread to pull. "Try the downtown DMV field office," she had said, slipping a sticky note onto the fridge before grabbing her suitcase. "Not the main one. This branch handles direct database flags. If your proposal got buried at St. James, maybe someone there will actually give a damn."

Nancy wasn't hopeful. She had stopped expecting anyone to give a damn weeks ago. But she also wasn't the same nurse who stayed quiet during administrative meetings and worked overtime to cover for system delays. Not anymore.

So she went.

The downtown DMV field office didn't look like the kind of place where national medical reform would take shape.

It was a beige building, boxy and bureaucratic, nestled between a bail bonds storefront and a shuttered travel agency. Inside, the air smelled faintly of toner and stale coffee. Laminated signs hung crooked over long lines of people waiting to renew IDs, update vehicle registrations, or argue fines. The kind of place where hope went to get processed in triplicate.

Nancy stood near the entrance for a moment, scanning the room. No one made eye contact. Everyone looked tired. Paperwork shuffled. Screens beeped. The line snaked toward indifferent windows where clerks answered questions with memorized phrases. She felt the familiar jolt of imposter syndrome.

But she tightened her grip on the manila folder and walked up to the "General Inquiries" desk.

The woman behind the plexiglass partition gave her a tired, skeptical glance. "Organ donation isn't handled here. You can update your donor status on your state health profile or online."

Nancy nodded, tone calm. "I'm not here for that. I'm a nurse trauma, transplant and I've been trying to flag some irregularities. I submitted a reform proposal to St. James Medical Center last week. It was rejected. But I think some of what I've documented... might affect DMV-linked donor processes."

The clerk looked unconvinced. She didn't even blink before sliding a small blue card under the partition.

"You can leave your concerns on this form and drop it in the feedback box."

Nancy didn't move.

"I have documentation," she said quietly but firmly. "And names. GPS logs. Surgeries that don't appear on UNOS systems. I believe someone may have been altering organ registration data through DMV override access. It's affecting real patients organs are being discarded."

That made the woman pause.

Nancy saw it a flicker of confusion, or perhaps recognition.

"You said... override access?" the clerk asked slowly.

"Yes." Nancy nodded again, lowering her voice. "A hospital tech forwarded me a memo. I verified some of the internal logs against state-level transplant data. Organs were rerouted. Others discarded after unnecessary delays. I don't think it's a hospital-level mistake anymore."

The woman frowned. She didn't ask to see the memo. She didn't challenge her claim. Instead, she picked up the desk phone and pressed a button labeled **DMV ADMIN: BACKLINE**.

She leaned in, whispered a few words, then hung up.

Nancy's heart beat steadily not racing, but with a pulse that came from long-ingrained medical alertness. Around her, the world carried on as usual. A teenager was complaining about a suspended license. A father in a business suit was frowning at his number ticket. The DMV clerk reached under her desk and pulled out a closed sign but didn't put it up. She just kept her eyes on Nancy's folder.

A minute passed.

Then another.

Nancy shifted on her feet. She caught herself staring at the peeling edge of a No Cell Phones sign. Everything here felt trivial and huge at the same time. She didn't belong here but maybe the problem had always been that nurses were only expected to save lives quietly, not question the system that wasted them.

Finally, a side corridor door clicked open.

A man in a navy vest stepped into view. His expression was unreadable firm, focused, and neutral in a way that immediately felt official. He scanned the waiting room, found Nancy, then let his eyes drop to the folder in her hands. He looked mid-fifties. His posture was straight, not stiff, and something about him felt like he knew how to move through bureaucracies without being erased by them.

He approached with measured steps, his posture precise but not unkind.

"You're Nancy Brooks?" he asked.

"Yes."

"Come with me."

The tone of quiet authority in his voice made her instinctively straighten. He wasn't hospital staff — that much was clear. His badge carried a federal emblem rather than the St. James logo, and the way others in the hallway subtly stepped aside confirmed it.

He led her through a side door that clicked shut behind them with a soft magnetic thud. No badge flash, no clipboard check-in. Just quiet tension and the cold hum of fluorescent light.

They walked in silence down a long hallway lined with locked cabinets, safety posters, and printer rooms stacked with boxed paper. The world back there felt different — unlabeled, functional, almost invisible to the public eye. The kind of corridor where truth was filed, not displayed.

He stopped at the end of the hall and keyed open a door. Inside, the room was modest but deliberate — two chairs, a desk, and a battered whiteboard covered in shorthand codes. A thick binder sat in the center of the table, its label clear: **Donor Intake Oversight Committee.**

Nancy hesitated near the door before taking her seat. She clutched her folder close, unsure whether to feel relieved or cornered.

"My name is **Dr. James Smith**," the man said as he took the seat across from her. "I'm one of the auditors for the regional transplant data reconciliation program. My wife and I run the field division."

He spoke with the steady calm of someone used to chaos — the kind of tone that could make an ICU nurse feel like a student again. His salt-and-pepper hair and slightly weathered hands hinted at years spent inside operating rooms before moving to oversight work.

He continued, "We've been working with hospitals across the Midwest since the early nineties, mostly post-incident ethics reviews. We step in when data and accountability start to drift apart."

He motioned to the woman entering quietly behind him. She carried a leather-bound tablet and the kind of composure only experience could shape.

"This is **Mrs. Evelyn Smith**, our clinical records liaison and lead auditor."

Evelyn offered a small, polite nod, her eyes steady and analytical. "We saw your name come up in our internal alert system yesterday. A few cross-tags in donor logs from St. James triggered a review."

Her tone was professional, but her gaze was soft — a balance of precision and empathy that made Nancy feel seen rather than interrogated. Evelyn had the presence of someone who had spent years in patient advocacy, a nurse turned investigator who still carried the quiet warmth of care beneath layers of procedure.

Dr. Smith leaned back slightly, folding his hands. "You've stirred quite a conversation in the compliance chain, Ms. Brooks. That usually means one of two things — either you've made a mistake, or you've found something worth protecting."

Nancy glanced between them. "I'm hoping it's the second one."

Evelyn exchanged a knowing look with her husband. "So are we."

Nancy opened the manila folder and slid the envelope across the table.

"I think some donor data's being rerouted," she said. "I compiled this under a working title EORP. Emergency Organ Reform Protocol. St. James's board rejected it. Said it was too political. Said it was too early to disrupt process. But every week we wait, patients are dying."

Dr. Smith began flipping through the contents typed observations, match logs, incident dates, charts, flagged GPS routes.

His brow furrowed. "These are clean notes. Precise. You've done your homework. This isn't just speculation."

Evelyn opened a thin side drawer, pulled out a single-page memo, and placed it gently beside Nancy's envelope. Across the top, in bold:

Internal: DMV Access Authorization Adjustments – Clearance B. Leigh.

"We've had this for months," Evelyn said. "But without a clear trigger, it sat dormant. We kept hoping someone would connect the dots."

Nancy leaned in.

The memo was dated four months ago.

It authorized Dr. Benjamin Leigh by name to temporarily bypass standard donor database lockouts and reassign compatible organs during any declared emergency.

Nancy looked up sharply. "But who declared the emergency?"

Dr. Smith tapped the heading. "That's the problem. It wasn't a federal or statewide emergency. That was internal language created by Leigh. He lobbied for override access citing 'local transplant urgency.' The DMV processed the clearance based on hospital assurance. No third-party review. No ethics board challenge."

Nancy's mouth went dry. "So... he had DMV-level control of organ reassignment?"

"Yes," Evelyn confirmed. "And while it may have looked efficient on paper, it bypassed national match alerts, compatibility verification, and waitlist fairness. It created a bottleneck and then a detour."

Nancy shook her head slowly. "I reviewed the transplant logs. Seventeen kidneys. Rejected over the past three months. They were viable. All of them."

Dr. Smith nodded. "And not accounted for through UNOS. Which means..."

"They were either destroyed," Nancy whispered, "or sold."

Evelyn looked grim. "Our suspicion is black market prioritization. But we don't have enough direct documentation."

Nancy stared at the memo. The red DMV approval stamp in the lower corner blurred briefly as her eyes burned. The initials were the same.

B.L.

Her hands curled into fists on her lap.

Mrs. Smith's voice softened. "Your EORP framework addresses the exact failure points we've been tracking. Secondary verification. GPS audit trails. Real-time accountability. It's good work."

Nancy looked at both of them, heat in her throat. "Then why hasn't anything changed?"

Dr. Smith closed the folder slowly. "Because we're auditors. We log it. We don't have jurisdiction to create change."

"But," Evelyn added, "someone else might."

She reached into the cabinet and retrieved another folder thicker, more worn. The tab read:

Senator Callahan – Organ Equity Drafts.

"He's been advocating for national transplant transparency for years," Evelyn explained. "But his office needs more than theories. They need hard evidence. Personal stories. Real people affected."

"We're meeting him tomorrow," Dr. Smith said, looking her in the eye. "We'd like to bring your EORP draft. With your permission."

Nancy didn't hesitate. She nodded once. Then again, more firmly.

"Bring it," she said.

But her eyes stayed on the memo.

The initials. The seal. The authority Leigh had managed to exploit under everyone's nose.

Dr. Smith studied her for a moment. "You look like someone who's seen what this really costs."

Nancy exhaled through her nose, then stood. Her voice came out low and steady.

"Seventeen kidneys. Three months. Every single one could've saved someone like Jim."

They didn't interrupt. They didn't need to.

She looked at them both, chest rising, eyes clear.

"I don't want revenge," she said. "I want to make this right. I want to encourage more organ transplants and reduce the wait time patients are currently dealing with. Because right now, the system isn't just broken it's suffocating people. Patients are dying on lists, not because organs aren't available, but because protocols are rigid, data is manipulated, and oversight is loose. Families are being told to wait months, sometimes years, while viable kidneys are tossed out or rerouted through loopholes. That isn't medicine. That's neglect with paperwork.

We need faster clearances. Smarter tracking. A system that protects patients not protects reputations. If one proposal, one framework, can push that change forward, even an inch, then I need to be the one to fight for it. Not just for Jim. For every name on that waitlist who deserves more than silence and statistics."

Dr. Smith sat back slowly in his chair, hands folded, studying her.

"You're not just speaking from loss," he said after a pause. "You're thinking like a reformer. Like someone who's still inside the system but isn't afraid to question it."

Mrs. Smith's eyes didn't leave Nancy. "We've been in this field for twenty-five years. We've seen policy memos come and go, good intentions buried under red tape. But what you've built EORP it's not just a complaint. It's a plan. Practical. Grounded. And it's backed by evidence."

Nancy nodded once, tight and deliberate.

Dr. Smith glanced down at the folder again, then back up. "You'll need to prepare yourself. If Callahan brings this forward, it won't be quiet. It won't be clean. But it could shift the conversation nationally."

Mrs. Smith added, "You may lose allies along the way. Especially those who benefitted from how things worked before. But if this is really what you want real change you have our backing."

Nancy looked at them both.

"I don't need it to be clean. I just need it to be real."

She reached for her folder, opened it again, and handed over a copy of the finalized EORP draft.

"Take this to Callahan."

Dr. Smith stood and took it without hesitation. "We will."

Nancy gave one last glance at the memo with Leigh's clearance signature.

And then she walked out of the office, not as a whistleblower or a grieving nurse but as someone stepping into a fight much larger than St. James.

Not to expose what was broken.

But to build something better.

Chapter 14:
The System Benders

The fluorescent light overhead flickered softly, humming in rhythm with the portable scanner Mrs. Smith had just plugged in. The DMV back office smelled faintly of toner and old files. Dr. Smith had cleared the entire morning schedule. This was not about renewing licenses anymore. This was about saving lives.

Mrs. Smith placed a thermos in front of Nancy, who had barely touched her own. She looked pale, her breath shallow but steady. Her fingers unclenched around the flash drive.

"This is what I saved from the offline logs," she said, her voice low but certain. "Leigh was smart. He never used hospital emails for the worst of it. These files show he had an alternate network, tied to shadow accounts. Some of the names might even match the transfer forms."

Dr. Smith gave her a long look, then plugged the drive into his encrypted laptop.

"You're absolutely sure about this?" he asked. "Once we open this door, there's no sealing it shut again. You'll be part of this investigation permanently."

Nancy didn't respond right away. Her gaze drifted to the muted TV on the wall. A local news channel scrolled across the screen. In the footage, healthcare workers in hazmat gear wheeled a ventilated patient down a crowded hallway.

"ICU beds overflow in Portland as post-COVID complications rise. Families wait weeks for organ match calls that never come."

"In Phoenix, a 23-year-old COVID survivor passed away last night. He was eligible for a double lung transplant. No donor match ever came through."

Nancy's fingers curled into her palm. She looked back at Dr. Smith.

"I don't want to watch another family beg for information while someone's playing gatekeeper behind a screen," she said. "This isn't about settling scores. It's about doing what we were all trained to do. If patients are dying while organs are being trafficked, what exactly are we still part of?"

She leaned forward, her voice firm now.

"I want to help fix this. We need to encourage more organ transplants. Not fewer. And if that means tearing out the rot first, then so be it."

Dr. Smith nodded, slowly closing the laptop lid.

"Then we start with protecting you."

Mrs. Smith clicked her pen and pulled out a legal form from a folder labeled *W-2 Civic*. She laid it in front of Nancy.

"This is your whistleblower affidavit. It states that you're submitting this evidence to prevent imminent harm. Your identity will be logged, timestamped, and verified, and we'll route copies to the Department of Public Health and the Senate Transplant Oversight Committee. One copy will live off-grid in a third-party cloud vault. Another goes to the civic blockchain."

Nancy picked up the document, eyes scanning the dense legal language. The page trembled in her hand. She had known what she came here to do. But reading it in black and white still sent a chill through her chest.

Dr. Smith didn't interrupt. He waited. And when she hesitated over the signature line, he said gently, "You know, medicine has always been a battle between right and wrong. Between healing and harm. You're not alone in thinking the system is failing the people it was supposed to serve. And you're not alone in wanting better."

He glanced at the paused footage on the TV. Another story was flashing in the ticker below.

"UNOS backlog crosses 100,000 patients nationally. COVID complications have added over 4,000 new transplant needs in the past quarter alone."

"We're not doing this to cause panic," he continued. "We're doing it because someone has to draw a line. If no one steps forward, the back door stays open."

Nancy steadied the pen in her hand. Her breath shook, but her grip didn't.

The scanner beeped. The room went still.

Nancy signed.

***

Later that afternoon, the small back office had turned into a makeshift war room.

Dr. Smith sat hunched at a dusty terminal plugged into the UNOS regional data mirror. The hum of the fan under the desk was barely audible over the rapid clacking of keys. His old clearance wasn't what it used to be, but it was just enough to pull logs tagged for donor reconciliation, the files that rarely saw a second glance.

He adjusted his glasses and squinted at a fresh batch of entries on screen.

"These logs aren't matching the standard route," he muttered, mostly to himself. "Here, this chain of directed donations. Way too many. That designation is supposed to be rare."

Nancy leaned in, her brow furrowing.

"Directed donation is... that's only when the donor family requests the organ go to someone they know, right? A sibling, maybe a parent?"

"Exactly. Specific relationships only. It's tightly regulated."

He tapped a few keys, dragging the record forward. A spreadsheet full of unfamiliar names opened up but what stood out was who wasn't on the list.

"They used it for strangers?" Nancy asked, voice rising slightly.

"Not just strangers," Dr. Smith said, scanning line after line. "They used it to divert organs away from high-priority patients and redirect them to people who aren't even in the official queue."

Mrs. Smith, who had been quietly flipping through a binder nearby, moved closer.

"They're all marked with the same internal override: BL-Override-A3."

Dr. Smith froze. His jaw clenched. He double-clicked the tag.

Nancy stepped forward, whispering, "That's Leigh's tag, isn't it?"

He gave a slow nod. "It's a shadow routing code. He created a workaround inside UNOS used the directed donation loophole to bypass the entire waitlist. This... this is why certain patients were mysteriously skipped."

Mrs. Smith frowned, tapping the screen. "These entries look clean from a legal standpoint. It's formatted just like a real donation   but there's no matching documentation."

"He exploited the only blind spot in the entire system," Dr. Smith said bitterly. "There's no automatic audit on directed donations. They just assume it's a personal request. And he used that assumption to run a second stream."

He leaned back in the chair, rubbing his face with both hands.

"I've seen bad actors before," he said. "But this... this was surgical. Hidden in plain sight. And no one caught it because it was all wrapped in the language of care."

Nancy crossed her arms, staring at the screen.

"And meanwhile, families are told their loved one died waiting. That there just wasn't a match."

Dr. Smith didn't answer. The silence was louder than any confirmation.

***

Mrs. Smith pulled open a shared drive on her tablet. "While you were tracing organ flows, I was checking the DMV's consent backend."

"Informed donor status?" Nancy asked, leaning over.

"Yes. Guess what? Over 9,000 active organ donors in our state never received the revised forms. The new ones that clarify how organs can be reassigned during emergencies."

Dr. Smith looked up from the screen. "You're saying they harvested organs from people who were never told they could be rerouted outside of UNOS?"

She nodded, eyes sharp.

"And that's not all," she continued, pulling up another tab. "I've launched a public campaign. Social media. Flyers. Email newsletters. The works."

Nancy blinked, surprised. "You've already posted about this?"

Mrs. Smith turned the tablet to show a Twitter post she had written earlier that morning. In bold text, it read:

'No more back doors. No more black market organs. We are calling on all medical professionals... doctors, nurses, residents...to join us in ending this corruption. Ethics over profit. Patient lives over manipulation.'

Below it, hundreds of likes, reposts, and replies had begun rolling in.

"It's gaining traction," she said, eyes scanning the notifications. "Young healthcare workers are responding. They're angry. They want to help."

Dr. Smith arched a brow. "You're building an army."

"I'm building a network," she corrected. "We'll need help tracing Leigh's phone activity, IP footprints, and cross-referencing encrypted hospital emails. These med students and interns know how to dig. We can't do this alone but with them, we can do this smart."

Nancy looked at her with a mix of admiration and awe.

"You're not just going after informed consent. You're going after the entire web."

Mrs. Smith gave a slight smile. "I'm tired of watching the news and pretending this isn't our problem. If we want the next generation of medicine to be ethical, we have to clean house now."

Dr. Smith nodded thoughtfully, then gestured toward Nancy.

"Speaking of problems..."

Nancy opened another folder on her flash drive.

"There's one more case I flagged. From St. James."

She slid a patient chart across the desk. Dr. Smith took it while Mrs. Smith leaned in from the side.

"DNR patient. Passed away last week. According to the records, no organ procurement team was officially assigned. But look at this."

Dr. Smith's eyes moved down the sheet. Then he froze.

"Kidneys and liver marked as recovered."

Nancy nodded. "No DCD authorization. No family consent. And no UNOS record of it ever happening."

Mrs. Smith put a hand over her mouth. "They harvested organs from someone with a DNR?"

"Illegally," Nancy said softly. "It wasn't a donation. It was a black extraction."

A heavy silence filled the room.

Dr. Smith set the file down slowly.

"They're not just gaming the system. They're breaking it. Quietly. Efficiently. Without fear."

***

The morning air was gray and silent, heavy with the kind of tension that follows revelations too big to bury. Mr. and Mrs. Smith had barely touched their coffee when the first email hit the secure inbox they had set up overnight.

The subject line read:

"Ma'am, My Mother Deserved to Live."

Mrs. Smith opened it. The message was from a young man, no name, just a username tagged to an online anonymity network. The words bled across the screen, raw and urgent.

"She had beaten COVID. She was recovering, slowly. But her lungs were wrecked. Doctors said she was eligible for transplant, just needed to wait.

We waited.

She coded three weeks ago. No match ever came.

I'm not a doctor. I'm just someone who stayed up all night, searching. I don't know how I ended up on your campaign page, but I saw your post and something told me to dig deeper. I found something. Maybe it's nothing. But maybe it's everything."

Attached was a zipped file. Encrypted, but crackable.

Dr. Smith downloaded it cautiously, scanning it offline.

Inside was a folder labeled **/BackdoorOps/**.

One document opened with a subject line that immediately caught his eye:

From: leigh.rx@consultsecure.com

To: ceo_private@vialbridge.org

Date: 03/15/20

Subject: Re: Asset Flow

"We control the back door. They won't even know what we took."

A chill ran through the room.

Mrs. Smith stood frozen beside him. "This is... an internal system message. Not hospital servers. Not government portals. This is their private exchange."

Nancy, now seated across from them, felt her throat dry. "He said 'we'. Leigh wasn't working alone."

Dr. Smith clicked for metadata. "Encrypted endpoint. Same one we saw reroute the DNR patient's record last week. The recipient... is the CEO."

Mrs. Smith whispered, "We have a chain."

A new message pinged into the inbox. From the same whistleblower:

"I don't need a reward. I just want this to stop. Use what I found. Please."

Chapter 15:
The Hospital Board Finds Out

The elevator chimed on the twelfth floor. Nancy stepped out first, her footsteps quiet against the plush carpet that muffled every sound like a well-guarded secret. This wasn't the part of the hospital where lives were saved. This was the floor where lives were weighed, measured, and sometimes, erased with a signature. Beige walls. Abstract art that said nothing. The smell of polished wood and corporate air.

Behind her, Romero emerged slowly. His shoulders slumped, his face pale and drawn. The cuff of his surgical mask clung damply to his chin, stained by breath and fatigue. He hadn't spoken much since they met in the lobby.

Nancy halted near the walnut reception desk where the secretary offered a tight-lipped, practiced smile. Before crossing into the boardroom corridor, she turned.

"Where the hell have you been?"

Her tone wasn't loud, but it cracked through the silence.

Romero blinked. His eyes were bloodshot, rimmed with exhaustion. He didn't flinch at the question. Instead, he sat heavily on a bench near the wall, the zipper of his coat catching slightly as he tugged it open.

"Quarantine," he said. **"Then three days at home. Thought it was over, but it wasn't. Felt like I got hit twice. I didn't want to bring it here... but I wasn't going to let you face them alone."**

Nancy's lips pressed into a line. The anger she held for his absence gave way to something quieter. Not forgiveness, not yet. But something close.

"You're sure you can do this?"

He looked up at her. His voice was calm, even if his hands betrayed a tremor.

"I don't think I can not do this."

The doors at the end of the hallway creaked open. The secretary said nothing. A man in a sharp blue suit stepped out and gave them a small nod   no greeting, no ceremony. Just a gesture that said, *you may now walk into the lion's den.*

Mrs. Smith joined them, stepping out of a side elevator with a sealed manila envelope clutched in her gloved hands. Her coat was buttoned to the top, her eyes forward. She looked like someone marching into battle with grief as her armor. Nancy noticed her knuckles were white from gripping the folder too tightly. These weren't political crusaders. These were parents who had outlived their child.

Nancy inhaled once and pushed open the boardroom door.

***

The conference room was colder than expected. The AC hummed steadily, but the real chill came from the people.

A long, gleaming table stretched across the room, flanked by high-backed leather chairs. Each board member sat like a statue, their bodies stiff, their faces a blend of calculated disinterest and quiet dread. White nameplates sat in front of them like shields.

Michael Grant, the hospital's CEO, sat at the far end. He didn't rise. He didn't speak. His eyes found Nancy's and held.

There was no welcome in them. Just a trace of something sharp control, pride, or fear disguised as confidence.

Nancy didn't look away.

On the left side of the room sat two representatives from the Department of Justice. One of them, a woman in a slate-gray suit, kept a legal pad open and a manila file laid neatly in front of her, as if daring someone to contradict her facts. Beside her was a UNOS official   younger, lean, with his arms crossed and an expression that flickered between skepticism and anger.

No one offered them a seat. Nancy, Romero, and the Smiths remained standing.

Mrs. Smith stepped forward. Her heels clicked sharply on the floor as she approached the chair of the board. She set the envelope down slowly.

"This is for the record."

Her voice was low, but it cut through the tension like a scalpel.

The chair a woman in her sixties with a silver bob and eyes that had probably witnessed their fair share of scandals didn't even touch the folder. She simply slid it toward the DOJ official, who opened it without asking.

Dr. Smith, quiet until now, moved toward the screen on the side wall. He removed a small USB drive from his pocket and inserted it into the panel with precision. The monitor buzzed to life, casting a cold glow across the table.

The first slide appeared:

"Internal Transplant Irregularities – St. James Medical."

Dr. Smith's hand hovered briefly over the laptop before he clicked to the first slide. The room dimmed slightly as the projector flickered to life, illuminating a spreadsheet lined with color-coded rows.

His voice was calm, but the weight behind it made the room feel smaller.

"Over the last eighteen months, your transplant program has departed from the ethical boundaries that are supposed to protect both donors and recipients. What began as emergency adjustments under pandemic strain has turned into a deliberate breach of national transplant law. We are no longer looking at clerical mistakes. This is systemic abuse."

A murmur passed through the far end of the boardroom. One of the hospital board members adjusted her glasses but said nothing.

Dr. Smith pointed to the spreadsheet.

"The green entries represent authorized and documented transplants. Fully logged, verified with updated consent, and reported in accordance with UNOS policy."

He tapped the remote again. Several rows flashed yellow.

"The yellow entries highlight cases with inconsistencies. Organs transferred without consent updates. Coolers rerouted mid-transit. Procurement logs missing timestamps. Many of these could be flagged as high-risk protocol violations."

Then the red rows glowed.

"But these in red... These are the ones that should never have happened. Organs removed and transplanted without a matching recipient on file. Internal audit trails wiped. Recipient profiles registered post-surgery or updated retroactively to appear compliant."

Nancy stepped forward. She spoke with quiet force.

"The red cases are not just breaches. They are evidence of a shadow distribution network. A parallel channel created inside this hospital to benefit specific patients   patients with connections, patients with offshore insurance packages, patients who bypassed the waitlist entirely."

The slide changed to a heatmap.

"These are the zip codes of recipients who received organs under the flagged operations. You will notice clusters near private recovery centers, political donor addresses, and corporate medical partners."

She paused. Her eyes locked on the DOJ representative seated across from her.

"These people did not just get lucky. They got access."

The DOJ rep, a woman with close-cropped gray hair and a dark charcoal suit, gave no visible reaction. She slowly flipped open her legal pad and began writing.

Nancy clicked again. This time, an email appeared onscreen.

From: <u>leigh.md@privatemail.com</u>

To: <u>ceo.mgrant@stjamesmed.org</u>

Subject: Back Channel

"We control the back door. They will never know what we took. Keep the UNOS team out of it. It's cleaner that way."

The words hovered heavy over the room. She read them aloud.

"We control the back door. They will never know what we took."

Silence followed. One board member whispered something under his breath. Another leaned forward and asked, "Are we certain this email is authentic?"

Dr. Smith responded without hesitation.

"The metadata has been verified through an independent forensic audit. Timestamped. Domain confirmed. This was not just internal miscommunication. It was a willful orchestration. Every name in these threads will be forwarded to the Office of the Inspector General."

Michael Grant, seated at the end of the table, finally spoke.

"You're painting a picture based on circumstantial correspondence. That email doesn't prove direct involvement in transplant manipulation. You're interpreting tone. That's not evidence."

Nancy's voice sharpened.

"If this were one case, you might have a point. But you are looking at seventy-four. With documentation gaps. Log overrides. Deleted security footage. Procurement tags that never made it to the national registry. And coincidentally, all routed through a small group of surgeons and administrators who share personal emails outside hospital protocol."

Dr. Smith added, "We also have internal call logs. Coordinators received text messages from encrypted third-party apps instructing them to override donor restrictions. In some cases, they were threatened with reassignment or dismissal if they raised questions."

A board member, younger than the others, raised a hand.

"Was law enforcement notified when this first came to light?"

Nancy nodded.

"Yes. After we discovered the cross-match discrepancies, we flagged the UNOS compliance board. When follow-up protocols were ignored by the hospital administration, we escalated to the Department of Justice."

The DOJ official looked up.

"The case is now under formal federal review. We are in the process of issuing subpoenas for all transplant data for the last two years. If it becomes clear that records were altered or intentionally deleted after the fact, this will extend into obstruction charges."

The UNOS representative, silent until now, finally leaned forward.

"You understand the consequences, correct? If even a portion of this is substantiated, your hospital could lose national transplant eligibility. Every single program under your registry could be suspended."

Michael Grant did not blink. He spoke quietly.

"We've saved hundreds of lives under impossible circumstances. If our methods were flawed, that should be reviewed in context. This board will cooperate."

Nancy tilted her head, watching him.

"Cooperation would have meant stopping this a year ago. Or last month. Or last week. But you didn't stop. You buried it deeper."

She pointed to the map still glowing on the screen.

"And every red dot on that map represents a life that may have been stolen."

Dr. Smith clicked the final slide.

"This is only the initial evidence packet. The full data set will be handed over at the end of this meeting. The names of the whistleblowers have been sealed, and multiple backups have been created to ensure chain-of-custody integrity."

He unplugged the USB stick and stepped away.

Nancy looked at the board chair, who had remained silent throughout.

"We are not asking for your approval. We are notifying you of an ongoing investigation. The time for discussion passed when the first backdoor transplant was signed off behind closed doors."

She turned and walked toward the door.

Dr. Smith followed, his eyes scanning the room one last time.

Michael Grant sat still.

He didn't flinch.

***

There was a long pause after Dr. Smith finished presenting the data.

Then the board chair looked up from her notes, her face unreadable. She adjusted her glasses and turned her attention to Nancy.

"Ms. Brooks," she said, voice steady, "you were among the earliest whistleblowers in this case. The DOJ has reviewed your initial emails. If you're willing, we'd like you to speak on the record now. Tell us what you saw."

Nancy's pulse kicked up. Her fingers curled slightly around the edge of the table, steadying herself. She hadn't expected to speak, at least not like this, but something in her chest tightened   the kind of pressure that doesn't let you sit in silence.

She stood, adjusting the sleeves of her blouse. The eyes in the room followed her, but it wasn't the kind of attention that sought to intimidate. It felt more like a challenge. Prove it. Prove what you know.

She exhaled.

"I've been a trauma nurse for sixteen years. I joined St. James during the height of the pandemic. It was chaos. We were all making impossible choices   triage in hallways, supply shortages, families begging us to keep their loved ones breathing a little longer. I saw good people break down, burn out, leave. But I also saw something else. Something no one wanted to admit."

She paced slowly behind her chair, not out of nervousness but to give herself space to think clearly.

"I started to notice inconsistencies in the transplant logs. Donor organs being signed out before paperwork was finalized. Coolers rerouted mid-transit. Recipients whose names weren't on the active match list getting priority over those who had been waiting for months, sometimes years."

She stopped pacing, now fully facing the board.

"I brought my concerns.... ummm, I was told the system was overwhelmed. Those protocols were being adjusted. But the adjustments kept happening   and only for certain patients... In reality, Dr. Elijah Leigh threatened me to shut my mouth or my license will be..."

She paused, then glanced toward the DOJ representative.

The room remained still.

Nancy walked to the edge of the screen where Dr. Smith had left the heatmap.

"I didn't know the full scale until I spoke to other nurses. Some were ordered to stay off the record. Others were told they'd lose their jobs if they asked too many questions. And one of them Laila Shah she's dead now. She was the first to send me a file. And that file led me to everything."

Her voice cracked, just slightly, but she held the line.

"I didn't want this job to be about secrets. I didn't sign up to be part of a machine that trades lives like commodities. And I certainly didn't ask to bury patients who never got a fair chance."

She pulled out a copy of her original anonymous report and set it beside the dossier.

"I kept notes. Emails. Cooler logs. GPS transport data. It's all there. Enough to prove this wasn't just a failure of oversight. It was a deliberate system. And it operated under the leadership of Dr. Elijah Leigh. With emails to Michael Grant. And with full knowledge of the risk."

She turned to face the board one last time. The silence felt heavier than walls.

"I know I'm not a lawyer. I'm not a compliance officer. But I am a nurse. And I'm standing here because my silence would have made me guilty too."

Her tone was even, but her words carried a quiet strength. "I didn't come forward to destroy a hospital. I came forward because I believe every patient deserves a fair chance at life, not a system that lets money and power decide who lives and who dies. This isn't about blame. It's about change. Organ transplant should not be boycotted, but the black market behind it should be dug out and wiped out."

She paused, her breath steady. "My husband's death taught me that saving lives means nothing if we lose our ethics in the process. This fight isn't about ending transplants. It's about restoring trust in the very system meant to save people."

Nancy stepped back, not dramatic, just done. The DOJ representative sitting at the end of the table nodded, jotting one final line in her notes. The silence that followed carried the weight of a system finally cracking open.

***

There was a long pause after Nancy's final words. The kind of silence that doesn't ask for response. It demands a reaction.

Michael Grant rose slowly, the tailored perfection of his suit contrasting the uncertainty flickering behind his eyes. He adjusted his blazer, pressing both palms flat against the table.

"This is absurd," he began, voice smooth, rehearsed, the kind that once filled conference halls and charity banquets. "What we're witnessing here is a mischaracterization. A handful of selectively extracted emails, chat logs, and vague allegations being spun into a conspiracy theory worthy of a courtroom drama."

He looked at Nancy and Dr. Romero, his gaze sharp and unflinching.
"I understand you've both been through trauma. Dr. Romero, I was informed of your recent hospitalization. Nancy, your husband's death was tragic. But grief can distort perception. Let's not confuse emotion with evidence."

The room shifted uneasily. One board member cleared his throat, another tapped a pen against the table. Grant's voice hardened.

"This is not a case. It's an ambush. Dragging the Department of Justice into this is reckless and undermines every professional in this building. We are a level-one trauma and transplant center that has saved thousands of lives. One misinterpreted email from a suspended surgeon cannot define our legacy."

Romero straightened, leaning on the table for balance. His voice carried the fatigue of months of silence and sleepless nights.

"I don't need to interpret anything, Michael. I saw it. We all did. We watched decisions shift from ethics to expedience. From patient need to influence. We watched donor records edited after the fact and cooler logs disappear."

He looked around the table. "I signed forms I wasn't supposed to see. I certified surgeries that broke protocol because someone higher up approved them. If I wanted revenge, I would have stayed home and let this place collapse on its own. But medicine means something. Or at least it should."

Nancy joined him, her tone calm but resolute.

"We didn't bring the DOJ because we were angry. We brought them because what we uncovered was criminal. Every report, every number we submitted was cross-checked by internal audit, verified by two independent compliance officers, and confirmed by transplant watchdogs. We didn't want to do this. We had to."

Her words settled over the board like dust in sunlight. No one moved.

***

The rear doors of the boardroom opened with a firm push. Heads turned in unison.

A federal prosecutor entered, calm and composed, his DOJ badge catching the light. Two federal officers followed, their presence silent but commanding. One held a sealed evidence folder marked "Federal Case File – St. James Medical Center."

The prosecutor walked to the head of the table and set the folder down. "Effective immediately," he said evenly, "Dr. Elijah Leigh will be taken into federal custody. He is charged with multiple violations of the National Organ Transplant Act, falsification of medical records, obstruction of justice, and financial misconduct."

A stunned gasp echoed. Phones vibrated across the table as notifications began to spread through hospital channels. The prosecutor continued.

"Michael Grant," he said, turning to the CEO, "you are hereby suspended from all operational authority at St. James Medical Center. Your access to hospital systems is revoked. You are ordered to remain available for federal inquiry. Evidence gathered under administrative subpoena shows you authorized unregistered donor exchanges, diverted medical funds, and knowingly concealed audit results."

Grant froze. The color drained from his face. "You can't be serious," he muttered, his voice breaking. "This is taken out of context. Those were administrative decisions. We were under pandemic pressure—"

The prosecutor raised a hand. "You'll have the opportunity to explain that in federal court."

The prosecutor raised a hand. "You'll have the opportunity to explain that in federal court," he said calmly. His voice carried no malice, only finality.

He paused before continuing, scanning the faces around the table. "For the record, Michael Grant is being placed under arrest on the basis of direct authorization and financial benefit tied to illegal transplant activities. The evidence includes signed correspondence, concealed payment trails, and policy overrides submitted under his executive credentials."

He opened the folder and read from the document. "Internal audits and independent reviews confirmed that these actions were not medical decisions made under emergency pressure. They were deliberate administrative orders that violated the National Organ Transplant Act and hospital compliance law."

Grant stared at him, expression hollow. "And the others?" he said, voice cracking. "You're letting them walk free after everything they did?"

The prosecutor turned slightly, facing Nancy, Dr. Romero, and the Smiths. "These individuals are cooperating witnesses," he clarified. "Dr. Romero and Nurse Nancy were whistleblowers who provided verifiable data, not participants in the financial misconduct. Their actions, though performed under your chain of command, were found to be in compliance with medical duty and patient advocacy."

He shifted his gaze toward Dr. and Mrs. Smith. "Dr. and Mrs. Smith are external reform consultants who submitted independent audits that exposed your violations. Their cooperation was instrumental in our federal investigation."

He returned his attention to Grant. "You, Mr. Grant, authorized falsified documentation, approved transfers outside

UNOS compliance, and obstructed internal investigations. That makes you criminally liable. Not them."

Grant's breath grew uneven. His jaw tensed. "You're making a scapegoat out of me," he muttered.

The prosecutor closed the folder with quiet precision. "No, sir. We are holding the person accountable who signed the orders, moved the money, and silenced the truth."

He looked toward the two officers standing by the door. "Proceed."

The first officer stepped forward and announced, "Michael Grant, you are under arrest for obstruction of justice, conspiracy to commit healthcare fraud, and violation of federal transplant compliance laws."

The sharp click of handcuffs echoed through the room. A board member gasped. Another covered her mouth. Cameras from the hallway captured the reflection of flashing lights across the glass.

Grant looked around, desperate for an ally. None came.

****

As the officers led Grant away, the prosecutor remained behind with two federal investigators. He turned toward Nancy, his expression calm but measured.

"Ms. Brooks," he said, "you'll need to remain available for follow-up questioning. You're not under investigation, but several procedures you assisted in are part of our evidentiary review. You were present during at least three unregistered transplant cases. We need your testimony to clarify intent and chain of command."

Nancy nodded slowly. "You'll have my full cooperation."

"Good," the prosecutor replied. "We're not here to punish medical staff who tried to save lives. But we do need to understand every decision made in those operating rooms."

He gathered his papers, offering a faint, almost weary smile. "Sometimes justice needs context before it can move forward."

Nancy watched him leave, her pulse still echoing from the chaos. She knew the questions would come. They had to. Truth always asked for proof before it settled.

Then she turned back toward the boardroom windows, where the reflection of flashing red and blue lights washed across the glass. For the first time, she felt the stillness of accountability filling the space where fear used to live.

Justice wasn't knocking anymore. It had walked in, taken its seat, and started writing names.

Chapter 16:
The Travel Nurse Could Expose Everything

The silence at home was finally starting to feel like her own. For the first time in weeks, Nancy had a full night of sleep uninterrupted by alarms, ICU beeping, or the tremor of guilt vibrating through her chest.

It had been three weeks since the federal arrests and her final questioning with the DOJ task force. The agents had assured her she wasn't under investigation, but that her statements would remain on record as part of the evidentiary chain. They had needed clarity—who approved what, who signed, who knew. She had answered everything.

Now, with the inquiries over and the headlines cooling, she was trying to rebuild something that resembled normal.

She had made a habit of turning off the news. Every headline for the past month had involved phrases like "organ ring," "hospital cover-up," "transplant abuse." But today, her kitchen was quiet. The sun spilled in through half-drawn curtains, dust floating like ash in the golden light. She stirred her tea slowly and let herself exhale. It had been so long since peace didn't feel like a betrayal.

She glanced at her phone out of habit. No texts. No breaking news. No updates from the DOJ.

Romero's name had finally been cleared at least publicly. His license reinstated, his face no longer plastered on conspiracy threads and local gossip blogs. He had called her last night, hoarse but smiling. COVID had weakened his lungs, but not his spirit. "I owe you a drink," he had whispered. "One that doesn't come in a hospital vending machine."

Nancy had smiled, but didn't reply. Even with the media moving on, her insides still curled tight with the weight of it all.

Evelyn's suicide had been reduced to a paragraph in a news scroll. A tragic nurse. A "possible link to organ smuggling." Buried beneath newer scandals, her death faded from headlines faster than it should have. But it hadn't faded from Nancy.

They had both been warned don't comment to press, don't stir anything, don't invite scrutiny. But the pot was already boiling. Nancy could feel it. A low pressure, rising every day.

So when her phone buzzed at 6:42 a.m. with an unknown number, she didn't flinch.

She answered before the second ring.

"Nancy Brooks?"

"Yes."

"This is Director Patel from the Department of Justice. We'd like you to testify before the Senate Oversight Subcommittee on Organ Transplant Ethics. Your presence isn't mandatory, but it's urgently requested."

Nancy didn't respond right away. The words hovered in her kitchen like fog. She stood still, letting the moment settle around her.

Patel's voice remained steady. "We believe your account could help shape real reform. Your file indicates you were on the transplant floor during multiple unrecorded procedures. We need the full picture on record."

Nancy turned toward the hallway where Jim's photo still hung. It had become a habit, this quiet ritual of looking for courage in his eyes before she answered anyone else. The image was grainy, taken on a camping trip in Colorado. He wore his favorite hoodie and that crooked smile she still caught herself expecting to see at home.

Her fingertips brushed the frame. She could almost hear him saying, Don't just stand there. Do something.

She swallowed hard. "I'll do it," she said.

***

That same day, she was called up to the transplant consult room at North Ridge Regional Hospital, a facility temporarily handling critical transplant cases after the federal freeze at St. James.

But nothing about the day felt simple.

A rare donor match had just come through—a healthy, viable lung. The kind that could make headlines or disappear under bureaucracy. Nancy scrolled through the files. Two recipients were flagged in the UNOS system.

Bradley M. Corman, age twenty-seven. Diagnosed with idiopathic pulmonary fibrosis. Private suite, sixth floor. Son of Senator Edward Corman. Political legacy. His family had three generations of transplants and influence to match. His chart read like a résumé—connections, privilege, access.

Janice Keller, age forty-one. Single mother of two. Diagnosed with the same condition five years earlier. No history of substance use, no comorbidities. Steady employment. Four years on the transplant waitlist. She had once called Nancy on Christmas Eve just to thank her—not for saving her, but for remembering her file.

Nancy read both profiles again. Then again. There was no clean choice, but there was a right one.

Before she could present the cases to the transplant review board, her badge pinged with a new assignment: **Admin Conference Room.**

The moment she stepped in, her pulse tightened. The room smelled like control — fluorescent lights, disinfectant, and a stack of paper packets too thick to read without consequence.

Dr. Meyer, now Acting Medical Director, sat at the head of the table. Two PR officers flanked him with tablets open. On the far side, Brianna, the CEO's assistant, greeted her with a polished smile that never reached her eyes.

Nancy didn't sit.

"We need you to triage in favor of Bradley Corman," Dr. Meyer said flatly.

Nancy blinked. "That's not how the system works."

"You know how things work here, Nancy," Brianna said smoothly. "UNOS can be flexible. Especially when a donor's family has... influence. The Senator's support would secure long-term funding."

Nancy folded her arms. "You're asking me to falsify a priority order."

"We're asking you to think beyond one case," Meyer replied, his tone controlled but persuasive. "Senator Corman sits on the Health Appropriations Committee. His backing could stabilize our funding, protect jobs, expand programs. That means more lives saved in the long run."

Nancy's voice cut through the quiet. "And Janice Keller? She has no senator. Just two children. One's in middle school.

You want me to tell them their mother was passed over again because she isn't powerful enough?"

Brianna's smile faltered. "If you go against the board on this, you'll be removed from the transplant team. Maybe from this hospital entirely. Be careful, Nancy. Sometimes it's not about one patient—it's about the bigger picture."

Nancy looked around the table. No one met her eyes.

She picked up Janice's file, tucked it under her arm, and turned toward the door. "I already have," she said. Then she left without another word.

Romero found her in the stairwell, her hands gripping the cold railing.

Later that evening, as the corridors dimmed, Nancy slipped into the empty staff lounge still wearing her scrubs. She hadn't planned on company, but Romero sat there nursing a half-cold coffee, flipping through a patient chart.

"You heard?" she asked quietly.

He looked up, exhaustion in his eyes. "Only rumors. Tell me it's not what I think."

Nancy sank into the chair opposite him. "They want me to assign the lung to Senator Corman's son."

Romero didn't blink. "Of course they do."

The bitterness in his tone wasn't loud—it was lived-in. The kind that grows after watching justice bend too many times.

"You going to let them?" he asked.

Nancy turned toward the window. Rain streaked the glass. Somewhere outside, an ambulance wailed and faded.

"I'm going to follow the list," she said finally. "Janice qualifies by every standard. I'll file a formal report with UNOS."

Romero exhaled slowly. "You'll be off the transplant team by midnight."

"Maybe," Nancy said. "But Janice will be alive."

A long silence stretched between them. Then Romero stood, walked to her side, and placed a hand on her shoulder. "I'll co-sign your report," he said. "You won't do it alone."

***

Janice Keller received the lung that night. The operation was delicate, but it went smoothly. When Nancy checked on her afterward, Janice's vitals were stable. Her two children were asleep on the waiting room chairs, their heads leaning together.

Nancy didn't cry. But her hands trembled when she signed the post-op notes.

By sunrise, North Ridge Regional's PR team had released a statement:
"Another life saved. Our staff continues to deliver critical transplant care during this unprecedented time."

There were no names. No mention of the nurse who risked her career to do the right thing. Only silence.

When Nancy returned the next morning, her badge light turned red. Security told her to report to HR.

In the HR office, a woman with a clipboard smiled in practiced sympathy.
"We're reassigning you to outpatient surgical pre-checks, effective immediately. You'll no longer serve on the transplant rotation."

"Can I ask why?" Nancy said evenly.

"There was a procedural review," the woman replied. "It's not punitive—just a staffing change."

Nancy didn't argue. She gathered her things and walked out.

That evening, Romero called. "You okay?" he asked. "I'm still breathing," she said. "They're trying to bury it." Nancy looked at the darkening sky. A quiet storm built in the distance. "Let them try."

***

Two days later, she was folding laundry when a slip of paper slid under her door.

An unmarked envelope. No stamp. No address.

Inside was a single page of heavy white paper. Clean type. No logos.

We saw what you did. We know why. The system needs people like you. The National Coalition for Transplant Accountability is hosting a public summit next month. We'd like you to speak — not as a victim, but as a reformer. Let us know if you'll attend. — M.C.

Nancy stood at the window. Rain tapped against the glass like faint applause. She read the letter twice.

Then she picked up her phone and sent a message to Romero. "They're giving me a mic."

His reply came almost instantly. "You going to take it?"

Nancy looked back at Jim's photo, then out into the rain. "I think it's time."

Chapter 17:
REAL: Reform, Reckoning, and Rise

The microphone offer wasn't the only thing that found its way to Nancy's quiet apartment that week.

Seven days after the anonymous envelope arrived, she noticed her name beginning to appear not in bold headlines or press interviews, but subtly, in the undercurrent of public opinion. Beneath an article about hospital reform on a mid-sized medical blog, one comment read:

"She's the nurse who stood her ground."

Another said:

"Quiet hero in a broken system. If you know, you know."

Nancy didn't reply. She never even clicked the like button. But she read every word. And then she read them again.

That was when her phone rang. The name on the screen made her sit up straight. Dr. Daniel Smith.

She hadn't spoken to him since the Mercy West donor chain seminar, nearly a year ago. He had been calm, articulate, ethical to the core. He wasn't the kind of man who made calls without purpose.

She picked up.

"Dr. Smith?"

"Nancy," he said, his voice exactly as she remembered measured, kind, serious. "Thank you for answering. I know it's been a rough few weeks."

She exhaled. "That's one way to put it."

"I'm not calling as a mentor," he said. "I'm calling with a plan. My wife and I are building a reform coalition. We're calling it REAL."

"REAL?" she repeated.

"Reform for Ethical Allocation and Life-saving," he explained. "It's grassroots. But we're not alone. We have support. A pilot program. And we want you on board."

Nancy leaned back on her couch, pressing the phone tighter to her ear. "You might not have heard. I've just been removed from the transplant floor. Badge access revoked. Officially reassigned to pre-checks. Unofficially, I'm being iced out."

"That's exactly why we want you," he said, not missing a beat. "You've seen what happens behind the curtain. You've watched policy get twisted into politics. We need people who understand what's broken, and more importantly, why it needs fixing. You've proven you won't stay quiet. That matters."

There was silence for a moment. Nancy closed her eyes and rubbed her temple.

"I'm tired, Dr. Smith," she admitted. "Really tired."

"I know," he said gently. "But tired doesn't mean finished."

He went on, voice steady and deliberate.

"The REAL protocol is not radical. It's what should've been happening all along. Here's what we're doing in the pilot rollout: Every transplant candidate and donor will give live recorded consent. Not a signature that can be hidden in files, but a verbal confirmation, stored offsite. Matches must be confirmed directly by UNOS. No hospital overrides. No political 'exceptions.' Every organ is matched by the book."

Nancy's eyes narrowed. "What about hospital admin interference? The soft lobbying. The donor shuffles."

"There won't be any," he said. "The protocol bans all financial involvement by hospital staff in the matching process. No incentives, no kickbacks, no nudges. And transparency audits will be conducted by third-party teams, not internal compliance."

He paused, then asked the question that had been waiting since the call began.

"You want to be part of the first implementation team?"

Nancy didn't answer right away. A notification buzzed on her laptop a new email. It was from Dr. Smith's assistant. Attached was a short digital pamphlet about the program.

She opened it.

Simple. Clean. White background. Black font. No logos. No marketing language. Just a title and three pages outlining the ethics and structure of the REAL program.

"This looks..." she began, then stopped. Her voice caught.

"This looks like how it was supposed to be," she finished.

"I'll take that as a yes?" he asked.

She looked out the window. The city skyline was blurry through the glass, but something in her chest felt clear for the first time in weeks.

"Yes," she said. "I'm in."

"Good," he replied. "Because change doesn't wait for permission."

***

250

REAL's launch didn't come with headlines or fanfare. There were no interviews, no social media campaigns, and no hospital lobby banners boasting about innovation. It began quietly deliberately so. Just a few patient files flagged for eligibility, a silent rollout in two partner hospitals, and a core team monitoring every step like guardians of a fragile spark.

But when a system that's long been corrupted suddenly functions with integrity, people notice.

In less than a month, three successful transplants had been completed under the REAL model. The cases weren't extraordinary in medical terms but their processes were revolutionary. Families of donors described feeling "protected" for the first time. One mother, whose son had died in a motorcycle accident, broke down in a follow-up interview and said, "They didn't just take his lungs. They honored his life. Every word I said was recorded, every signature explained. No pressure. No rush. Just clarity."

Recipients, too, reported a shift. They were no longer just names on a waiting list, shuffled in and out of eligibility based on factors no one explained. Instead, they were given full access to selection records, timestamped UNOS confirmations, and an open-door policy to request review. For the first time, the *entire journey* of an organ could be seen from donor to surgery.

A post-transplant public trust survey, quietly piloted alongside the protocol, recorded results no one expected. Respondents gave the new system an approval rating that soared past traditional models. What had begun as a grassroots prototype now felt like a rising standard.

Romero returned around this time frail from his recent illness but visibly energized by the mission. He stepped in as a medical advisor, overseeing clinical applications and working closely with the legal team to reinforce the integrity of each case. Nancy saw him during a virtual case review call one afternoon. His face appeared grainy on the screen, but his smile was unmistakable.

"You look like you actually believe in this again," she teased.

Romero chuckled. "It's been a while since I've done medicine that didn't feel like politics. This? This feels right."

Across the network, whispers turned to inquiries. Hospitals that had once dismissed reform began requesting protocol copies. A few asked to send observers into upcoming REAL surgeries. Others more cautiously sent administrative emails with subject lines like *"Exploratory Interest"* and *"Model Review Request."*

One midwestern facility went a step further. They invited Dr. Daniel Smith and Claudia Smith, his wife and co-architect of REAL, to conduct a formal two-day training workshop. Claudia, once a quiet policy analyst overlooked in boardrooms, now stood at the front of packed sessions, breaking down case flow charts and guiding chief surgeons through the mechanics of ethical allocation.

Nancy, now fully embedded as the project's ethics coordinator, watched each success with quiet resolve. But even she knew what was coming.

Because in healthcare, success especially ethical success never goes unnoticed.

And not all attention was friendly.

Not all eyes were grateful.

Not all hands reaching toward the protocol wanted to protect it.

Behind the scenes, resistance was already taking shape.

***

Nancy was halfway through patient readiness reviews when Dr. Smith entered the temporary REAL command center in Cincinnati. He wasn't carrying his usual laptop or clipboard just a plain manila folder in his left hand and something far heavier in his expression.

"We have a problem," he said, closing the door behind him.

Nancy paused mid-keystroke. "What kind?"

He handed her the folder.

Inside were documents from a third-party investigator they had retained weeks ago to monitor international logistics vendors. But the deeper she flipped through the report, the more familiar it became.

There it was buried halfway down page six.

Elijah Leigh.

Or rather, *Elias K. Langston* his new alias.

He had registered a company in Arizona: "Future of Transplant Logistics, LLC." The address was fake. The license photo doctored. But the paper trail didn't lie.

Nancy's breath caught. "He's trying again."

Dr. Smith nodded grimly. "Same vendors. Same signatures. Same shady donor match patterns. But he's moved the operation offshore."

Nancy flipped to the last page. Her eyes locked onto a customs scan dated three days ago a medical transport container flagged in Doha, Qatar.

"He's laundering donor tissue through the Gulf."

"And franchising the model," Smith added. "He's already submitted pre-authorization paperwork to a medical tourism hospital in Dubai."

Nancy's hands balled into fists. "How is this man still breathing free air?"

Just then, Claudia rushed in, holding her phone.

"You need to see this."

She turned the screen toward them.

It was a live news feed grainy, probably shot on a civilian phone but the scene was unmistakable. Airport tarmac. Emergency lights flashing. And in the center, a man in a navy-blue blazer being pushed against the hood of an unmarked black SUV by Interpol officers in plain tactical gear.

Nancy leaned closer. The face was blurry but the posture, the arrogance, the haircut

It was Leigh.

Claudia narrated what was unfolding. "Interpol intercepted his inbound charter flight from Muscat. Tip came from a whistleblower inside the logistics vendor he was using. They flagged inconsistencies in organ tracking logs. Qatar passed it to Dubai authorities, who passed it to Interpol."

Dr. Smith exhaled. "About damn time."

The camera panned awkwardly as Leigh was pulled upright and walked toward a waiting van. He didn't resist. He smirked still convinced of his invincibility. But even he looked smaller than before. No press team. No hospital lawyers. Just him and the cold metal cuffs clamped around his wrists.

Nancy stared at the screen.

Justice didn't always come in full color. But this? This was close enough.

"We'll get confirmation within the hour," Claudia said. "They're flying him to The Hague. Charges pending include organ trafficking, falsification of medical documents, international health code violations…"

Dr. Smith sat down slowly, as if his knees had finally given in. "It's not over. But it's the beginning of the end."

Nancy nodded, still watching the screen.

"The system let him operate for years," she said quietly. "But he finally got caught by the very transparency he tried to outrun.

***

The news of Elijah Leigh's arrest traveled faster than anyone expected.

By evening, international headlines had already begun cycling the footage across major outlets. Phrases like "Black Market Transplant Kingpin Caught" and "Surgeon at the Center of Global Scandal Arrested in Gulf Sting" dominated news tickers. Former patients of St. James recognized his face instantly. Investigative reporters started piecing together the puzzle Nancy, Dr. Smith, and Claudia had been unraveling for months.

Nancy watched it all unfold from the REAL command center's small lounge, her eyes fixed on a wall-mounted TV as anchor after anchor described the fall of a man who had once controlled entire transplant floors with little more than a smirk and a signature. She did not speak for a long time. She simply stood there, arms folded, jaw clenched.

Romero was seated beside her, a steaming cup of tea in his hands. He had not touched it.

Claudia was pacing near the window, phone in one hand, earbuds in the other, shuffling through interview requests and press inquiries that had begun flooding their inbox.

Dr. Smith entered the room, phone pressed to his ear. He listened quietly, gave a sharp nod, and then finally disconnected the call. He looked around at the others.

"It's official. He has been transferred into international custody. They're not wasting time. Preliminary charges include illegal organ trafficking, falsifying medical records, and human rights violations. More will follow. They're already tracing payments to his offshore accounts."

Nancy let out a long breath. "He's really going down."

"He is," Dr. Smith said. "And this time, there will be no deal. No anonymous legal team swooping in to clean up. No university cutting a backroom settlement. This is different. This is global."

Romero leaned back slowly, the tension in his shoulders beginning to ease. "So what happens now?"

Claudia stepped in, lowering her phone. "Now? Now, the floodgates open. Every hospital that ever worked with him, every donor file he ever touched, every patient whose outcome didn't make sense   all of it will come under review."

She looked directly at Nancy.

"And REAL just became the alternative everyone is looking at."

For a moment, the room was silent. Then Nancy finally sat down, rubbing her hands together.

"People died because of him," she said softly. "Families waited. Others were pushed up the list for a price. And we let it happen because the system didn't want to look too closely."

Dr. Smith knelt beside her. "We are looking now. And we're not just watching. We're acting. The next stage is ours, Nancy. It has to be."

She nodded, slowly at first, then with conviction.

"Then let's give them a reason to believe we are different."

***

REAL's rollout expanded beyond the two original pilot hospitals within weeks. The protocol, once considered overly idealistic, began gaining traction. Hospitals that had never questioned their own transplant processes were now requesting to observe REAL-trained teams. The training sessions, once limited to Zoom calls and downloadable guides, turned into live seminars.

Dr. Smith and Claudia began traveling one week in Minnesota, the next in North Carolina, then Texas. Every stop brought packed auditoriums, curious surgeons, skeptical hospital executives, and, more often than not, tearful family members who had lost loved ones during the years of chaos.

Claudia's voice began to carry weight in policy circles. As a former researcher who had seen corruption from the sidelines, her journey into reform made her a compelling advocate. When she spoke, senators listened.

Nancy stayed in Cincinnati, working with Romero and the implementation team. She led simulation sessions, reviewed consent training modules, and oversaw the independent data archiving system. But despite the growing momentum, Nancy remained cautious.

The stain of what had happened at St. James still clung to her memory.

Sometimes, in the middle of an otherwise calm day, she would remember the sound of Leigh's shoes on the hallway tiles. The clipped rhythm of power. The way silence used to fall when he entered a room.

It would pass. But it never truly left.

***

It was nearly midnight when Nancy received a call from Claudia.

"I just got off with the committee," Claudia said, her voice calm but shaking with restrained excitement. "They're inviting me to present at the National Transplant Oversight Committee hearing in Washington. And they want someone from the implementation team to join me."

Nancy sat up in bed. "What does that mean?"

"It means the REAL model is being considered for nationwide adoption. Not just as a recommendation, but potentially as a federally supported framework."

Nancy was quiet.

"You helped build this," Claudia continued. "You helped expose the cracks. You risked your license, your job, your reputation. Come with me."

Nancy looked over at the cluttered nightstand beside her bed training manuals, highlighted protocols, notes from families who had written to thank her. She placed her hand gently over a worn photo of Jim, her late husband, tucked just behind her lamp.

Then she smiled, small but certain.

"Tell them I'm coming."

Chapter 18:
A Tragic Turn of Fate

The email came in just after 4:00 p.m. The office was quiet, the kind of quiet that settles in after the day's rush has passed but before the lights start going off. Claudia Smith was still seated at her corner desk in the Cincinnati satellite office, her screen aglow with the final edits of the REAL protocol pamphlet. She had been fine-tuning phrasing for over an hour, tweaking sentence structure and clarifying bullet points, her focus razor sharp. Then, without warning, the notification appeared a gentle chime, a blinking dot. She blinked once, as if her eyes needed confirmation, then hovered her finger over the trackpad and clicked.

The subject line stopped her breath.

"CONFIRMED: REAL Approved for Federal Hearing Slot – November 4."

For a long second, she just stared at the words. The noise of the office dimmed around her. Her hand floated toward her phone on instinct, snapping a screenshot as though the email might disappear if she didn't preserve it immediately. Then she stood. Not dramatically, but with the kind of motion that carried weight the kind of motion that said, finally.

Across the room, Dr. Daniel Smith was hunched over his laptop, reviewing logistics reports. He looked up at the sudden shift in energy, the slight tremor in the air around her. His voice was low but expectant. "Good news?"

Claudia turned her screen toward him without a word, her expression lit from within. "We're in. Washington. Full slot. Oversight Committee hearing next month."

Daniel stood up slowly, not rushing the moment. He took two steps forward, processing the weight of what she just said. "That's it then. This is the start."

She nodded, unable to hide the soft laugh that bubbled out of her. "You still got that bottle you've been saving for a day like this?"

He was already halfway to the kitchenette. "I'll open it tonight."

But Claudia waved a hand in mock protest. "Not now. I've got twenty files to cross-check tonight and barely enough focus left for twelve."

Daniel leaned on the counter, opening the mini fridge. "Then we celebrate with Trader Joe's and sparkling water."

"Read my mind," she replied, slipping on her coat and wrapping a scarf loosely around her neck. The wind outside had picked up, but inside, something had lifted from her shoulders.

He came back over, touched her cheek lightly, then kissed her forehead. "Text me when you're close."

Claudia gave a mock salute, the kind only long-married partners share. "Always," she said, smiling as she headed for the door.

The air outside was sharp with the bite of early winter. Her breath fogged as she walked toward her car, but the cold didn't reach her. Inside, she carried warmth the kind born from knowing that something you've built is about to become real. The REAL protocol wasn't just a document anymore. It was on the path to national legislation. Change was no longer hypothetical. It was scheduled.

She pulled into the Trader Joe's just off the expressway, parking in her usual spot under the flickering lamppost. Inside, she moved with muscle memory vegetable wrap, sparkling water, and this time, a small bouquet of wildflowers. Something celebratory, but not loud. Not yet. At checkout, her phone buzzed. She glanced down and saw Daniel's name flash on the screen.

"Home in 20. Be careful. Roads look slick."

She smiled and replied with a single thumbs-up emoji. Her hands were full, and words didn't feel necessary. They would talk soon. They always did.

In the car, she placed the bag carefully on the passenger seat and buckled her seatbelt. She turned the heater up, letting it melt the frost from her windshield. The radio came on automatically soft classical music, violins drifting through the cabin like a private score to her life.

She drove with practiced ease, exiting the parking lot and merging onto the highway. The city lights faded behind her, replaced by quiet wooded stretches and the occasional passing car. Her mind was already halfway home. She imagined setting the table. She pictured Daniel unwrapping the wrap and pouring the sparkling water like it was champagne. Her mind was full, but it was full of ordinary, beautiful things.

And then, near Lake Roland, it happened.

The turn was familiar. She'd driven it hundreds of times. But tonight, the temperature had dipped just low enough. The sun had disappeared just early enough. And the road shiny in the lamplight had turned to glass.

Black ice is always quiet. It doesn't announce itself. It doesn't shimmer like danger. It waits.

The tires lost grip without warning. The car drifted, the steering wheel light in her hands. Her reflexes kicked in. She twisted the wheel, trying to compensate. For one suspended second, it seemed like she might pull it back.

But it wasn't enough.

The front right tire caught the edge of the guardrail with a grinding scream. The metal peeled. The momentum didn't stop.

The car tipped, then fell.

Over the edge. Through the thin metal barrier. Down the sloped embankment that led straight to the lake.

A moment later, the night was silent again.

Then came the splash.

A single, terrible sound that broke the cold.

And then nothing.

***

The first call came in just minutes after the crash. The lake was still again, silent in that deceptive way winter water always is. Nothing stirred except the ripple trails moving outward from where the car had disappeared.

Across the lake, a jogger had paused to tie his shoelace near the trailhead when he saw something strange a sudden flash of metal, a sickening twist of headlights, and then a sound he couldn't place. A distant splash. Not the kind made by a rock or a bird. Something heavier. Human instinct pulled his head up, eyes straining in the dimming light.

He fumbled for his phone and dialed 911 with trembling fingers.

"There's been a crash," he told the dispatcher, breath catching. "Something went into the water. Near the north curve off Roland Lake Drive. I think it was a car."

Within minutes, emergency services were en route. Red and blue lights cut across the darkening sky. Fire engines, medics, and rescue trucks pulled up along the guardrail, their tires skidding slightly on the same hidden ice that had sent Claudia's car over the edge. A dive unit arrived shortly after, hauling on cold-weather suits before descending toward the shore.

By the time they reached the water's edge, most of the vehicle was submerged. The lake had swallowed it quickly, its surface now calm again, as though nothing had happened.

But the rescue crew moved fast. Flashlights scanned the shallows. Ropes were lowered. One diver plunged beneath the surface while the others stayed ready at the bank.

A few agonizing moments passed.

Then the diver resurfaced, breath ragged, visor fogged. He gave a nod.

"The driver's still inside," he shouted. "Window's cracked. There's a badge visible. It's a hospital ID."

They hauled the vehicle partway up with a winch and a harness, enough to reveal the shattered glass on the driver's side. One rescuer pressed his face to the window, angling his flashlight just right. The beam hit fabric first then a glint of plastic.

A badge. Still clipped to a dark coat, soaked but unmistakably visible.

He leaned closer, squinting at the name behind the droplets.

"Claudia Smith."

Silence hung around the realization like frost in the air. The team didn't speak for a moment. Not out of confusion, but out of recognition. The name wasn't just familiar. It belonged to someone whose work had been reshaping the very system they all lived in.

Back at the hospital, the world had not yet caught up.

Dr. Smith was still in his office, lights low, laptop half-closed. On the small kitchenette counter, two glasses of sparkling water waited patiently. He had just poured them a few minutes earlier, one for him, one for Claudia. The bouquet she had promised to bring was already in a vase near the window. They had done this before celebrated little wins. But this one had been bigger. Washington. The federal hearing. They had said it together, aloud, for the first time in months: "We made it."

The trauma pager vibrated against his hip.

He didn't look right away.

Then the hospital PA system crackled to life, its tone more urgent than usual. The voice that followed was steady, but clipped at the edges.

"Medical command requesting nearest physician to Roland Lake crash site. Unconfirmed ID on victim."

Dr. Smith froze. A hollow expanded in his chest, the kind that knew before his brain could confirm.

He looked down at the pager, the screen glowing against his scrub top.

The crash site. Roland Lake.

Unconfirmed ID.

He didn't ask anyone else to go. He didn't wait to ask questions. He ran.

***

He arrived just as they were pulling her from the water.

The crash site was a flood of urgent motion. Flashing red and white lights cut through the thick gray dusk. Emergency responders in bright reflective jackets moved with trained precision, their radios crackling, boots sinking into frozen mud as they hauled equipment and issued commands.

Somewhere beyond the organized chaos, a quiet grief was forming like frost.

Dr. Daniel Smith stepped out of the second emergency transport vehicle, his steps slow at first, then purposeful. The wind slapped the hem of his hospital coat as he approached. Mud caked his shoes within seconds, but he didn't notice. His eyes were locked on the stretch of shoreline cordoned off by caution tape and guarded by silence.

One paramedic glanced up, recognition flickering across his face. He tapped the shoulder of another responder. No words were exchanged, but when Dr. Smith crossed the perimeter, no one stopped him. He wore his credentials openly. But it was the look on his face that let them know. This man was not here to ask questions. He already knew the answer.

He moved past two medics who instinctively stepped aside. They understood. This wasn't just another physician on call. This was a husband answering the worst page of his life.

The figure on the ground was still surrounded by trauma staff. Her body had been lifted gently from the half-submerged vehicle moments earlier. Her clothes were soaked, her coat waterlogged and torn. They had laid her down on an insulated tarp, just above the tree line, away from the frigid slope where the guardrail had given out.

They had followed every protocol. They had done their jobs.

But there are no protocols for grief.

The body bag was unsealed, left open while final documentation was underway. One of her arms lay just outside the lining, stretched slightly outward as though reaching for something that would not return.

Her skin was pale, fingers bluish from the icy water. Her wedding ring had been removed by the dive team for preservation. But there was one thing they had not touched. Around her wrist was the thin gold bracelet engraved with a phrase familiar to every transplant coordinator in the country.

Donor. Advocate. Leader.

Claudia Smith had never taken it off.

Dr. Smith dropped to his knees in the thick slush beside her. His scrubs, already damp from the van, were soaked through instantly. He didn't flinch. His hands, gloveless, hovered above her arm. He couldn't bring himself to touch her yet.

He simply stared.

Not at her face, not at the full outline of her body he couldn't. His gaze stayed on her hand. The same hand that had once tugged his tie during lectures. The same hand that had helped him edit proposal drafts late into the night. The hand that had signed every REAL protocol revision with fierce precision. A surgeon's wife with a policy brain, always five steps ahead.

There was a small scar near the base of her thumb, a kitchen knife injury from years ago. She had laughed about it after the bleeding stopped, but then cursed for a week because it ruined her pen grip. He stared at that scar now, the memory slicing sharper than any wound he had ever treated.

A paramedic stepped forward, voice low. "Doctor... we need to finish sealing..."

Dr. Smith raised one hand without looking up. It was not a command. It was a request. The kind of request that bends time.

No one else moved.

Then, slowly, he reached for the zipper tab on the body bag.

His fingers trembled. Not from cold, though it was bitter. But from the unspeakable weight of closing something he had no will to close. Inch by inch, he pulled the zipper upward, over her chest, past her collar, and finally to the edge of her chin.

His hands lingered on the fabric once he finished. He pressed his palm flat against the bag, as if steadying it. As if steadying himself.

He remained there for a long time.

Kneeling. Breathing. Saying nothing. Crying.

The light changed around him, shifting from dusk to something darker. But he stayed unmoving until one of the medics asked softly, "Sir... should we prepare the transport?"

Dr. Smith stood slowly, his knees stiff, back damp from the icy wind.

"She flies back with me," he said.

The field commander, clipboard in hand, looked uncertain. "Doctor, we can arrange proper escort…"

"She's going home," he repeated. This time, his voice had an edge. Not raised. Not emotional. Just… absolute.

There were no further objections. The commander nodded once. The others moved quickly but quietly. Transport was arranged. Paperwork exchanged hands. Protocol bent in quiet recognition of something larger than policy.

Because sometimes grief rewrites the rules.

***

The helicopter lifted with a low mechanical whine, its blades slicing through the night air as the ground fell away beneath them.

Inside the cabin, there was no speaking.

No briefing.

No prayer.

Only silence.

Dr. Smith sat beside the stretcher, still in the same scrubs, still soaked to the bone. He had refused to change. Refused to rest. Refused to let anyone else sit beside her. His posture was rigid, but his expression was unreadable. Like glass under pressure. Not yet cracked. But close.

His hand lay flat on the sealed body bag, fingers spread across the center of her chest. It was not a comforting gesture. It was anchoring. A man trying to keep something from drifting too far, too fast.

The sky outside the window was dark, layered with purples, greys, and the soft flicker of distant city lights. But inside, the cabin held no time. No past or future. Only this unbearable now.

He thought about her words just days ago. The conversation they had after finalizing the slide deck for the upcoming federal hearing.

"Daniel," she had said, half-joking but serious at the core, "if we ever make it to the committee floor, you're not the one who should speak. Nancy should. She's the one who risked everything. You and I? We're just custodians of the truth."

He had smiled, reminded her that she had practically invented the protocol structure they were now defending in Washington. She rolled her eyes, the way she always did when he tried to give her credit. "We don't matter," she had said. "The work does."

Now her voice played like a phantom through the whir of rotor blades. Over and over. We're just custodians of the truth.

She had fought for integrity in a system known for bending. She had sacrificed her name, her sleep, her peace. And now, she had given her life.

Not in a blaze of heroism.

But in the quiet fallout of doing the right thing over and over until the weight of it wore her thin.

She had saved more lives than she ever counted. Had written more letters to grieving families than anyone should have. Had caught irregularities that no one else bothered to check.

And now she would never sit before that committee.

Dr. Smith clenched his jaw. More tears. And only silence.

As the helicopter began its descent toward the hospital, the cabin lights flickered faintly. He looked down at her wrist one last time. The donor bracelet, though partially hidden under the edge of the fabric, caught a sliver of light and glimmered.

His hand closed into a fist over the zipper line.

There, in that moment, the emotion shifted.

Not just grief.

Resolve.

Not just heartbreak.

Purpose.

She had walked this path not for glory. Not for recognition. But for change.

Now, the burden passed to him.

She was gone.

But her work was not.

And he would see it through.

Chapter 19:
From Grief to Giving

The pager buzzed at 5:12 a.m., just before the first trace of daylight broke over the city. Nancy stirred on the couch, the blanket falling from her shoulder as she sat up, groggy but alert.

She had fallen asleep in her scrubs again. Not out of carelessness, but because lately, it felt safer that way like being ready for whatever came next was a kind of armor.

She rubbed her eyes, reached for the pager on the coffee table, and read the alert through half-blurred vision:

Organ Alert: Female, 60s, Brain Death Confirmed. Viable Heart/Lungs/Liver/Kidneys. Consent Registered. Prep in 45.

No name. Just numbers. No story. Just organs.

She exhaled, slow and practiced. Death meant life again, at least for someone else. Nancy swung her legs to the floor, pulling her hair into a quick knot as she moved. The apartment was quiet. The city outside, quieter still.

She left without coffee. The air was sharp and cold when she stepped into it, a different kind of wake-up call. As the hospital came into view, she felt the familiar tightening in her chest. The transplant floor always had a strange energy. Half hope. Half gravity.

Romero was already in pre-op when she walked in. He gave a quiet nod from across the room. He still moved slower than usual, the virus having left its own trail through his body, but his eyes were sharp again.

"Good to have you back," she said softly, slipping into gloves.

He smirked. "Don't get sentimental. You still owe me a bad coffee."

They scrubbed in side by side, and for a moment, it felt like the world hadn't changed so much. The rhythm of protocol, the click of gloves, the tightening of masks   it gave them structure when emotions didn't.

Nancy glanced once more at the surgical chart. Still no name. Just the code. Female donor, early sixties. All organs viable.

She said nothing. Just nodded to the OR tech. "Let's begin prep."

They entered the room.

The donor was already prepped and covered, the surgical sheet draped neatly over the chest. The rhythm monitor beeped faintly beside them, tracking nothing but absence. Machines were silent. Time felt suspended.

Nancy stepped to the table and reached for the overhead light, adjusting the angle with practiced ease. As she moved toward the donor's upper torso, she paused. Something glinted faintly from beneath the edge of the sheet.

A bracelet.

Thin. Gold. Inscribed.

Her blood chilled.

She reached down with one gloved hand and lifted the sheet slightly.

There it was not just any bracelet, but the one she had seen a hundred times on Claudia Smith's wrist. A small, delicate band she never removed. Nancy had joked about it once during a meeting, calling it her "good luck charm."

Her fingers froze mid-air.

Everything around her receded... the beeping, the humming, the sounds of tools and metal. Her eyes locked on the wrist.

She didn't speak. She stepped back, one step, then two.

Romero noticed the shift in her breath before he saw her face. "Nancy?"

She didn't answer. She pulled off one glove and turned back to the donor record station. She keyed in the code. Hit enter.

Name: Claudia Ann Smith.

Age: 63.

Consent Date: Pre-registered, October 10.

Condition: Non-survivable injury. All organs cleared for transplant.

Nancy stared at the screen.

Tears came from her eyes. She didn't collapse. She could not process the situation...

She stepped out of the OR quietly, the door swinging shut behind her.

Just outside, in the corridor dimmed by early morning shadows, Dr. Smith stood waiting hands folded, eyes tired but steady.

"She signed the release herself," he said quietly. "Two weeks ago."

Nancy couldn't speak. Her breath was stuck somewhere between her ribs and her throat.

"She would've wanted this," he added, voice barely above a whisper. "You know she would have."

Nancy swallowed. Nodded. But how did this....

"Accident. Tragic accident...who took my wife's..." He could not speak further, putting his hands over his mouth as he closed his eyes and turned towards the door.

"Scrub me back in," she said to the nurse waiting nearby.

And then she walked back into the OR.

This time, her hands didn't shake.

***

Back in the operating room, the temperature felt colder than before, though no one had touched the thermostat.

Nancy stood still for a moment, her gloved hands hovering over the surgical field. Romero looked at her once, briefly, but said nothing. He knew the look in her eyes   focus with a pulse of something heavier beneath. Grief that had no time to grieve.

She reached down and adjusted the light again. Her voice was calm when she spoke.

"Let's start with the heart."

The nurse confirmed. "Recipient is prepped. Sixteen-year-old female. End-stage congenital defect. She coded twice this week."

Nancy didn't reply. She began the incision.

Each movement was precise. She didn't hesitate. Her hands moved the way they always had, but sharper, tighter   as if she was no longer just a surgeon but a guardian of something sacred.

Romero assisted where needed. He was quieter than usual, almost reverent. No small talk. No jokes. Just the weight of what they were doing hanging in the sterile air like unspoken prayer.

When the heart was removed and preserved, the team stepped back.

One nurse whispered, "Vitals steady on the recipient's end. They're ready."

Nancy gave a slight nod.

Next came the lungs. "Recipient?"

"Thirty-two. ICU. Eight months pregnant. On ECMO. No time left."

Nancy paused for a breath. Just one.

Then she began again.

They worked in silence, the kind of silence that didn't feel empty   it felt full. As if the room itself was holding its breath.

Each organ, when removed, was handled with careful, almost ceremonial grace. Wrapped. Tagged. Documented.

Claudia's liver and kidney were the last.

"Donor matches confirmed," the nurse said quietly. "Firefighter. Forty-one. Post-COVID complications. Liver failure and collapsed lung. Long waitlist. This is his only shot."

Nancy blinked slowly.

She remembered Claudia talking about firefighters once, after a meeting. How underappreciated they were. How she wanted to include occupational priority data in the next draft of

REAL. Nancy hadn't understood the urgency back then. She did now.

The liver came free without complication. The kidney followed.

And then it was over.

Nancy stepped back, covered her tools, and pulled off her gloves.

Her hands didn't tremble. Not until she was outside the OR, in the hallway, away from the hum of machines and the rhythm of scalpels and steel.

She leaned against the wall. Breathed in.

Out.

Then she walked to the conference lounge, sat down, and opened her laptop.

She knew what she had to write.

Not a report.

Not a chart.

A letter.

***

The first line came easily.

Her name was Claudia Smith. And everything we built only exists because she refused to let silence win.

Nancy stared at the words for a long time, letting the sentence settle before continuing.

The hospital was quiet. Most of the surgical team had gone home. Only a few night-shift nurses moved quietly down the corridor outside the glass-paneled lounge. Inside, she sat alone

with her laptop, a cup of untouched coffee growing cold beside
her.

Her fingers moved slowly across the keyboard.

*She believed in process, but she believed in people more. She
taught us that doing it right, not fast, was the only way to protect both
the living and the dead.*

Nancy paused, her throat tightening. She didn't want to
make the letter about grief. Not entirely. This wasn't just
mourning it was a map forward.

She kept writing.

*Today, I stood over the body of my mentor. My friend. A woman
who gave more to the cause of ethical transplant reform than any memo
or policy could capture. And I did what she asked of us all. I followed
the truth.*

*We performed four transplants today. Four lives saved. Her heart
now beats in a young girl who had forgotten what it felt like to breathe
without pain. Her lungs now expand inside a pregnant woman who
will live to hold her child. Her liver and kidney now belong to a
firefighter who has spent the last two years saving others while his own
body failed.*

Nancy stopped typing for a moment.

Then she wrote:

*We did not rush. We did not cut corners. We followed the REAL
protocol she helped write with her own two hands. Because of that,
those lives were saved without lies, without fear, without shortcuts.
This is what it means to do it right.*

Her hands hovered over the keyboard again.

She thought of Claudia's voice   steady, never theatrical. Her ability to walk into a room of skeptical men in suits and dismantle their objections with one line of logic.

Nancy's next paragraph was the hardest to write.

If you are reading this and you work in medicine, in policy, in regulation   ask yourself how many lives you are willing to lose before you admit the current system is broken. Ask yourself what it will take before you stop protecting the problem and start protecting the patients.

She hit return twice.

Then typed the final words.

Her last gift was not her organs. It was her example. May it teach us how to choose better while we're still alive.

Nancy didn't read it again.

She hit send.

To Romero.

To Dr. Smith.

To the internal press office.

To three trusted names in medical policy networks.

And to one inbox marked: **Public Statement – REAL Advocacy Distribution.**

Then she closed the laptop and leaned back.

The wind outside howled faintly against the windows. Somewhere down the hall, a phone rang. The world kept going. But something had shifted.

***

By morning, the letter had spread like wildfire.

Nancy had barely finished her first sip of coffee when her phone buzzed with the fifth alert of the hour. At first, she thought it was another patient update. But as she unlocked the screen, her inbox flooded in real time. Subject lines piled on top of one another like waves:

"Powerful words, Ms. Brooks. Thank you for speaking up."
"Sharing this across our transplant coalition immediately."
"My daughter received a kidney last year. Please know your letter reached her surgeon."

"We're with you. REAL is the future."

Across the country, it was being reposted by nurses, physicians, residents, survivors, and family members of those still waiting for a call that might never come. It hit medical Twitter before lunch. LinkedIn by noon. Then came the articles. Small at first   local news blogs, advocacy newsletters   then national outlets.

Romero called first.

"I just saw it," he said, his voice thick. "I didn't know words could do that."

Nancy was sitting on the bench outside the hospital, her coat wrapped tight against the wind. "It wasn't mine," she said. "It was hers. I just wrote it down."

He didn't argue.

Ten minutes later, Dr. Smith messaged her directly: **"She would have been proud. I am."**

The hospital PR team reached out next. They wanted to feature the letter on their website. Then a policy think tank requested permission to include it in their upcoming brief to the House Committee on Health. Another message came from a transplant ethics journal editor, asking for a longer reflection piece.

By late afternoon, the letter had been translated into three languages.

Nancy sat back from her desk, exhausted but still. She wasn't overwhelmed. She was waiting.

She knew the real call was still coming.

And it did.

Her phone lit up with a blocked number just before six.

She answered without hesitation.

"Dr. Nancy Brooks?" The voice on the other end was deep, firm, and unmistakably familiar. "This is Senator Callahan."

She stood instinctively, like she was back in med school, responding to a supervisor.

"I read your letter," the Senator continued. "Twice, actually. The room went quiet both times. Your words are going into the federal record, just so you know."

Nancy blinked. "Thank you, Senator. I didn't write it to ...."

"You wrote it to tell the truth," he interrupted gently. "And you did. Better than any lobbyist or lawyer ever has."

She could hear papers shifting on his end, then a breath that meant something bigger was coming.

"The final vote is scheduled for next month. You'll be speaking for all of us, Ms. Brooks. I need your voice in that room."

Her stomach dropped.

"You're inviting me to the hearing?" she asked, barely above a whisper.

"Inviting you?" The Senator gave a dry laugh. "No, Doctor. I'm telling you. Get your remarks ready. And don't hold back. Not now. Not after what she gave."

Nancy didn't respond right away.

The wind outside pressed against the windows again. Somewhere, someone was paging for a nurse. Life went on in steady chaos.

But something inside her had changed.

Not just from grief.

Not just from the surgery.

Not even from the letter.

Something deeper. A switch had flipped.

Her fight had always been about justice, about correcting a system twisted by money and silence. But now, with Claudia's name echoing in policy rooms and medical forums, Nancy realized this was no longer about reform alone.

It was about remembrance.

It was about truth finding breath in every saved life.

"I'll be ready," she said finally.

The call ended.

And in the silence that followed, Nancy stared at the hospital floor like it was the starting line of something enormous. Her hand hovered over her laptop again. Not to edit the letter.

To write her speech.

Chapter 20:
A Future Rewritten

The yellow tape had been taken down.

For weeks, the front entrance of St. James Hospital had stood sealed, guarded by federal agents and tight-lipped administrators. The headlines had faded from prime time, replaced by newer scandals and shifting politics, but inside these walls, the echoes of betrayal lingered.

Now, for the first time since the DOJ investigation, the glass doors slid open on a Monday morning. No reporters. No ribbon-cutting. Just a short internal memo circulated days earlier:

Subject: Reinstatement of Transplant Operations under Interim Federal Oversight.

Nancy stood in the lobby, coat still buttoned, her ID tag freshly reactivated. The badge scanner lit green. A small mechanical chirp confirmed entry. No applause. No speeches. Just a soft sigh behind the reception desk, as the day's first nurse clocked in and offered a quiet nod.

St. James was no longer privately run.

A coalition of federal and state administrators had assumed operational control, backed by a temporary ethics board and multiple rotating compliance officers. Every transplant request, every donor match, every surgical report would be reviewed by at least two external entities.

Nancy walked slowly through the halls. She half-expected to feel haunted. But what met her was something else: structure.

New signs hung over the transplant wing. Bright blue labels pointed toward clearly marked **Consent Verification Bays** and **Family Advocacy Rooms**. There was now a permanent **Donor-Recipient Audit Station** set up just outside the OR wing, staffed 24/7. Every checklist had a countersignature. Every form had a digital backup.

Romero passed her near the staff lockers, fresh out of rounds. His mask hung loosely around his neck. "You believe it?" he asked.

Nancy looked around, then back at him. "I believe they'll never make the same mistake again."

He gave a small smile, not cheerful but steady. "That's enough."

The whiteboard still listed **COVID-positive: 7**. The virus hadn't vanished. It never truly would. But the panic was gone.

What had changed wasn't the numbers it was the **system's response**.

Nancy stood just outside the transplant ICU wing, reviewing the updated intake protocols. The new rules had slowed everything down at first double-verification, PCR testing on both ends, mandatory family Zoom sessions before consent but the outcomes were different now.

Better. Cleaner. Safer.

There were still patients on oxygen. Still fevers that spiked in the middle of the night. But the difference was what happened after.

The high-stakes transplant cases the pregnant women too weak to fight on their own, the teenagers with failing livers post-COVID, the elderly who couldn't risk waiting another month **they were getting second chances**. Because the organs coming in weren't stolen, hidden, or rerouted through corrupted systems.

They were real. They were verified. And they were saving people.

Nancy passed one of the observation windows and saw a young woman   twenty, maybe twenty-one   asleep under oxygen flow, chest rising steady. A heart transplant, just four days ago. The match had come through in time because the donor consent video had been validated within twenty minutes.

In the old system, it would've been flagged. Delayed. Or worse, misused.

She looked down the hallway at the donor ledger screen blinking green.

"Verified: One Heart, One Match."

The ICU wasn't quiet. Machines still beeped. Nurses still moved with urgency. But **no one was guessing anymore**. Every decision was traceable. Every life saved had a documented path behind it.

Nancy's phone buzzed.

Oversight Committee testimony: T-minus 3 hours.

She exhaled, tucked the device away, and glanced one last time at the board.

COVID wasn't over.

But because of this reform, **it wasn't a death sentence anymore**.

***

The hearing room was chilled with silence. Overhead lights buzzed faintly, and a single government-issued camera adjusted its lens with a soft mechanical whir. The panel of senators sat in heavy chairs, faces unreadable. But everyone was watching the woman in black.

Nancy Brooks sat at the center witness table. In front of her lay a leather folder, carefully opened. Inside it were three things: the viral letter she had written days after Claudia Smith's death, the gold donor bracelet she had found beneath the surgical drape, and a thick binder of notes and research compiled over years by Dr. Daniel Smith and his late wife.

She wasn't in scrubs today. There was no white coat. No stethoscope around her neck. Just a plain black blazer, her hair tied back, and a steady expression carved from weeks of loss and resolve.

This wasn't mourning.

It was memory. Purposeful. Sharp-edged.

Senator Callahan cleared his throat and gave her a nod.

"Ms. Brooks, you have the floor."

Nancy leaned forward, resting her fingertips on the folder as if steadying something larger than paper.

Then she began.

***

"My name is Nancy Brooks.

I am a trauma nurse by training. A transplant specialist by necessity. And a reluctant reformer by force of circumstance.

I did not come here to read statistics. You already know them. You know how many people die on the waitlist every year. You know the disparities how certain names in certain zip codes rise faster. You know that paperwork doesn't always tell the truth.

What you don't know what the data won't show is what it feels like to watch someone you love die waiting for a match that existed. A match that was simply… rerouted.

So I won't start with a graph.

I'll start with Jim.

Jim was my husband. Not a doctor. Not an executive. A civilian. He was quiet, grounded, the kind of man who brought coffee to nurses during snowstorms and never complained about missing holidays because his wife was on call. He had a respiratory illness long before COVID. It made life careful, not small. We adjusted. We learned to cherish everything.

When COVID hit, Jim got sick.

We did everything right. Monitored. Isolated. Prayed. His lungs failed. He needed a transplant.

We were told there were no matches. But later, I found out there were.

They had just gone… somewhere else.

I want to be clear. This wasn't some technical glitch. This wasn't a tragic delay.

This was theft.

Organs were rerouted. Consent was skipped. Matches were forged. Paper trails vanished. All under the supervision of people who were supposed to protect patients, not trade their lives like currency."

Nancy paused, her voice steady, but her breath catching for just a second.

"I was part of it, in ways I hate admitting.

I scrubbed in on those surgeries. I doubted, but I said nothing. I looked away from inconsistencies because I was grieving, because I was scared, and because the man orchestrating it Dr. Elijah Leigh knew how to keep people quiet.

He was smooth. He didn't threaten openly. He didn't need to. He used logic as a weapon. 'One silence, a thousand benefits,' he told me once.

I carried that silence like lead.

And then, I met two people who didn't.

Dr. Daniel Smith. And his wife, Claudia.

They were working in the margins. Quietly, methodically, building something they called the REAL protocol Review, Ethics, Accountability, Ledger. Simple words, but somehow radical in a field where urgency had erased caution.

Claudia didn't have a title. She didn't need one. She had spreadsheets. Data logs. Email trails. She found donor records that had been altered, matches that were fabricated, and a pattern of quiet crimes hidden under the cover of emergency.

We filed affidavits. We submitted evidence. We were granted a hearing slot. This hearing.

And then she died.

Claudia was in a car accident the same night we received confirmation.

The next morning, I got paged.

A female donor. Anonymous. Brain dead. Age 62.

During prep, I saw it. A gold bracelet under the sheet. Her bracelet. Claudia's.

My hands froze. I stepped out of the room. I couldn't breathe.

Dr. Smith was waiting in the hallway.

'She would've wanted it,' he said.

He was right.

Her heart saved a teenage girl who had been in and out of heart failure since birth. Her lungs saved a pregnant woman fighting both pneumonia and panic in an ICU bed. Her liver and kidney went to a firefighter whose own lungs had collapsed post-COVID.

Even in death, Claudia refused to be silent.

She gave her body to the cause she had fought for.

And that moment… that unbearable, unspeakable moment… is why I am here."

Nancy slowly opened the folder, pulled out the bracelet, and placed it on the desk. The gold caught the light a small glint of memory.

"I want to talk to you now about courage.

Courage is not pushing through flawed systems to maintain output.

Courage is not covering for your department to avoid scandal.

Courage is stopping a surgery because a consent form feels off. It is pulling a file when no one wants you to. It is being the only voice in the room saying, 'This isn't right.'

Claudia Smith had courage.

She was not a surgeon.

She was not a politician.

She was not wealthy. Not loud. Not verified on social media.

She was a wife. A volunteer. A reformer. And the most ethically grounded person I have ever known.

She didn't get to give this speech.

But I am here, wearing her bracelet, holding her notes, and standing on her shoulders."

Nancy looked each committee member in the eye, one by one.

"Don't tell me we can't change this.

We already did.

We've already saved lives by doing things the right way.

The Emergency Transplant Ethics Act does not ask for miracles. It asks for a system that can be trusted again.

Make real-time video consent mandatory. End anonymous redirections. Use a transparent national match ledger.

No more shadows. No more whispers. No more rerouted lives."

She closed the folder. The chamber held its breath.

"Claudia's last gift saved lives.

May her final act teach us how to choose better while we're still alive."

The room remained quiet. There was no applause. No immediate fanfare.

But in the first row, Senator Callahan leaned toward his aide and whispered something that changed history.

Within the hour, the **Emergency Transplant Ethics Act** passed by majority vote.

It became **LAW**.

And across the nation, a system began to heal; not just in policy, but in spirit.

***

Life happens in silence sometimes. Not with announcements. Not with applause. But in the quiet aftermath, when the storm has passed and you are still here, catching your breath.

Nancy Brooks sat at a corner café two blocks from the Capitol, hands wrapped around a warm cup of tea that had long gone cold. Outside the wide glass window, late autumn sunlight painted the sidewalks in soft gold. Inside, the table was scattered with empty coffee cups, half-finished pastries, and the hum of shared exhaustion.

Romero sat across from her, coat off, sleeves rolled to his elbows, the smallest glimmer of peace finally settling on his face. To his left was Carla, laughing with two young nurses from the new transplant oversight team. Across from them, Dr. Smith, eyes tired but clear, nodded along as someone told a story about the early days of chaos in the ICU.

No one here had slept much in the past year. They had buried friends. They had signed affidavits that could have ended their careers. They had scrubbed in for surgeries that pushed the limit of science and morality. They had wept privately and testified publicly. And somehow, they had made it through.

Nancy leaned back, exhaling slowly, letting the warmth of the moment sink in.

This was not the celebration she once imagined. No speeches. No press. Just a table of people who had carried each other through the fire now sitting shoulder to shoulder, finally breathing without fear.

She glanced at the TV behind the counter. A health segment scrolled across the bottom ticker: **"Transplant Wait Times Down by 18% Since Passage of Emergency Ethics Act."**

No anchor read it aloud. No one in the café seemed to notice. But Nancy did.

She reached into her coat pocket and ran her fingers over a thin bracelet still tucked inside Claudia's bracelet. The clasp had broken during surgery, but she kept it close anyway.

She thought of Jim then. Not with sorrow this time, but with a quiet gratitude. He never got his second transplant. But he had sparked the fight that helped hundreds more receive theirs. The boy in Texas. The teacher in Maine. The grandmother in Kansas who woke up today with a working liver because someone said, "Let's do this the right way."

Nancy smiled faintly.

They had done something that mattered.

And in the end, that was enough.

As laughter swelled around the table   Romero cracking a joke about their first day back, Carla pretending to be the ethics enforcer with a mock-serious glare   Nancy let herself join in. The sound was unfamiliar on her tongue, but it felt good.

Tomorrow would bring more work. More patients. More lives to hold steady through uncertain storms.

But today?

Today, the system held.

Patients were being matched faster.

Organs were arriving with verified consent.

And no one... no one...was dying in the dark anymore.

Nancy looked around the table one last time. She closed her eyes briefly and whispered inwardly, for Jim, for Claudia, for every donor whose name was never read on TV.

"We're ready now."

The End.

www.ingramcontent.com/pod-product-compliance
Lightning Source LLC
Chambersburg PA
CBHW070528310726
48976CB00002BA/568